The Forsaken Pearl

Broken Water Series

Book 2

Wentworth-by-the-Sea

Jennifer W. Smith

Published by Ó Apple House Publishing
ISBN: 978-0-9966954-5-9

Editing by Sue Ducharme of TextWorks

Printed in the USA

DEDICATION

For my parents

Steve and Diane

A true love story

Novels by Jennifer W. Smith

Contemporary Romance

Flying Backwards

Landing in Love Series

Defying Gravity

Holding Pattern

Ground Control

Turbulent Kisses

Flight Plan

Falling in Love at Christmas: Holiday Special I

Protecting my Love at Christmas: Holiday Special II

Rescuing Love at Christmas: Holiday Special III

Paranormal Romance

Broken Water Series

The Rare Pearl: Book 1

The Forsaken Pearl: Book 2

The Vanishing Pearl: Book 3

Wiccan Haus Series

Legends Mate

Join my Book Squad – Facebook Group

Do you love sweet and sensual romances, and learning about the author who writes them? Join me!

Jennifer W. Smith's Book Squad

By joining you'll get access to early release Book Squad content and specials, learn the inside scoop about my books, and get to weigh in on my work-in-progress. Join Now!

THE HUMAN REALM

New Castle, New Hampshire

Harmony Parker — heroine

Pearl — Harmony's Great-great grandmother

Margaret Parker — Harmony's grandmother

Stanley Parker — Margaret Parker's husband

Harry and his wife — Friends of the Parkers, boat owners

Brook Parker — Harmony's mother

Eric — Harmony's father

Samantha Finch — Harmony's best friend

Mike Coombs — Acquaintance of Harmony's

David — Samantha's boyfriend

Rudy — Samantha's boss

Mary Falk — Finn's human mother

THE AQUAPOPULEAN REALM

The Coastal Clan on the Sacred Island
{New Castle, New Hampshire seashore}

Kodiak Night — Clansman Diver

Calder — Clan Linker

Nami — Calder's daughter

Binda — Calder's granddaughter and Linker

Rio — Calder's grandson

Morie — Keeper of the Wellness-by-the-Sea

Lynn — Wellness-by-the-Sea attendant

Deniz — Linker

THE AQUAPOPULEAN REALM

The Forest Tribe on the Great Falls
{Niagara Falls}

Finn Falk — Current Chieftain

Nakoma — Previous Chieftain

Umiko — Tribesman

Taura — Tribesman

Catori — Tribeswoman

Gale — Tribal Linker

Amadahy — Chieftain's room attendant

Bo — Farmer's son

Ren — Flower vendor's daughter

THE EARTHLY REALMS

Suijin — Water God

1

The Aquapopulean Realm

Finn crouched, his fingers brushing the dusty soil. The sun's rays penetrated his dark hair, intensifying the heat; there was no cooling breeze. The grasses a few feet away stood as tall as his shoulder and stretched for acres, their delicate flowers creating a sea of purple. Indeed, as the farmers had claimed, the dry weather had affected the crops. Finn squinted against the scorching sun as he scanned the faces of the children who had followed their chieftain up the hill to the field.

"Boy." Finn singled out the wildling whose chin rose a notch mightier than the others. The farmer's son strutted forward. His arched neck made him look like he was trying to appear taller than his mates. His disheveled hair matted around his ears, and dirt shadowed his neck. Finn's expression was impassive, but he felt a mixture of admiration and empathy toward the child's tough persona. Neglect was indeed something to overcome. At age twelve, Finn had been forced to look out for himself. After he was taken from his family, he ended up in a boy's domicile within the city walls. He was a displaced human in a strange world who had to overcome the obstacles of being different from the other children. Every civilization had its foundlings. The Linker who had brought him through the portal had been exiled, orphaning Finn. In those early years he'd learned harsh lessons: to hunt for his food or starve and to stand up for himself to prove his worth. The city of plenty rewarded its productive citizens, and Finn strived to contribute, despite his situation. His diligent efforts had paid off. He was the chieftain now.

Finn tipped his head; the boy followed his gaze down the hill to where the farmhouse stood. The stone structure next to the large barn was modest. The farmer's wife was hanging the wash on a line. She glanced over her shoulder up the hill, no doubt to catch a glimpse of the new chieftain. "Tell your mother to bring in her linens. I will summon the rain."

The boy beamed, revealing his incoming front teeth, white against his tanned skin. Eager to do the chieftain's bidding, the boy dashed away. "It's happening! The chief will summon the rain!" he yelled ecstatically. The boys had been desperate to witness their chieftain's amazing ability. They had heard stories of the human man who lived in the city and could control the weather.

Finn stood and inhaled the floral sent mingled with earth. He nodded at the farmer and the men who worked the field. He called, "Take shelter if you wish. I will bring a drenching rain."

The workers moved toward the nearby woods. The small group of trees offered little protection, but this was the first chance they would get to watch this miraculous show. The leather-faced farmer puffed with pride, and his respect for his leader shone in his dark eyes. "It's good of you to help us, Chief. Thank you," he said humbly, before turning to yell at the neighboring children who'd gathered. "Get to the house—all of you!" His harsh command sent the lot dashing down the hill.

Finn watched the farmer join the workers in the woods and then glanced down the hill. The woman had collected her linens, the full basket on her hip, and swung her free arm at the children, shooing them toward the door.

The sky above the farm was clear and blue. Finn looked to the east as he raised his bare arms. He would draw the moisture clouds from the ocean. He worked his fingers as if coaxing the energy around him. Soon dark clouds appeared on the horizon and then rolled overland ominously. A vibrating roll of thunder announced its arrival, and the air temperature cooled. Raising his powerful arm perpendicular to the earth, Finn reached skyward and curled his fingers into a fist, harnessing the energy of the rainstorm. The clouds were overhead now. Fat drops smacked the dust. Quickly, random drops became a downpour.

Finn didn't hear the cheering of the workers or see the children, who'd refused to go inside and instead jumped in the puddles. He stood with his eyes closed, concentrating on the isolated rain. At the sound of thunder, tremendously close, Finn opened his eyes. His soaked hair plastered his cheek and neck. Water droplets bounced off his bronzed skin. The leather belts he wore around his shoulder and waist darkened as they became saturated. Releasing his fist, he slowly relaxed his arm. The spongy earth told Finn this soaking would prove sufficient for the crops.

Reaching the wood's edge, Finn gathered the reins of his elk, tethered to a branch. To the farmer, he said, "You may send your boy to me in the city to keep me abreast of the crop's progress."

"I will do so, Chief. Thank you," responded the farmer, who seemed surprised by Finn's request.

Finn swung into the saddle and headed north toward the walled city. The elk trotted past the farmhouse through the puddles at the end of the hill. The children ran to follow him, but Finn extended his hand and swirled his wrist, dropping snow in the valley. The snow stopped the children in their tracks. They thrust their heads back to stick their tongues out and catch the drifting snowflakes. As Finn spurred the animal on, the snowflakes again became rain.

When Finn had taken over the leadership of the tribe,

he appointed two high-ranking members of society and the greatest of the male warriors, Taura and Umiko, as his closest councilmen. These men had survived the earthquake at the coast at his side. Their support proved valuable when they assured the city dwellers that their previous chief, Nakoma, had wanted Finn to be leader. They attested to his character, which had already been proven to the people by Finn's heroic hunting expeditions. It was no secret that the female chieftain Nakoma favored the human, and not exclusively for his power to manipulate the weather. Nakoma had appointed him lead hunter, an honor.

The domineering female hunters with their gigantic pet lions disputed their replacement. But they settled in, waiting to see what this human could do for them. In Nakoma's reign, the female hunters had dominated the council, but now many were gone—perished in the earthquake. The earthquake, followed by a tidal wave, had taken the lives of one-hundred-eighty-four warriors, as well as Chief Nakoma.

The first time Finn had traveled east was when he left with Harmony and Kodiak after he had helped them escape from Nakoma. Seeing the ocean was an experience he wouldn't forget. The force of the powerful rogue wave that caused many to die was beyond anything. Finn felt he was to blame. Nakoma had followed them and come to claim him—and his abilities—that critical day. She wanted Harmony as well, but Finn wasn't going to let that happen. Many said his ability was a blessing from god. It was more like a curse, he thought.

When he reached the city the sun was shining. The majestic Romanesque city, high and sprawling across the land like a stone mountain range, had a powerful waterfall at its gate. The rain Finn brought in for the farmer's crops had been an isolated shower. His hair had mostly dried now, wavy at his collar. The elk instinctively slowed as it crossed under the gate. Immediately Finn was surrounded by the crowd awaiting his return. Before his departure that morning, the council had argued that a chieftain shouldn't leave the city unattended, but Finn had assured them he could manage without further protection, as he always had. He reasoned that the hunters could better serve the people in the forests while he rode alone to investigate a farm in need.

He dismounted, and his elk was immediately led away by an appointed groom. A woman hurried to match his pace, her big golden cat skipping along beside her. She oversaw the raw materials from the farms being transferred to the mills for processing. Finn brought her up to speed on the status of each farm he had visited that week and the follow-up he expected from her.

"One more thing," he said as he reached the base of the staircase. "If a farm boy comes looking for me, I want to see him. If I'm unavailable, see he gets a proper meal, is outfitted with new boots, and sent home with some provisions. The items are to be billed to my personal account."

Finn watched confusion cross the woman's face, but she agreed without question. His eyes dropped to the panting lioness; Finn imagined the creature probably hoped her busy owner would stop rushing from place to place. Finn turned away and mounted the steps. He never did care for the cats.

In the chieftain's quarters, Finn sat on his bed. A young woman stepped up, waiting for instruction. She'd been appointed room attendant by the old chieftain.

"Shall I bathe you in the pool downstairs?" the girl named Amadahy asked, eager and somewhat breathless. She inched forward. "I've wanted to say for some time…that is, after the escape I never thought I'd see you again. And here you are, our leader. I'm glad you're back and that you've allowed me to serve you these several weeks." She caught her bottom lip with her teeth, her hands clasped behind her back.

Finn smiled at both Amadahy's comment and the desire that softened her young face. He knew that when he'd kissed her in the woods a month ago, the day she helped him escape with Harmony and Kodiak, that she'd wished there were time for more between them.

"I could use a swim." He stood, running his hand through his damp hair. The mineral spring in the cavern below would give welcome warmth. She demurely lowered her lashes and grinned.

Amadahy obediently followed him down the stone steps. Finn considered what kind of warmth her body could bring him. The sound of the rushing falls grew louder as they reached the chamber. A balcony offered the only natural light in the underground room. All Aquapopuleans enjoyed private pools large enough to swim in, but the mineral bath in his new quarters was the largest Finn had seen. The geothermal waters helped calm the mind and body, increased circulation, and relaxed his sore muscles.

Amadahy helped him strip away his heavy belts. The belt that curved across his torso and around his broad shoulder held several short knives. The thicker one around his waist held other blades, plus pouches of various survival materials. She unbuckled the leather cuffs that protected his forearms from the sting of the bowstring. Kicking his worn leather boots aside, he finished discarding his clothing. He walked into the sunken pool, sighing as the hot water surrounded his bare skin. *Just as I like it,* he thought. Although the Aquapopulean race could withstand the coldest of temperatures, his warm-blooded human body appreciated all things heated.

6

He swam several laps to burn off his anxious energy. With every lap he mused at the progress he'd made so far. His tribe had returned to the city within a fortnight of the quake. The great hall had filled with tribe members who wanted to know everything that had transpired. The remaining council members announced that Finn Falk was their official chieftain. His first order of duty would be the numerous water burials. He attended the funerals of every tribe member who lost life and offered support for the families they left behind. After that, he had spent many long hours, the best part of a week, listening to the petty disputes of the city dwellers. He meted out each decision with tolerance and swift decisiveness—just the way he hunted.

He reached the edge of the pool and draped his muscular arms over the lip, extending them wide. He focused on the wisps of steam that wafted from the surface. Finn sensed when Amadahy knelt behind him. She poured scented liquid into her palm and started to rub his shoulders. She slid her hands along each hill and valley, stretching as far as her slim hands could reach toward his forearms. Her cheek was near his, and she whispered softly, "Would you like me to come in?"

Finn understood what she was offering. He hadn't had the pleasure of knowing this particular girl in that way, but more pressing thoughts weighed heavily on his mind.

"Perhaps another time. You are dismissed," he said without turning around. He heard the scuff of her sandals as she stood and as she sashayed toward the stairs. He closed his eyes—not even the soft shuffle of her sandals on the stone steps penetrated his thoughts.

Exhaling deeply, Finn thought about the pivotal choice he had made to remain in this realm. A month ago he could have crossed through the portal to the human realm with Harmony Parker—he corrected his thoughts: Harmony Night, now that she was married to Kodiak. He had considered going. The question still lingered: had he made the right choice? He pondered whether his human parents were still alive. If so, would he have been able to find them? If he had, how would he explain where he'd been all these years? Humans had no knowledge of a second realm, so his story would seem…absurd at best. Furthermore, he'd lived in this city for more than fifteen years, working hard to make it his home. Conflicting emotions aside, he was chieftain now, and he resolved to improve the city's relations with the coastal clans in the east and use his unique and powerful ability to control the weather to make his city prosper.

It was time to stop thinking about the past—*again*—and look to the future.

2

A warrior keeping vigil alerted Gale of Umiko's arrival. Weeks had passed since they had last spoken, before Umiko had left alongside two hundred heavily armed warriors to invade the coastal clan.

Gale, the tribe's exiled Linker, watched Umiko's elk leave tracks in the dusting of snow that had fallen overnight. It was late in April for snow. By now the early crops were knee high. With a shrewd glance at the sun, Gale estimated the snow would be gone by noon. The Linker's gaze returned to the hunter as he dismounted. Umiko's steady, unhurried pace added to Gale's anticipation. Finally, the isolated Linker would hear some news. Umiko greeted the two men as he marched up the steps of the old hydropower station. The station was built according to plans brought back by Gale's master, a well-traveled Linker in the previous century. After the technique proved successful at producing power for the tribal city, this station was abandoned and a larger facility built closer to the falls. Gale, who leaned heavily on the railing, straightened and eagerly asked, "What news do you have, Umiko? Was Nakoma successful in returning Finn and Harmony to the city?"

Chief Nakoma had come to him squawking because Finn had helped the mixed-race human girl, Harmony Parker, and her clan husband, Kodiak Night, escape the tribal city. Gale was furious that Nakoma had allowed Harmony to marry a clansman after he'd advised the chieftain to facilitate a union between Harmony and Finn. Finn and Harmony were the first of their kind— both possessed fantastic and powerful abilities. Gale could only image what their offspring would inherit.

After that debacle, Gale agreed to give the chieftain two hundred battle-trained hunters to retrieve the pair. Though Nakoma was a pawn in his overall plans, she had proved to be a disappointment. Now he was anxious to know if his grand scheme could be rectified so that he could continue as planned.

"This is the first opportunity I've had to slip away," Umiko said; his high cheekbones were emphasized by his flat nose. He continued in his deep monotone. "There has been a turn of events. Our army made haste chasing Finn, the girl, and her husband to the coast. However, when we arrived and surrounded the great temple, an earthquake came upon us." Umiko drew in a shallow breath, his face stern. "We lost one-hundred-eighty-four hunters, as well as our chieftain. Nakoma is dead. Finn has taken her place as chieftain. I suggested his takeover and swore fealty to him."

After Umiko related these events to the older man, Gale's weather-worn face crinkled. Laughter rumbled from his chest. "A waste of warriors...truly a terrible waste, but...Finn is chieftain." Umiko apparently didn't see the humor; he nodded curtly. Gale wondered about the other asset, and asked, "And what of the mixed-race girl?"

"Harmony and her husband Kodiak used the herbs to pass through the portal. They're gone."

Narrowing his eyes, Gale growled, "Kodiak Night is no Linker! He may be a renowned Diver, but he is *no Linker*! Did Calder allow him to pass through?"

"According to Finn, Calder warned that it was forbidden." He shrugged a shoulder. "No one knows if he survived."

Damn! Harmony is gone! We still need her—she is the key to defeating the water god. But however much they infuriated Gale, at least these events had led to Finn's leadership. Finn's survival during the earthquake and his new position were better results than Gale could have expected under the circumstances. One problem remained—Harmony Parker shouldn't have been allowed to leave. Nakoma was supposed to secure the asset. Nakoma had been incompetent, and not only in this matter; her feeble attempt to get him reinstated as the tribal Linker had never come to fruition. He'd provided a trained army in exchange for his freedom, but she'd held him at bay. He'd secretly vowed that following the attack on the clansmen, which should have been successful, that he would make his move and rejoin the tribe. Not even Nakoma would have held him back this time.

"And what of the coastal clans? Do they think their water god, Suijin, brought forth the quake, or do they think it was a disturbance from the other realm?" Gale had been in the human realm many times. He had his own ideas concerning the unique connection between the dual realms, believing a stronger energy could tip the scales of the delicate balance linking them.

"The clan Linker, Calder, was certain it was because of some forespoken destruction on the human side of the realm. Apparently Harmony Parker had prophesied a building was to be torn down, wobbling the energy. Calder sent her back to stop further disturbances." Umiko shifted. "Before she could leave, the sea serpent came, taking its vengeance out on whomever it could. It was Finn who struck it down with a lightning bolt, although the mixed-race girl had some ability that affected the sea serpent. She was somehow able to shield herself from it. I saw her from the bluff and again briefly later as she passed by me on her way to the temple." Umiko raised his eyebrows at Gale. "Her golden hair was remarkable."

Another warrior who joined them on the platform looked up at the mention of golden hair. He leaned against the railing that Gale gripped.

"Yes, there is something to be said for blonds," Gale smirked, but the light quickly left his eyes. "Finn's ability will transform this city into an empire. His legacy will change our future, making this the greatest kingdom in all of Aquapopulean history. It will rival the god's prestigious city from long ago. But I wanted Harmony to fight off Suijin's minions, the sirens."

"You would pit a half-human against our god?" Umiko tested.

Umiko's question didn't shake Gale's faith. Passion fueled his next words. "With Finn's abilities, he practically *is* a god. What has Suijin done for our people? Suijin is nothing in the human realm but a minor deity, hardly recognized among so many other idols. He will soon be nothing to the Aquapopulo."

Gale glanced around the makeshift home where he'd lived for the last fifteen years—an abandoned power station miles upriver from the falls. The platform they stood on held little more than a shed with a door. Inside the dinky shack, deep within the earth, lay a labyrinth of facilities stocked with technological and medical advances that Gale had brought back from his travels in the human realm, a deeper and darker secret down every stairwell. The outbuilding contained a barge with a large cage on the deck. The barge had been built to Gale's specifications and was ready to voyage downriver.

"Let's prepare for my return. It's time for me to reenter Finn's life and resume my role as tribal Linker. The time is upon us," Gale said to Umiko, his trusted spy.

While Umiko departed to gather Gale's supplemental warriors, who'd been recruited from the southern tribal villages, Gale visited the outbuilding. Watching the beast in the cage, Gale believed fifteen years was too long an exile—although his banishment for bringing

Finn Falk over from the human realm had been a life sentence, Gale knew his punishment was temporary. He had planned to return all along. After all, it was because of him that the tribe had a new ruler with the gift of controlling the weather. How could the tribe not accept their Linker back, with Finn as their leader? They should welcome him with open arms—and he would see to it that they did. With Nakoma dead, Finn would now be his instrument of supremacy.

Weeks later the barge floated its way toward the city. It carried Gale and a dozen warriors, including Umiko, who was also Finn's trusted friend and confidant. The fortified cage containing a mammoth beast dominated half the aft deck. After traveling miles downriver they maneuvered the barge into a manmade port built hundreds of years ago by the tribe. It was efficient for the easy import of goods such as wood, food from orchards and fields beyond the city walls, and animal meat and pelts. The river was their highway. Gale used it now to infiltrate the city.

***

Finn sat among several councilmen and women on an open-air platform, discussing the working conditions of the salt miners. The man who oversaw the operation assured the chieftain they were an industrious population but limited by a lack of numbers. Improving conditions, like shortened work hours and more compensation, would only drive up salt prices, he argued.

The overseer's obnoxiously loud voice was laced with arrogance. "Nakoma said she'd get clan workers—I don't see any clan workers."

Finn critically examined the man before him, whose rounded shoulders and soft abdomen revealed his leisurely life. *Productive citizen* was practically a tribal creed. Finn's gut told him this man was shady. He needed to see the mines for himself before he negotiated further. A girl who'd been circling around the council members with refreshments offered the man smoked fish on bite-sized crisps. When he removed the entire tray from her hands, taking what was left, the girl gasped in shock. He followed his rude behavior by directing an insinuated kiss at the girl before he stuffed his mouth. She swirled away, wrinkling her nose. Others glanced in Finn's direction; expressions of exasperation abounded. Finn struggled to control his anger. The council, the crowd, the insolent overseer before him who challenged his authority—they all watched him, waiting to witness the kind of leadership he'd adopt, lenient or heavy-handed.

"Your observation is noted." Finn leaned forward, elbows on his knees, his fists pressed together. "Tell me, what percentage do you make from my personal account? My household account," he clarified.

The man paled. "A modest amount, I assure you." The man's laugh was high, nervous. Indeed, a large portion of this overseer's salary came from the percentage for salt he sold to customers.

Finn cast a pointed look at his record keeper, who could barely contain a smirk. "Fifty percent," said the man wielding the pen.

Blowing a long whistle, Finn lifted a brow. He leaned back and stretched his legs. Finn acknowledged the record keeper. "Thank you for your immediate response," and then he added, "Suspend all purchase of salt until a new percentage is negotiated."

The overseer tossed the food tray on a nearby chair, his face a bright shade of red. "I earn that money," he bristled, shaking his fist.

"I will see for myself when I visit the mines. Make

14

no mistake, I will resolve this salt issue with resourcefulness and justice. This will be a major issue for discussion at the upcoming summit."

Before the man could respond, the noise from a growing ruckus outside tempted many to abandon Finn's diligent ruling for better entertainment.

"Someone approaches on the river…and he has captured a short-faced bear!" Gushes of astonishment swept through the crowd. They scooted around each other for better views over the balustrade. Finn leaped from his seat, the overseer forgotten, and people parted to offer him a view.

It was true—a short-faced bear filled the confined bars of its cage, its black fur gleaming in the sun. Finn's eyes narrowed on the tall figure who stood cloaked, a hood covering his face, at the front of the barge. Something in his posture told Finn who he was. *It can't be!*

Finn turned, shouting, "Gather your weapons!" He jogged down the granite steps that spiraled to the central courtyard, his hunters soon on his heels with weapons in hand. Finn followed the corridors that led to the cove, which was lined with warehouses and vessels tied at the docks. Brawny men were unloading pelts into carts.

The barge floated closer, and the rowers skillfully bumped it against the dock. Umiko jump off first, greeting Finn. "I bring someone of great importance who has come to see you." Umiko glanced up scanning the faces that had gathered along the entire length of the enormous balcony that connected several city buildings, which afforded them a vantage point and kept them clear of the danger.

"Listen up," Umiko shouted. "I have returned to you someone who has been wronged, someone who can offer this city a great service. We can finally have a Linker among us again. I give you Gale the Linker."

As murmurs broke out, Finn's jaw clenched. When Gale slung back his hood and advanced, his slight limp almost went unnoticed by Finn, who could only think about killing the man before him. Gale had ripped him away from his human home when he was a twelve-year-old boy. He'd suffered greatly because of this man. Finn's hand hovered over his blade as he waited for Gale to come closer.

However, Gale kept his distance and allowed Umiko to stand between them and play the diplomat. Finn exclaimed through clenched teeth, "Umiko, why have you brought him here? He's exiled, never to return!"

Umiko, a permanent crease between his eyebrows and wearing a serious frown, beseeched his friend to listen. "It is time to make peace, for the sake of the tribe. You are chief, well respected and needed. At one time we didn't know your true purpose, but it's clear to us Gale brought you here because he knew you would bring us into a new era, as he has said all along."

"It is true, I have returned to help you." Gale spoke directly to Finn. "I apologize for the circumstances of your long-ago journey here, but my intentions were just. I have watched you all these years, and in your honor I have brought you a gift—a short-faced bear." As if on cue, the bear stood on its hind legs to reach the top of the twelve-foot cage.

"Please, allow Gale to stay and talk with you, with the council," Umiko reasoned.

Suddenly, Taura spoke at Finn's shoulder. "I agree with Umiko. Let's hear him out." Taura projected his voice, engaging the dockworkers, who joined in.

"It would be good to have a Linker again," a worker commented. Several more voiced agreement.

Finn felt just as caged as the bear that now huffed and sniffed, its black eyes watchful. Finn's mind raced with questions; foremost was why Umiko of all people would bring this untrustworthy Linker back into the tribe. No matter his reasoning—he'd broken the law.

Feeling deceived but knowing he must keep his cool and stay rational despite what the Linker had done, Finn said, "Very well, we will speak privately." Finn turned, and without hesitation his hunters, excluding Taura and Umiko, surrounded Gale and escorted him inside. Finn refused to allow his apprehension and annoyance to show. Instead he met the eyes of his people and winked at several females who caught his attention as he walked past.

Outside, the enormous cage was being maneuvered off the barge. It took a dozen men and a rolling mechanism to lift the cage carrying the monstrous bear onto the dock. Gale's warriors were directed to roll it to a nearby courtyard for all to ogle. Finn was well known for hunting this species, the largest of the bears, but he'd never returned with a live one. Teeth and hides where all the crowd had ever seen.

Rattled by the excitement, the bear roared from its prison, causing onlookers to cheer and whistle.

3

The Human Realm

Kodiak stood with his hands on his hips looking out at the ocean, the breeze ruffling his hair. This was the first chance he'd had to return to this site on the bluff since they had crossed the realms. He tried to pinpoint exactly where the portal lay under the sea, where two weeks ago he'd passed through the human threshold. He hadn't understood how the smoke from three herbs could physically warp a body to another place—and, more strangely, to a place underwater. Perhaps, he thought, that was why humans didn't cross. Humans couldn't hold their breath as long as the Aquapopulean coastal clans. *Like me—like I was before.* He'd left his home choking and feeble, thinking he was going to die, only to wake up in a human realm, where he found he couldn't hold his breath underwater for long. That terrified him. He sighed in wonder at how it all worked. Would his condition eventually change? *Who am I without my Diver's ability?*

That eventful day when Kodiak and Harmony had passed through the portal and swum safely to shore they'd clung together, grateful just knowing they had survived the perilous trip. When they reached the hilltop they learned what had caused the earthquake and massive chaos in his realm. The hulking yellow construction equipment that loomed behind him on the bluff was to blame, not only for the partial demolition of an abandoned hotel but for sending a pulse of destruction that penetrated the portal, killing hundreds of people.

Within a day after the crossing Kodiak had taken ill, a bizarre sickness he'd never experienced before.

Harmony nursed him, staying by his side for days. After the fever broke and his dizziness and nausea were under control, they'd discussed his symptoms. Harmony's great-great-grandfather, Calder, had warned them about the ill effects the portal had on the body. They presumed Kodiak's illness was a result of the crossing, though Harmony hadn't experienced any adversity.

Back on his feet, Kodiak felt revived and more like himself. Late one afternoon, Harmony suggested they return to the Wentworth-by-the-Sea. She said, "We will go inside the hotel after the construction workers go home for the day."

Turning away from the sea, he searched for his wife, Harmony, who had wandered over to take pictures of the teardown with her camera. Most of the hotel was gone; flattened piles of splintered wood and rubble remained. Kodiak's brows drew together when he saw her standing on the bucket of an excavator, hanging on to the hydraulic cylinder, stretching her arm to get a better angle with the camera she held. *She is going to fall. Her obsession with this place is going to get her hurt*, he thought as he trudged across the grass in a huff. His thoughts flashed back to the time when Harmony had fallen from a tree branch into a swamp and was nearly eaten by a gigantic alligator. Kodiak had dived in to rescue her.

Rushing now into the street, he was forced to jump back, startled by a passing car horn. Kodiak hadn't been in this realm long enough to learn he must look both ways before crossing the street; these fast-moving vehicles were infinitely more dangerous than the bikes in his realm.

At the blast of the car horn, Harmony jumped down, landing in mud. The late April rain had left dimples of mud puddles everywhere. She hopped from dry spot to dry spot, calling his name as she went.

"You have to be careful crossing the street, Kodi!" she scolded when she reached him.

"Right. You be careful too. I saw you up there." He rebuked.

She waved at him, whether to get him away from the road or dismiss his comment, he didn't know. He followed her past several chain-link fence sections that were stacked up like flapjacks. They skirted around them, keeping their distance from their spiky edges. The investment company that had recently purchased the hotel had torn away eighty percent of the edifice. Efforts to board up the gigantic hole in the building's side were underway. It was no problem for the two of them to slip through.

"So this is what's left?" Harmony's voice was solemn and dejected.

It appeared to Kodiak that gutting efforts had started. "You said this part is going to be rebuilt, right?"

Harmony retrieved two flashlights from her jacket pocket and handed one to Kodiak. When he just stared at it, she reached over and switched his on before turning on her own. "Yeah, according to my friends at the preservation group, this big conglomerate proposes to reopen the hotel. I only hope it's true." She sighed.

"Why wouldn't it be true? It would solve the problem of future disturbances with the portal so close, wouldn't it? Calder said this land should remain sacred so positive energy will help maintain the balance between the duel realms. Perhaps a new building would be a positive addition."

Harmony lifted a shoulder and made a face. "I don't know, Kodi. I think there is more to this mysterious energy then we know." She poked her toe at some crumbled plaster on the floor. "You know, this isn't the first company to propose this idea. Every company that gets its hands on this property wants to divide it up and build condos. They just don't get it," she griped. "This place is a historical gem."

Kodiak remembered the evening they came ashore after crossing the realms. When they had crested the bluff, he had watched shock and agony contort his wife's beautiful face. This Victorian-era hotel, the Wentworth-by-the-Sea, had essentially brought them together. Harmony had found a satchel hidden in its decaying walls, a satchel containing the herbs that gripped her very essence and warped her through the portal into Kodiak's world. Somehow she had found her way to him, into his heart. He knew they'd both struggled to find a way to make their unusual relationship to work.

"I'll show you where I found Calder's satchel. This way."

She chattered about the past glories of the Wentworth-by-the-Sea. Kodiak plodded along beside her, listening to her history lesson in silence, hearing the nostalgia in her voice. They avoided loose debris on the stairs and aimed their flashlights around the dark hallways. Harmony paused outside a doorway, identical to several they'd passed already. On the upper floor she turned to look at him. Her hair, tousled by the wind, rested over the bulky jacket she wore. The last rays of evening light caught the outermost strands, illuminating them in gold.

"The satchel was in this room, in the wall," she said, her voice small in the silent room. She moved out of the sunlight into the shadows.

At the wall, Kodiak angled his flashlight to reveal the hole. "So Calder stashed the bag in the wall for safekeeping?"

"Yes, he said he traveled in the human realm with the herbs on his person at all times. The herbs can be used over and over again. Somehow they don't fully burn away. These were extra, you know, in case he lost or something happened to the ones he carried." Harmony drifted to the window, and Kodiak moved there with her.

"Hey," he began, hesitation in his voice. "I know there is so much more to your realm and I'm curious to see it, but if this place is now secure—if the threat is gone—we could go back." When her eyes widened at his suggestion, he reached for her and pulled her into his arms.

Harmony's eyes were full of concern, and she spoke with fervor. "You were so sick after... It's too dangerous." A long blink seemed to shift her thoughts. "And besides, Kodi, this renovation will take time. We can't even think about leaving before it is finished. What about the rest of this island? What if something else causes other disturbances?"

He was instantly sorry he'd worried her. "Of course. I didn't mean right away. We'll take this one step at a time. And in the meantime we can get to know one another much better." He dropped his mouth to hers, taking extra care to coax away her anxiety and replace it with ease and pleasure. Her stiff lips spoke volumes about her worries, but he persisted. Sliding his fingers down the back of her thick coat, he gave a soft groan when his hands contacted the backside of her jeans. He clutched her to him. Harmony yielded and slipped her arms around his neck.

Tasting her mouth again after several weeks was rapidly driving his arousal. He broke free of their intensifying kisses and said, "Let go back to your dwelling."

She laughed, and he captured her mouth again, but she eased away long enough to suggest, "Let's get dinner in town first. I want to show you around."

The side of his mouth lifted and he said suggestively, "I'm famished." She laughed again and shook her head, landing a playful punch on his chest.

"I'm serious, Kodi. You've been here two weeks and haven't even left my house until now."

Over the next several weeks, Harmony took him around the area, touring small towns and big cites. Kodiak Night found living in the human realm vastly different from life in the Aquapopulean realm. The population density was staggering, overwhelming. His race only inhabited a fraction of their earth. Riding in a car took some getting used to, and he gripped the door handle during highway driving, especially when they were surrounded by city traffic in Boston. The humans reminded him of the people of the Forest Tribes, always building, hunting, taking from the land. In this realm glass and steel skyscrapers replaced stone fortresses. He commented, "Humans seem ambitious, eager to gain riches while ignoring the sacredness of the earth and a simple life."

"We're not all bad!" she jested, but humor didn't reach her eyes. She promised he would like the next place on her tour. The famous eatery, Faneuil Hall, served up a variety of foods, including assortments of meat that made him wrinkle his nose in distaste. The clans were vegetarians, unlike the tribespeople. However, something called fudge tasted amazing. When they toured the well-known sites in Boston later, Kodiak confessed he liked the swan boats best.

Each evening, after a day full of mindboggling information, Kodiak settled into bed with his wife. Those hours made the crossing and his personal sacrifice worth it. He was with the woman he loved; now he needed to adjust to her world.

Kodiak was eager to get back into the water again. Fortunately, Harmony's house backed up to the bay, so he consistently slipped out for early morning swims. These excursions only proved what he feared. He had lost his most valuable ability, the ability to hold his breath for twenty-four minutes, the ability that meant everything to him. It was who he was. Because of it he could stake his claim in his clan community as a Diver, the best-skilled underwater performer. His ancestral coastal race shared this natural ability, though many could only hold their breath half as long as Kodiak could.

Every day for months he tried and tried to remain under, but something was wrong. It was as if he were merely...human. He wondered why. Had a god cursed him? Two months passed before he finally brought his loss up with Harmony.

On a warm June morning, Kodiak watched his wife arranging breakfast dishes on the porch table while he was toweling off. Earlier, when he'd left for his swim, Harmony was putting the corn muffins in the oven, a human recipe he'd come to love. His words tumbled out. "Harmony, I don't know why or how, but I seem to have lost something of myself."

She looked up with concern. "What is it, Kodi?"

For a moment he wasn't sure he wanted to say anything more—he almost regretted bringing it up. He liked their simple routine of a back-porch breakfast, watching the birds; he didn't want to ruin it. He'd read about birds, but they didn't exist in his world. They'd only evolved in the human realm. He glimpsed a tiny finch and paused to collect his thoughts.

He mustered a smile for her sake, but as he sat in the white wicker chair, he let out a harsh sigh. "I can't seem to hold my breath for very long. Only a few minutes. Something happened to me when I crossed."

"When you crossed? But you've been swimming for weeks." He could see she was trying to understand why he'd kept this from her.

"I didn't tell you before because I was hoping it would come back or redevelop. I felt different right after we came through the portal. But after all this time nothing has changed. I don't know what else to try." He shrugged.

Harmony's eyes filled with tears, and she swallowed hard before whispering, "I'm so sorry. This is all my fault. If you had just stayed—"

"No, this is not your fault." He leaned in, placing his hand over hers, the webs between his fingers visible. "You need to stop blaming yourself for everything. Things happen. I just wanted you to know, that's all."

She nodded, and he asked for a muffin and changed the subject. He was here now, living in the other realm with a new wife. He had to adjust to everything. Losing his ability was like losing a part of his heritage, and it made his home seem that much farther away. But he resolved to put that behind him for now and focus on the beautiful woman who sat across from him. After all, he'd crossed a realm for her.

4

Late one evening, Harmony bustled around in the kitchen making dinner while Kodiak flipped through the television channels. Kodiak was fascinated with television. She'd convinced him to take another trip into the city, and they had gone back to Boston to visit the New England Aquarium. She explained to him that this was a place for people to learn about underwater animals and aquatic life, but Kodiak's experience of the true meaning of captivity left him frustrated and solemn. They had argued on the ride home. He thought it cruel, but she pointed out humans weren't adapted to underwater breathing, nor were they impervious to the cold like the Aquapopuleans. Although she knew it was hard for Kodiak to adjust to this crazy overcrowded human world, at the same time she was tired of feeling like he believed where he came from was superior. Normal couples fought, but their differences were complicated. How would they work through them? He was right that she needed to stop blaming herself for his crossing. She did love him, and she wanted him here with her, no matter the cost.

Arriving home, they'd walked through the door after a long silence and regarded one another. Her eyes roved over his handsome face; his copper-flecked eyes glowed intently at her.

"Kodi, I'm sorry we argued." Her passionate voice seemed to do him in, and they rushed together, kissing, clinging—forgiving.

After an hour or so of make-up time, they retrieved the bedding that had slipped to the floor and untangled the sheets so they could put the bed back together. Kodiak tugged at the bedpost, shifting the bed back into place. Harmony gathered papers that had scattered across her floor. The folder that had held them had been knocked from her desk when a shirt was flung across the surface. She pranced around in her underwear until she finally discovered her shorts out in the hallway.

Relaxed and sated, they grinned at each other, holding hands as they walked down the stairs. "I'll make some dinner. You find us something to watch." That was twenty minutes ago.

"Harmony! Come look at this!"

"What is it, babe?" Harmony appeared, concern on her face.

"It's a shipwreck. They're running a special on a rig carrying iron ore that sank in Lake Superior. Have you ever heard of the *SS Edmund Fitzgerald*?"

"Yeah, there's a song about it." She stood watching him engrossed in the program. She saw in him, at that moment, a glimpse of his old self. He was as giddy as a child with a new toy. This television special about a sunken ship seemed to open up the possibilities to him of what could be hidden in the waters of this world.

"You know, I'd love to be able to do that, to find stuff underwater like I used to. What's cool is that this realm has machines that can go much deeper than I could ever swim. Look at that equipment!" He muttered to himself.

Harmony sat beside him. Hardly glancing at the broadcast, she tucked his shaggy hair behind his ear and leaned her torso against his arm. His hand instinctively found her thigh. "Babe, I'm sorry if you miss what you left behind."

Kodiak swiveled his head to look at her and reached to caress her cheek. "Don't be. I'd do it again in a heartbeat." He stretched to press a tender kiss on her mouth. "It's just I need to find something to do here. Doing something like *that*," he pointed to the screen, "would be incredible."

"Okay. Well, I just happen to know someone who was part of the *Titanic* diving expedition, Mrs. Coombs from the preservation group. Well, not her, her son. I can make a phone call if you like."

"Sure, but what is the *Titanic*?"

***

That evening, Kodiak watched Harmony as she moved around the bedroom. She had not been his wife for long, and as far as the rest of the humans in this realm knew, they'd met and eloped while Harmony was away on an extended vacation. The lavender pearl ring she wore, had always worn, was now her wedding ring. He'd gotten more than he'd bargained for that day when she solicited his help on the beach. He'd risked his life on that journey, gathering the herbs from sea-serpent infested waters, the dangerous swamp, and the bear-guarded field. Eventually, he'd earned the ultimate prize, his beautiful wife.

True, he had not wanted to leave his realm and take the perilous journey into the human world, but he'd had no choice. Harmony was going back, and he couldn't be without her. No woman had ever made him feel the way she did. He'd had his fair share of girlfriends, but Harmony was the most beautifully exotic and sweetly loving woman he had ever known.

Harmony finished her shower and now wore her fluffy pink robe. He frowned, unable to see any part of her alluring shape. Her voluminous hair was dry and piled on her head. He was about to call her to bed, but she released her hair and picked up her hairbrush. He loved watching her brush her long blond tresses. Mesmerized, he pictured running his fingers through it. Catching him staring at her in the mirror, Harmony lifted the corners of her pouty mouth.

He lay back, waiting for her to come to him, allowing the anticipation to build. When she turned toward him his heart squeezed with emotion. "Take that thing off and come over here." His voice was husky; he could feel the rise and fall of his chest quicken.

Laughter rumbled in her throat. She abandoned her hairbrush, setting it on the dresser. Stepping to the bed, she placed her hands on the end of the mattress at his feet. Lifting one knee onto the bed, she moved forward slightly and placed her other knee on the bed. She poised on all fours, straddling his long legs in her small bed. He lifted his foot, and his big toe managed to loosen the tie of her belt. The robe was dangerously close to opening, threatening to reveal her flawless skin. At her outraged huff, he smiled gleefully. She advanced like a prowling cat, stopping with her head above his bare chest, her knees straddling his thighs. He lifted his hand to touch her soft hair, but she eased back on her heels, dropping her head to his belly. His hand paused in midair, heart thudding, waiting for what she was going to do next.

Her sweet, innocent eyes held his. But soon the innocent look evaporated, replaced by a wicked gleam. She parted her lips and dropped wet kisses onto his stomach. His body was slightly lifted as if doing a crunch, allowing her to kiss each rippled muscle. Her hair tickled his smooth chest. More kisses scorched above the band of his boxers. Her kisses torturously moved up his torso. When he felt her heavy breasts against his chest, he groaned and plunged his hands into her hair, trying to drag her mouth closer to his. She wiggled, slithering against him. He sucked in a breath.

She held herself above him, again on all fours, pressing her hands into the soft mattress and framing his handsome face. The pink robe hung open. All was his for the taking. He repositioned his hands in the hair that hung on his chest so his fingers slipped deeper through it. She shuffled her position slightly so she could lean down and kiss his mouth. The kiss was soft and slightly hesitant. He liked the way she made him suffer. It made his blood boil more ferociously. His hands reached to touch where her robe was parted. She sat back at his touch, pressing against his lap. He watched her grin wickedly, knowing and loving what she was doing to him. *The minx!* He slid his hands inside the robe, filling his palms. The robe slipped from her shoulders, and she slithered her arms free. While his eyes feasted on her, his hands moved over her ribcage, feeling every bone. They traced the flare of her hips and the slender curve of her belly. His finger outlined her belly button then slowly, steadily rose through the valley of her breasts until his hand held the column of her neck. His other hand captured hers caressing his thigh. Her back was slightly arched.

He pulled her down to him, capturing her mouth again. As he clung to her for dear life, he moaned her name between broken kisses. Maybe she sensed his urgency and longing—something made her lift her head. Her lips were parted and swollen from his assault; her eyes questioned him.

There was something he wanted to say. Though they were wed and would be building a life together in this realm, they hadn't spoken much of their feelings for each other. Meeting and marrying someone in scarcely a week's time was unusual, yet the attraction they'd felt for one another from the start was undeniable. He'd known for a while that he was in love with her. Coming here and getting to know her better only confirmed it. He slid his hand into her golden locks again, caressing her back.

"Harmony." She became still, waiting for him to continue. "You are so exquisite," he whispered. She lowered her lashes at his praise.

"Hey," he coaxed, and her eyes met his again. "I want you to know, crossing a realm for you was nothing compared to the way I feel about you. I love you."

A wide smile filled her face. "And I love you."

5

Harmony's heart was pounding as she descended the stairs. Someone was milling around in her kitchen and it wasn't Kodiak, who was sprawled, asleep, in her bed. As she tiptoed closer, the squeak from an old floor board in the hallway gave her away.

"Good, you're up." Samantha Finch sniffed, setting a frying pan on the stove with a clank.

"Sam, holy shit! What are you doing here? I thought you were shooting in Malaysia?" Harmony clutched her chest, as if to slow her pounding heart. She was relieved; her oldest and dearest friend wasn't a burglar. Samantha's eyes were red rimmed, and the corners of her mouth turned down. A grocery bag sat on the counter along with a gallon of milk, a carton of eggs, and a loaf of English muffins.

"I was!" Samantha replied indignantly. She added flippantly, "And good morning to you too."

Harmony collected her frazzled nerves and moved to hug her best friend. "I'm sorry, Sam, you just scared me." She mumbled the half-truth. Her brain was racing for answers to questions she knew Samantha would soon be asking, like "Where have you been?" and "Why haven't you returned my calls?"

Sensing something was amiss, Harmony pulled back from their lingering hug. Samantha usually sprang back first, always eager to talk directly. This time, Harmony was asking the questions; the tables had turned. "What's going on? Why *are* you home?"

Samantha turned toward the stove, adjusting the pot she'd just set there. Her composure slipped, and her expression crumpled. "When I got back to the shoot after my visit home, I caught David hooking up with someone. When I went to Rudy, the producer, to tell him I couldn't work with David after what had happened, Rudy made a pass at me! When I *refused* him—he fired me!"

Harmony embraced her friend again and called the producer unladylike names until Samantha laughed at her vulgar vocabulary.

Separating from her friend, Samantha produced a genuine smile and reached for a tissue. "I tried calling you, but I couldn't seem to reach you." After a loud blow she gave Harmony a questioning look.

Harmony sighed. "I've been in another world." The real meaning of that statement was lost on Samantha, who nodded and reached for the coffeepot. Harmony watched her pour, realizing she'd smelled coffee brewing when she came down the stairs. *What burglar would brew coffee?*

"I can't believe that asshole cost me my job." Handing Harmony the mug, Samantha suddenly went still, and her eyes grew round. "What was that?"

Harmony held her breath as she listened to Kodiak trot down the stairs. When Samantha's eyes cut to Harmony's face, her expression changed from concern to wonder. All Harmony could do was smile sheepishly. She was caught with her hand in the cookie jar; her friend's jaw dropped when Kodiak entered the room.

"Hello." He seemed surprised to see a guest but recovered with an endearing smile.

"Aahh, I see why you were so hard to reach," Samantha said slyly to Harmony. Then she sidestepped her friend and thrust her hand out. "Hi, I'm Samantha Finch, Harmony's *best* friend."

"This is Kodiak Night." Harmony slipped her hand into the crook of his elbow. "He is… Well, he's my husband."

"Ha. Ha. So funny."

Kodiak slung his arm around Harmony's shoulder and bent to kiss her good morning. She stretched her arm around his waist, and their mouths touched with familiarity.

"First of all, I've been gone for less than three months, hardly enough time to meet someone, fall in love, and get married. And secondly, I will kick your ass if you got married and didn't invite me to the wedding." Samantha ended this statement with her arms crossed over her chest.

"It's complicated," Harmony apologized. She could see hurt and confusion written all over Samantha's face.

"Try me."

After Harmony loaded the toaster with English muffins, and the trio sat at the table.

Sipping her coffee, Harmony glanced at Kodiak, hoping he'd let her do the talking. She started off in a shaky voice. "So... Remember that satchel I found inside the wall at the Wentworth-by-the-Sea? Remember you thought those dried herbs were tea leaves?"

"Of course." Samantha set her elbows on the table, intent on what Harmony was saying.

"Days after you left, I was looking at them, and I accidently set them on fire. They smoked oddly, and I blacked out."

The toaster popped. Kodiak moved around the kitchen. He placed the forgotten milk and eggs into the refrigerator and took out the orange juice. Harmony's eyes followed him while she spoke.

"What were they?" Samantha sounded surprised. Her eyes also followed Kodiak around the kitchen.

"Sam, this is going to sound strange. I wasn't hallucinating." Harmony paused, not sure if she could tell the bizarre story. Her eyes drifted to Kodiak, leaning against the counter as he chewed his muffin methodically.

34

"The herbs are a blend of three very hard to gather ingredients found in a world separate from ours. *The herbs* somehow transported me through a portal into another realm. There are dual realms. The other is similar but different, and that is where I went for six weeks. After I blacked out here I woke up in the ocean of the other realm. So much happened." Her mind racing for the right words, she rushed on. "It took a while, but eventually I was able to come back here." Harmony waited for a reaction.

Samantha turned her head slowly over her right shoulder to gaze at Kodiak, and then she turned back to Harmony. She flung her hands in the air as she said, "Okay, you got me! I'm no stranger to practical jokes." She stood and reached for the refrigerator handle.

"Samantha, she is not jesting. My home was in the other realm, where we met. Harmony is special. Special for many reasons, but one way in particular links her to my realm."

"It's true!" Harmony said, leaning back in the chair, hugging her elbows. "He's talking about my other family. And there is something about all the drownings—my grandmother and my parents. I would not joke about their deaths." Her last remark seemed to ring true with Samantha.

"What about your other family?" Samantha raised her eyebrows.

Harmony was relieved when Samantha gave her the opportunity to continue. "Two things. I am distantly related to the people in the other realm. It turns out one of them was here in 1905 during the peace treaty signing. He stayed at the Wentworth. As you know, my great-great-grandmother, Pearl, worked on staff at the Wentworth at that time. Apparently they fell in love and she got pregnant, but he left to return to his world."

"So there is another world, with other people, and

35

they come visit us, like aliens?" The corner of Samantha's mouth turned up as she tried to put a light spin on Harmony's story.

Harmony rolled her eyes at Samantha's assessment. "Not like aliens! And only a select few have journeyed over throughout the ages. They aren't supposed to have relationships with us. They are here as observers." Harmony caught Kodiak's stiff movement out of the corner of her eye at her comment about *them* not having relationships with humans. She blurted, "But it's different for Kodi and I." She moved from her chair to stand at his side and slipped her hand into his. His reassuring smile immediately set her at ease. He'd sacrificed so much for her, the thought of hurting him left her feeble with worry. Especially after he'd endearingly pronounced his love for her last night. She gazed into his copper-flecked eyes. Samantha couldn't miss how luminescent they were.

"And...the other thing? You said there were two things." Samantha's impatience brought Harmony back to her explanation.

"Yes, that's right. There is a god, a water god—he's the mystery in my nightmares."

Samantha nodded, acknowledging the nightmares.

"He's real, Sam. That day when my mother fell through the ice and drowned—I was there. I fell in too, though no one ever told me. I had repressed the memory. The newspaper never printed that a five-year-old girl also fell into the river. They only reported my mother's drowning." Kodiak ran his hand up and down her arm, hoping to soothe her. "I saw him, that day, under the ice. He reached for me, but he couldn't take me. I saw him swim away and take with my mother deeper. And then someone pulled me from the river."

Samantha held her hand to her mouth and choked, "That's awful. I'm sorry."

"I think he has taken all my family members. It explains why each one of them drowned." She knew that as strange as it sounded that a water god had drowned her mother, father, grandfather, and finally her grandmother last year, it just couldn't be a coincidence.

The girls hugged. Feeling secure that Samantha believed her, Harmony suggested Kodiak go for his morning swim. She could handle the conversation from here without his hovering.

"Take out the eggs, and we'll make breakfast," she directed Samantha before she walked Kodiak out to the porch. He gathered her close, and her arms slipped around his neck.

"I won't be long." He planted a lingering kiss on her mouth.

Harmony buried her nose against his neck, inhaling the salt and sand scent that was her husband. "Take as long as you like. We'll probably talk for a while."

"Maybe just to the Isle of Shoals and back."

She snapped her head back and eyed him beseechingly. "Be careful." She knew his ability was gone; there were many boats, too many dangers in those deep waters.

The smile tugging at his lips drove her mad with desire, and she greedily kissed him. "Or...I...could...stay," he said between kisses.

"No! I'll see you later." She stole one last kiss before she watched him trot down the porch steps and slip behind the overgrown bushes where, undetected, he could enter the river that flowed into the sea.

Inside, Samantha stood waiting for her at the stove; eggs sizzled in the pan. "Wow," she said, "I can see why you married him—what a hottie."

Over fried eggs, Harmony recounted a vague version of her experiences. She left a considerable amount out because it just seemed too unreal—swamps with alligators in New York, sea serpents and sirens she could burn or deflect. No, instead she told Samantha about falling in love with Kodiak and how they'd married in a majestic Romanesque-style city built completely of granite. And that her precious lavender pearl ring now had a deeper meaning as her wedding ring.

"I can't believe you're married."

"I'm surprised your dad didn't mention it."

"We haven't talked much over the phone. He's busy with his girlfriend, and besides, when he picked me up from Logan last night, the conversation was all about whether or not I could sue the production company for harassment." Samantha rolled her eyes. "I don't want any more drama. I just want a fresh start."

"I'm glad you're home, Sam, I missed you. With you living next door it will be easy to hang out again—that is, until something else comes along to whisk you away." Harmony floated her hand in the air, knowing her friend wasn't one to linger in this small town.

Samantha shrugged and half smiled.

"So what happened with David the dickhead?"

Samantha drew in a long deep breath before she poured out her saga with David and why she was now home with no prospects.

6

The Aquapopulean Realm

More than a decade had passed since Gale last stood in this cozy council chamber. He had served two tribal chieftains before his exile, and now he hoped to serve his last. Life expectancy for the average Aquapopulean was one hundred forty years, and he estimated he had little time left. Though he should have another ten years or so to prosper, that wouldn't be his fate. He was dying. He persevered to stay strong until the end and prided himself on his physical health, endurance, and dexterity. Even now he was able to spar with the warriors and not be beaten too badly. At his age he considered himself more the tutor, drawing from his experiences when he'd fought in human combat at one time or another.

A large trestle table dominated the room, a surface previously used for map making. The maps aided the expansion of the fortress city and its assets. Finn stood behind the table, making clear the space separating them was necessary. They were alone in the wood-paneled room.

"Why have you returned from exile? What is it you want from us?" Finn's baritone voice projected throughout the room.

A natural commander, thought Gale.

"I know you harbor hatred for me, Finn. But I couldn't leave you in the human realm. I knew one day you would grow strong, capable, and you would rule. With my help we can build a world better than any human city or nation. I've got the technology we need and you have the loyalty of the tribe and coastal clans, and of course there is your miraculous ability."

"Why would I want your help, especially after you abducted me from my family? I was alone here, a child...with no protection," he accused.

Gale paused, giving him a long, hard look. He remembered when he'd taken the boy, how he'd imagined raising him, educating him, and bonding with him, but the tribe forbade it. They were already exasperated that he'd been intimately involved with a human woman. And they couldn't send the boy back—humans couldn't know about their society. They feared Finn would tell.

Gale revealed his thoughts. "It's a miracle you were conceived. A miracle you were gifted with great powers."

"Why me? What made me so special?"

"Finn, you must remember me. You must know why you are different."

Finn's hands rose in defense. "Yes, I'm different—I have the ability to control the weather. I can only figure the reason is because I'm human in the Aquapopulean realm. But I didn't know about the ability when you first brought me here. You're telling me what...you knew I'd develop this powerful energy?"

"No. I only knew that you were conceived by a human woman with an Aquapopulean man. Such a birth had never been documented." Gale watched emotions buckle Finn's brow and tug at the corner of his mouth. Finn was remembering *something*.

"I had human parents," Finn insisted.

"Your mother was human. That man wasn't your father."

"That day you took me, you argued with my mother," Finn said. Gale watched anger flash in Finn's green eyes, his voice gruff. "That day...I know you hurt her. Did you kill her?" His lips pinched in pain, but his glare never faltered.

"Ahh, the lovely and fair Mary Falk." A vision of the only woman who ever meant anything to Gale flashed before his eyes. Her flaxen hair gleamed, wrapped like an abundant shawl around her narrow shoulders. The tall beauty had green eyes, a green the color of northern pine trees. Freckles lightly spattered the bridge of her nose, and the corners of her mouth rounded at him in a way that promised him something. She had bewitched him from the moment he saw her. Gale had first laid eyes on her in Stockholm, where he was meeting with Swedish scientists. He became involved with Mary despite every warning his conscience flagged. He didn't have the luxury to stay with her because of who he was…what he was. Everything changed when she became pregnant with his child.

"Your mother betrayed me, Finn." Gale began to pace while Finn maintained a defensive stance, white knuckles propped against the dark wood table.

"You see, at one time I loved her very much." Gale paused, but Finn didn't so much as blink. "She knew I traveled for my *elusive job*, though she didn't know fully what I did or where I came from. Mary tolerated my constant absences for a while. But after you were born she became more demanding. When you were four she told me not to come back if I wasn't interested in being a father." He continued to pace, ignoring his stiff leg, the one that caused his slight limp. "As a Linker I was marked, selected by nature, to serve the Aquapopulo. I had no choice. I had to go. However, after we argued, I went back within the week to tell her I'd bring her to my home, where we could always be together, but she was gone. She took you and left Sweden. Left without any information about where she was going. I looked for you for eight years." His voice lowered, and he bit out, "Mary hid my son away from me for eight years!"

"Lies!" Finn growled.

"No, Finn—she was the liar!" Gale roared back, fists clenched at his sides. His next words were quieter, but still harsh. "She told me she loved me. When I finally found you she was with another man. She told me she didn't want me any longer, and when I tried to explain again that I would take her home with me to this realm, she called me crazy. The man you knew wasn't your father—he was a pretender. A pretender with my mate. I returned several times to see you, but she didn't want me in your life. So finally that day…that day I took you home… Well, when that pretender rushed in when your mother screamed, I wounded him. I wanted to hurt her then, but I left her there, crying over the bleeding body of a thief."

"There is no way I'm your son."

"You are, Finn, and I know you can feel it. Your abilities are strong because of your mixed blood. You are capable of so much. Let me help you, *my son*." They stared each other down, until Gale tried another tactic.

"You have her eyes. And when you were little you had blond hair like hers." Gale noted its darkness now. "She called you 'scout' because you were always curious, scouting about in the woods." Gale's mouth twitched at the painful images. Those memories were locked away for a reason.

Finn spun away, knowing his expression betrayed his determination to lock this man out of his past. Gale had provided the key to unlock his memories. Finn moved across the room and looked out the window, not seeing the views, instead picturing his mother calling for him; "Scout, time for dinner." Though he'd lived in a small American town, his mother always spoke with an accent, different from others, though he never heard her speak another language. His hardworking and kind dad taught him to play baseball and cheered him at games. But those memories were hazy after so long. Finn now recognized the demon that led him astray. *My father is Gale the Linker!* Maybe it explained the feeling in his gut that told him he was beyond human—beyond the race of the Aquapopulo. When he became aware of his ability, he'd envisioned himself elevated to the level of Suijin, the water god. He struggled all his life not only to fit in but to become something worthy.

"If what you say is true, then my mother could still be alive." Finn chose not to mention Mary's husband. And he was again haunted by his decisions. He could have gone back with Harmony and looked for his mother.

"I don't know whether or not she still lives. I have not passed through the realms in many years. One suffers greatly with each pass, sometimes with long-lasting sicknesses or pains. There are many dangers. This," Gale ran his index finger along the scar that stretched from the corner of his left eye to the missing lobe of his left ear, "was caused by materializing too close to a shark as I passed through the portal. I managed to gut the shark with the knife hidden in my boot, before my face was bitten off."

Finn's darker thoughts pulsed. *If you'd died, then at least I would have believed a good man was my father.*

"With you as chieftain, the half-human boy *I* brought to the tribe, there is no longer just cause to keep me in exile. We mustn't allow the past to hold us back, Finn. Tell the tribe who I am. We can reunite and make a powerful duo."

Finn hated to admit that Gale's case couldn't be held against him any longer. The council members wanted to hear him out, and after all was said, Gale the Linker was a legend. His knowledge was vast, his insight keen, and his methods got results. It was because of him that the tribal grounds grew to become the great city that it was today. The main stone fortress had stood for thousands of years, but the innovations within its walls were credited to Gale and the knowledge he had brought from the other realm. Many people at the time, after the exile sentence was past, wanted their Linker back and had taken out their frustrations on Finn, excluding him, shorting him on goods, or ignoring him altogether—until later, when he'd earned his place among them.

After everything that had happened between them, could he tell the tribe that Gale was his father? Gale had kept his paternal secret, but why? Finn figured Gale had broken one law by bringing over a human. He would have broken two laws if they knew he was involved with a human woman. He wondered how often these cross-the-realm love affairs had happened. They weren't documented—this behavior rarely was. After all, Harmony Parker was proof that pregnancies were viable between mixed-race parents.

"Just because it's true it doesn't mean I accept it…or that the tribe will accept it. However, I will call a council meeting immediately, and you will have a chance to speak. After that, your fate will be decided," Finn said. He strode to the door and called in a young man who awaited instruction.

"Escort Gale to the main hall, where he can have refreshments, and inform Umiko to gather the council posthaste."

The council gathered later that day. Finn drew his brows together as he surveyed the councilmen and women. Not one seat was empty; they buzzed like springtime bees. The council met for hours, but it only took minutes for Gale's persuasive tongue to convince them of his value. He masterfully steered the conversation to why Finn was brought here in the first place. The Linker spoon-fed the compelling tale, eloquent and epic, to his listeners.

"My son belongs here. It is proven by the extraordinary abilities he possesses. It is time for a son to exonerate his father, now knowing what I've sacrificed for him and for the people of this great city!" Gale grinned triumphantly at their applause. No one seemed to care that Gale had relations with a human woman. The miracle trumped the misdeed.

In other matters, Gale was aided by Umiko and Taura, who boosted issues that were relevant to their people and that Gale had the answers to like advancing their technology. He promised medical advancement in fertility which interested the people. While humans could produce large families, the Aquapopuleans delivered one male and one female.

Finn sat back, brooding, wanting to discredit this man. But he saw the excitement and trust in the eyes of the council. Nakoma, their last leader, had set these people along a path leading to more…more riches, bigger city, more control and influence over the coastal villages. They were now primed for Gale. And Gale knew it.

"I make a motion that you make Gale a councilman, Finn. We could use his wisdom," Umiko urged.

Finn leaned in, and everyone quieted. "I understand your enthusiasm, but a councilman must prove himself. Gale has been away for fifteen years, and much has changed. I'll grant him a trial period to be sure that you, my sensible councilman and women, will approve. I'm sure you understand the wisdom I speak."

Murmurs of agreement rumbled through the assembly. Finn caught the glimmer in Gale's eye, a worthy adversary.

Finn instructed that Gale be giving a room in a common housing area, far away from Finn's own chambers. The man in charge of lodging escorted Gale away. After the majority of the council members left, eager to tell their friends of the incredible return of their Linker and the miraculous discovery that he was their chieftain's father, Finn was approached by Umiko and Taura.

Umiko suggested they head to the pools for a swim and some refreshments. Finn sighed, certain that both the water and spiced brew would help ease his tension. Besides, he wanted to understand why Umiko had a hidden relationship with the exiled Linker. As the three men entered the cool water, it didn't take long for Umiko to speak his mind.

"I am glad that after so long I can tell you what I know," Umiko said honestly. "When Nakoma placed you in the boys' domicile she enlisted me to watch over you. She made me swear to protect you with my life and promised that if I proved myself worthy I would not only continue to be compensated but I'd be fulfilling my ultimate duty to our tribe. I was privileged to know, and sworn to secrecy, that Nakoma and Gale remained in contact. It wasn't until about a year later that Gale took me under his wing. After that, my orders were to report directly to him, both about the tribal affairs and about you and the progress you made as a hunter and citizen. When your abilities became known throughout the tribe, Gale revealed to me that you were his son. He counted on me to ensure your success."

Finn wanted to be mad at his longtime friend. But he knew Umiko was an honor-bound individual. Finn was certain Umiko thought what he'd done was for the ultimate good of the tribe. Still, he had kept secrets. On the fence over what to do about Umiko and his accomplice, Taura, Finn wavered before he decided he would let things lie. Right now, he had more important things to consider, like the upcoming summit hosted by Calder at the Wellness temple on the seacoast. As the thought that Gale would want to attend occurred, Finn sank his head under the water, reveling in the silence.

After their long swim, they lounged on blankets spread in the grass to dry off. Taura remained quiet while Umiko had more to confess. "Nakoma wanted warriors because resistance from the coastal villages was inevitable. They have refused to work the salt mines since our tribes found them thousands of years ago. They want the salt, but they don't want to work for it. That has to change."

Finn sympathized. "They are the original descendants of the water dwellers. They don't want to leave their seacoast area. They are dependent on that lifestyle. We can raise the price of salt. They will have to understand that they need to pay more. I know both councils have spoken about this matter, and price negotiations are being considered." Finn rolled over on his stomach, feeling the glorious heat from the sun's rays penetrate his skin.

"When Nakoma brought hunters to train as warriors, they weren't only taught by the tribes in the south. Those southern tribesmen and women were taught by Gale, who brought the techniques from the other realm," Taura said from his cross-legged position on the blanket next to Umiko's.

Finn felt his blood start to boil. Nakoma allowed Gale's soldiers to train her army, an army *he* was trained in!

7

The Human Realm

The storm that barreled up the east coast had gone out to sea and spared the little New Hampshire town from potential damage. The remnants of the hurricane left lingering showers and cooler temperatures on this late July evening. Harmony and Samantha took Kodiak into the seaport town of Portsmouth, where bars lined the streets. Their favorite bar was jammed with people elbow to elbow and gave off a cheery vibe despite the rain. Samantha knew the bartender, who winked at her as soon as he saw her. He ignored other patrons while he got whatever drinks she wanted. Harmony smiled, remembering the years past. Samantha had always been popular and well known around town.

Samantha waved to some locals hanging out at a corner table. Grabbing their drinks from the bar, the group snugged up to the table. Her friends seemed surprised and excited to see that Samantha had returned. They wanted to know where her exotic travels had taken their resident weather girl. A meteorologist, Samantha had become a local television celebrity before her career took off and she was *discovered*. Harmony was pleased her friend found her calling, but when Samantha was off jet-setting the globe making her dreams a reality, Harmony was often melancholy. Samantha brought light to every room she entered, and when she wasn't present the room sometimes grew dim.

Samantha hugged the other girls and made introductions. Harmony noticed one girl tugging on her boyfriend when his eyes lingered on Samantha. Harmony understood how that girl felt, now that she noticed the girls' lingering stares at her handsome husband. She told herself perhaps Kodiak's strangely luminescent eyes gave them cause.

Harmony turned to one guy, who reached forward to shake her hand and then Kodiak's.

"Mike Coombs." He repeated his name over the din. "I think we've met before. At a Preservation meeting." He scratched at his clipped beard. "Yeah. It's been awhile, but I remember you."

"Right—of course. I know your mom! Mrs. Coombs has done so much for the group." Suddenly Harmony threw her hands in the air remembering she had recently left a phone message for Mrs. Coombs to ask for her son's number but hadn't heard back. "*And* I was just talking to Kodi about you the other night! I told him you were on the *Titanic* expedition a few years ago. He might be interested in doing something like that, something to do with diving." She shrugged.

Mike Coombs seemed thrilled to talk Kodiak's ear off about the experiences and discoveries made on his last *Titanic* expedition in 1986. While Harmony chatted with the girls across the table, she kept an eye on Kodiak. Seeing his continuous cheerfulness made her pleased and relieved. They'd had a rough start.

She overheard Kodiak mentioned that he'd watched a special on the sunken ship the *Edmund Fitzgerald*. Mike went wild with excitement.

"My buddy is gearing up for an expedition for the *Edmund Fitzgerald*. It's happening in the next couple of weeks. I'm trying to go myself. Those guys plan on using the ROV—a highly technical remotely operated vehicle. Hey, if you're interested and looking for work, I'm sure my buddy can get you on that crew too," Mike offered.

"That would be amazing. I'm definitely interested."

Mike raised his beer glass. Kodiak gave Harmony a

sideways glance before raising and clinking his in their private toast. She didn't want to be a killjoy, but she felt it necessary to warn Kodiak to go easy on the beer. After all, he was still a rookie about drinking alcohol in her world.

Later that night, he staggered up the steps to their bedroom. Her warning had gone unheeded. Kodiak was snoring loudly by the time she came out of the bathroom. She slid into bed next to him and reached to smooth the hair from his brow. In the car on the way home, he had said over and over how much he enjoyed hanging out and meeting people, especially Mike. Harmony wondered how much of this enthusiasm was the alcohol talking. The night had been fun for her too, reminding her of old times. It had been awhile since she and Samantha had gone out. The last time was before Samantha left for Malaysia. Yawning, she thought what a lucky coincidence it was that they had run into Mike Coombs. However, the thought of Kodiak going off on an exploration so soon gave her pause. *Surely he won't leave me right now.* She drifted off, thinking about deep water and the ships that lay broken at the bottom of the sea.

It was late morning when Kodiak came into the kitchen, holding his head. "I feel awful." His overgrown hair stuck up in all directions, and his lovely eyes squinted to block the sunny morning.

"You drank too much. You have a hangover." Harmony tried not to smirk; she pressed her fist to her lips.

After pulling out his chair and indicating he should sit, she said, "Don't worry. I'll make you something to feel better."

Soon enough she set black coffee, greasy fried eggs, and toast in front of him.

She kissed his temple. "Eat up."

He looked doubtful at first, but he dug in and eventually finished every bite. After the alcohol was absorbed and his second cup of coffee slurped, Kodiak seemed to return to normal.

Buttering her toast, Harmony listened to Kodiak ardently retell the expedition details that Mike told him last night. "This is exactly what I hoped to find— mysteries and treasures beneath the human sea."

"That's amazing, Kodi," Harmony said supportively, but her heart was twisting. She remembered Mrs. Coombs complaining that her son was gone for months at a time when he'd worked on these expeditions. Kodiak had just crossed into her realm, and he had scarcely experienced life here. She was certain he needed more time to acclimate and adjust to society. They needed more time together. Without her guidance, she worried how he'd handle the vast differences in this realm. *Maybe Mike's connection won't work out,* she thought, *and I am worrying over nothing.*

Suddenly the phone rang. Harmony moved to pick up the receiver. She lost all hope when Mike said, "Hey, Harmony, I've got great news! Is Kodi around?"

Over the next forty-eight hours, Harmony was on edge. Mike's buddy had gotten Mike and Kodiak minor jobs on the expedition; nothing exciting, but it was a foot in the door. She desperately tried to keep her nauseating feelings of impending loneliness, jealousy, and resentment at bay. Despite telling herself she was being ridiculous, she inwardly seethed. *How could he go so soon?* Now that she'd returned to her own realm, she realized she had been clinging to him. Her grandmother's death had left her without family. She *desperately* wanted to belong to a family. It felt like Kodiak was setting her adrift once more. *I don't want to be left alone—again.*

At the airport, the guys booked one-way fares.

Standing by the window, a jet plane looming outside, Harmony tried to hold back her tears. No aircrafts existed in the other realm. Kodiak would first experience flying without her. She thought about going with him, but what would she do when the ship left port? *She* didn't have a job in the expedition.

While turmoil churned inside her, she faked a smile. "Kodi, I want you to be happy. I realize this opportunity gives you access to that underwater life you miss." She knew instantly that Kodiak recognized her diplomatic approach to their farewell.

"*Please* don't worry about me. It's only a few weeks, and I'll come right home to you. I'm not abandoning you. I'm not Calder," he said pointedly.

She blanched. *Abandon* seemed a strong—but accurate—word.

His voice softened. "I just mean… Look, I need to do this. But Harmony, I love you, and nothing will ever change that."

A female voice announced over the intercom that his flight was now boarding.

"I know." Those two words seemed to mend both their apprehensions. She felt his familiar hands slide into her hair. "Be careful. I love you too," she said before she was invaded by his kisses.

Their kissing lasted well into the boarding process. Even Mike gave up on waiting for Kodiak. He waved good-bye to Samantha, who had tagged along, and turned to follow the other passengers down the jetway. Samantha waited for Harmony inconspicuously, leaning against a column, giving the lovers relative privacy. Eventually, Kodiak disappeared down the jetway.

Harmony, her arms crossed tightly over her chest, shuffled across the patterned carpet toward Samantha. "Let's go," she grumbled. Harmony put up a good front before they reached the gate, although tears sparkled in her eyes during their good-byes, but she didn't break down until they sat in her car.

"I know you're worried. But he's a big boy, and he'll figure it out. Kodi loves you. Let him find his way, and he'll come back to you," Samantha cooed. She tried to cheer her. "Besides, I'm here to keep you company while I search for my next gig."

Her words sunk in and spurred a new perspective. Harmony placed her hands on the steering wheel with new resolve. "You're right. And I need to focus on me. I've got to figure out what to do about school—I only have one semester left before I graduate. And I've wanted to work in Boston since I left for architecture school. I should get my life in order," she said emphatically.

"Looks like we're both in transition in our lives," Samantha commented. "Our futures may be uncertain, but for now, how about we go get a drink and toast to new beginnings."

"Well said, my friend." Harmony pulled from the parking lot as they discussed which establishment to drink at.

8

The Human Realm

Passing through the realm was hell on the body, even for the young and strong Linkers. Gale knew passing through at his age could prove disastrous, but bringing Harmony Parker to his son Finn would be worth the chance. Harmony and Finn were the *only* breathing mixed-race people in either realm.

The girl had been afforded tremendous abilities. Harmony's gift to kill sirens and hold off sea serpents would prove valuable, especially since the water god Suijin of their realm commanded them. Perhaps Suijin could be controlled. It was said that the water god could take human form and he had lived among the Aquapopulean people after they began to dwell primarily on land. Those were days long before Gale was born, long before the tribe was formed.

During his long life of one hundred twenty-nine years, Gale had passed through the realms a couple dozen times, probably more than anyone had ever crossed. Most Linkers endured the passage for knowledge, and their egos often led to their demise. He felt he was the exception, destined for greatness. He'd witnessed countless historic events, and love and loss.

He opened his eyes, awareness coming back into his body as he kicked to break the surface. Confirming the familiar coastline, he again slipped under the waves and began the long, mechanical strokes that would bring him closer to land. Although he was a *tribal* Linker, he possessed the ability to hold his breath underwater for about ten minutes. He hadn't lost the evolutionary trait, as the tribesmen had. In the early years, when he'd first passed through, he had panicked, thinking that he'd lost the ability to hold his breath. It took time, but with enough training he was eventually able to reschool his ability. He employed full control now as he glided underwater to a secluded spot along the shore.

Dragging himself out of the water, he dared sit on the beach a few moments catching his breath. Not wanting to be seen, he picked his way through the thick underbrush. Trees secluded the area. Sharp pains, like daggers behind his eyes, caused him to drop into the leaves, where he stayed until he was dry and the pain subsided. Now all he had to do was find a phone book. He already knew Harmony Parker's name and what town she lived in, so it would be easy to find her.

The residential streets were quiet, and he followed them to the only main road in town. There was a phone booth outside the quaint general store, the only retail building on the island.

In no time, Gale stood in the shadows, watching the house when Harmony entered through the back door, her blond ponytail swinging. He ran his palm over his pocket and felt the bulge from the pouch that contained the herbs that would allow him and his guest to return to the other realm.

She made it easy for him by leaving the door unlocked. He slipped inside and prepared to capture her.

***

Samantha Finch let herself into Harmony's house with the hidden key. Harmony wasn't home, Samantha knew, because her car wasn't in the driveway. Last night, Samantha had accidently left her purse there and wanted to retrieve it. In the last two weeks, since Kodiak left, Samantha had kept Harmony company most afternoons, which often stretched into rather late evenings, like last night. Her purse was on the kitchen counter, but she left it untouched as she moved farther into the house. In the living room, she was suddenly overwhelmed with sadness. She plopped onto the worn sofa, surrounded by the décor the couple who'd built a life together in his house had collected. *I miss you, Mrs. Parker.* What Samantha deeply missed was her motherly advice. She'd practically grown up in this house, and Harmony's grandmother had looked out for her. Today was a low point; Samantha had received yet another phone call telling her she wasn't the right fit for a news station. Tears slid down her cheeks. She bent forward, crying into her palms.

When the moment passed, she trudged up the stairs to the washroom. After splashing water on her face, she looked in the mirror. Her eyes were red and puffy. How had her life changed from international television personality to unemployed and broken-hearted in one day? Here she was, back in her small hometown, reliving the day of destruction in her mind for the hundredth time.

That day the weather had been postcard perfect. They were doing a piece on beaches and jungles. She felt confident, rocking her new bikini while shooting her segment in Malaysia. One afternoon, finished with wardrobe earlier than expected, she returned to the hotel room she shared with her boyfriend, David. Samantha walked in to find David in bed with the chunky makeup girl. The startled girl had bounced from the bed, grabbed her dress, which she tried to cover her nakedness with— to no avail—and exited through a connecting door. Apparently David had conveniently arranged for adjoining rooms.

"How could you do that to me!" Samantha practically choked on the bile that rose in her throat. To be so disrespected...insulted...deceived! She stared at him as

David rose from the bed, slipped on a pair of shorts, and ran a hand through his tousled hair. The artsy guy with trendy hair and an indifferent attitude shrugged, making her wonder what she'd ever seen in him.

"Look, Samantha, I'm sorry. I think we need to see other people." After his casual response the pounding in her ears was so loud that when she yelled at him, she didn't think her voice was voluminous enough.

"You *bastard*! You could have told me before you cheated!" Through the lens of her red rage, she saw him wince.

His hands went up in defense as she sent choice words in his direction. "Okay, okay, I get it. You're upset. I'll get my shit and go next door."

Samantha watched him scoop up his travel bag, the one he lived out of because he never bothered to unpack, and then he waltzed to the adjoining door. He tapped with his knuckles. "It's me." The lock clicked, and the door opened an inch. He pushed through without a backwards glance and closed the door. She heard the lock reengage.

The pounding in her ears became a throbbing in her head. Each exhale produced a low sob. Samantha collapsed on the floor, crying. Her runny nose forced her to her feet in search of a tissue.

As if David's betrayal wasn't bad enough, when she went to the producer and told him she wouldn't be able to work with David, she got her second blow of the day.

"Look, Samantha, I had to jump through hoops to get David for this job. He's incredibly talented," said Rudy, the producer.

True, he was a sought-after cameraman; his passive-aggressive personality and open-minded thinking gave him an edge when filming. But this was not what she wanted to hear. While her mind raced, trying to figure out how to make this work, her boss put his arm around her. When she sagged with a heavy sigh, he moved to encircle her in an embrace. His clingy hug felt inappropriate, and when she tried to disengage he held on tighter.

His raspy voice whispered in her ear, "There are a lot of weather girls out there, Samantha, but none as fine as you."

Her skin crawled when his hands skimmed down her back. Suddenly he cupped her behind, and then his fingers reached between her legs, trying to slip into her shorts. She shoved and twisted to get away, but he was quick to clamp his meaty hands around her biceps, jerking her until her head snapped.

"I see this new breakup as an opportunity for you."

"I don't think so!" She swung her fists outward and down in one swift motion, breaking his hold on her. She silently thanked her dad for making her take self-defense classes. "You better stay away from me, Rudy!"

"Now hold on," he warned. "If you want to keep your job... Well, we can work something out. I'm in charge of this production company, you know." She cringed at his smile. His teeth were yellowed from years of smoking, and one tooth tucked strangely behind another. Surely he would apologize for his unprofessional behavior, but instead he raised his eyebrows and offered her a sleazy, crooked smile. She turned and headed for the door, remembering warnings other girls had given her about *both* these men.

Suddenly Rudy grabbed her retreating form, swinging her around, and landed his wet mouth on hers. She reacted. A swift knee thrust to his groin dropped him like a stone.

"You're fired!" he wheezed.

Repulsed, she spat out, "You and this production company can go to hell!" She strode out of his office, shaking with fury.

Telephoning her dad from the airport overseas, she told him what time her flight was coming in and what time to pick her up. She returned to her dad's New England home with her tail between her knees, at a complete loss what to do next. She had taken a hit. Suitcases in hand, she returned to the narrow street that hadn't changed much since she was a little kid.

She'd been home for weeks, and the job search was turning up empty. Samantha pulled the ponytail holder out of her hair and ran her fingers through the wavy blond locks. She had been growing it out for a while, and now it reached her shoulders. It was time to take a hard look at her life. She'd lived in the spotlight for some time, and most of those years had been great—amazing even—but it was urgent she get something else soon, while she was still marketable. In her prime, at age twenty-five, she was also ready for a serious relationship. She wanted to meet her *forever* guy.

She eyed herself in the bathroom mirror, wondering why she was no longer good enough for David but still desired by a man her father's age. Tears began to build again. "Be strong, Samantha Finch!" she said sternly to her image. "Your life can't get any worse!"

She heard a sound downstairs and figured Harmony had returned home.

"Hello!" she called, coming out of the washroom. "Hello?" Samantha stood still, listening at the top of the stairs. *That's weird.* She was sure she'd heard something. Needing a fix, she headed to the kitchen to grab a Pepsi. Opening the refrigerator, she reached in, and her fingers curled around the bottle's slim neck.

Suddenly she was grabbed from behind. Strong arms clamped around her torso, and she screamed, throwing her weight to get free. The refrigerator door swayed but stayed open as her foot bumped it. With all her might she launched the glass bottle she held at the assailant behind her. It missed its target and smashed when it hit the floor. Her attacker was tall. He managed to drag her kicking, bucking, and twisting down the hallway into the study. In the confined room she felt him shift her in his grasp. She soon heard what sounded like a flame igniting.

She arched to get a good look at what smoldered on the desk—dried leaves! Harmony's story flashed into her mind about the dried leaves she'd found in the walls of the Wentworth. These looked the same!

As a bitter smell filled her nose, she frantically wondered, *Who is this stranger? And how does he know about the herbs in Harmony's house?* She remembered that she had left the back door unlocked, intending to stay only a few minutes. *He must have seen me come in. What is he doing! Why is he burning those?* Harmony said that's how she'd crossed into the other realm. Was he from the other realm—was he taking her there?

She started to choke, as did her attacker, which caused him to loosen his hold on her. Now was her chance! Samantha broke his grip and straightened to dash away, but instead she doubled over, violently coughing. Her lungs burned. Unable to stand, she dropped to her knees, trying to suck in air. She crawled, attempting to escape, and glanced over her shoulder. The man she saw through the black spots in her eyes sat on the floor. Samantha could feel herself sinking. The air around her seemed tangible as she clawed at it. When her cheek met the carpet fibers she saw that the man toppled next to her. He lay on the floor, almost face to face with her. She wanted to scream—but there was no oxygen. The woolen rug was rough against her cheek. She stared at the face inches from hers before blackness overtook her.

The Aquapopulean Realm

Every muscle in her body throbbed like a toothache. Samantha struggled to open her eyes; she felt something clamp on her arm. Her lids opened; her eyes burned in the blackness. She quickly realized she was underwater and that she was being dragged by her arm toward the surface. She immediately kicked her feet to speed her progress. Thrusting her head into the glorious fresh air, she inhaled sharply and deeply.

She stared at the man next to her, just making out his features in the dim moonlight. He was the same man from Harmony's house. Frantically, she tried to swim away, but her throbbing limbs wouldn't cooperate. She could barely stay afloat. The man, ignoring her attempts, let out a loud, long whistle.

How did we get in the ocean? Samantha tried to make sense of what was happening.

Suddenly she was lifted from the water and dropped into a small row boat. On her back, she slipped around and tried to sit up as the boat dipped to the right. The man from the water climbed in. Two other men, the ones who had pulled her from the water, picked up their paddles.

"Welcome back. We see you were successful," one remarked to her abductor.

"And we waited here, just like you said," said the other rower.

"Who the hell are you? What are you going to do with me?" Samantha quivered.

The man who abducted her still hadn't said a word. He slumped over on the middle seat, his knuckles pressed to his brows. The rowers mostly ignored her, but one studied her curiously for several moments. A visible shiver violently shook her, and she wrapped her arms around her knees.

"Did you bring the blankets?" her abductor asked, glancing at the man seated in front of him.

"Yes. Here."

Samantha eyed the blankets greedily as one of the men handed them to her abductor. She was surprised when her abductor turned and handed them both to her. Her frozen fingers shook them out, and she wrapped them around her shoulders and legs. Warmer, she eyed the man who'd taken her from Harmony's house. She squeezed her eyes closed, trying to remember. It was the middle of the day when he'd attacked her. Now it was night, the moon high in the sky. "Where am I? Why were we in the ocean?"

Her abductor was clearly older than the other two men; he looked haggard and breathed heavily.

"Why are you doing this? Who *are* you?" she continued to demand, but she felt her own breathing become shallow. She felt lightheaded.

"Don't be frightened. I will take you to my son," her abductor finally announced.

His son? Who the hell is that? Samantha fought to stay conscious.

"A lot has changed over the several months since you left," he added mysteriously.

"What are you talking about?"

"My son has successfully taken over the tribe. He is accepted by the people and council members. They would have been foolish not to recognize his gifts and abilities. But he was missing one thing—a partner of equal strength who can give him a new race of children—you, Harmony, were meant to be that person. Together you will carry out his legacy."

"Oh no!" Samantha whispered, terrified what would happen when she told him that she wasn't Harmony. She huddled deeper in the blankets and didn't say another word. Maybe he took this as acceptance or defeat. Either way, he seemed satisfied to remain silent until they reached the shore.

9

By the time they reached the shore, Gale felt stiff. His head pounded. If that wasn't enough to worry him, he scowled down at Harmony's slumped, motionless body. When Gale tried to rouse her, her low moan cautioned him, and he immediately reached to feel her face. He had seen fevers, and he was certain she had one. His hand against her brow, warmed by her flushed skin, he said urgently, "We need to hurry. We need to get her in dry clothes."

While Taura tied off the rowboat, Gale instructed Umiko to carry the unconscious girl. Umiko lifted the bundle easily, careful to conceal her hair in a fold of the blanket.

Gale brooded while they traversed the web of interlocking docks. He thought it odd that Harmony was feeling ill effects from the crossing. He'd heard from his spies that she was perfectly healthy when she'd passed before. He willed her to live. This couldn't be a wasted trip; he knew it would be his last.

Entering unseen through a side door, the men followed Gale into the Wellness-by-the-Sea. His men had secured several rooms while he was gone to the human realm to acquire Harmony. They indicated their rooms were on the upper floor, and they led Gale quietly down the hall.

Inside the suite, Umiko carried Samantha to the bedroom and gently placed her on the bed. He drew the blanket away from her face. Gale stepped up beside Umiko, and both men studied her. Wondering about the best course of action, Gale finally said to Umiko, "Go fetch an attendant to undress her." Umiko nodded once and left the room.

"Taura, did you bring my medical case?" Gale asked as the tribesman as he entered the bedroom.

"It's in the next room."

"Fetch it."

Taura scurried off to do his bidding and returned within a couple of minutes. Gale was glad to see the worn leather box had made the journey from the falls intact. Inside were ingredients he needed to feel better. Also, he was eager to see if there was something in there to help Harmony. Umiko returned with a girl to tend to their guest. The three men left the bedroom to wait in the outer sitting area. After the human girl was dry, the attendant was dismissed. Gale settled by the bedside and turned his administrations to her.

Gale tried every herbal remedy he knew to break the girl's fever. While he waited for Finn and the tribe to arrive for the summit, he stayed in his room and moved in the shadows, avoiding being seen for two days. He sent his men to fetch what he needed and allowed only the one attendant to see to his human guest as she changed her clothes and bathed her hot skin. He scared the young female attendant, timid but capable, into secrecy. Gale wanted no one to know his plans until he was ready to reveal them. Bringing the human girl back to their realm would be sensational news, and intimidation tactics with the attendant were necessary.

However, with Finn due to arrive any day now and the situation with the human quickly becoming dire, Gale had no choice but to seek Calder's help. His old friend had always been more experienced with the healing herbs than himself.

The meeting arranged, Gale strode confidently, despite his limp, down the corridor to the great library on the uppermost floor of the Wellness. Everyone he passed stepped out of his way, staring in awe. He was well known as the Linker who had brought over the human boy. Flyers posted with his picture had been plastered around every coastal village and trading post. Parents told their children the remarkable tale, which surely left them wondering if humans were bad.

Times were changing for them, especially since the mixed-blood human, Harmony Parker, had come. After all, destruction had followed. Many superstitious people thought she had angered their god by being in their realm, and that god had caused the earthquake and sent his sea serpent to ingest them. Still others thought that, instead of punishment, their god had sent the earthquake to protect them, killing off the tribe's men and women who threatened them.

Gale planned to use this time of turmoil and doubt to his advantage. He glanced at the wide eyes of onlookers as he entered a room where books and Linkers' journals were stacked on freshly polished floor-to-ceiling shelves. He had heard the tidal wave had spared the top floor, washing out the lower two floors. Sparing the vast library had been lucky indeed.

The professors, wearing distinctly cut tunics, looked on wide-eyed when the Linker entered. Gale sensed their curiosity and nodded, acknowledging them. He thought his diplomacy would be important with professors because they were the storytellers of their future—a future Gale was taking control of. He was escorted to a private room. Entering, he halted the escorts from following. They shut the door behind him. The two old Linkers faced each other.

"It's been a long time, Gale. Welcome back to the Wellness temple." Calder respectfully nodded to his old comrade.

"Indeed it has. You are looking old, my friend." Gale's eyes swept to Calder's white hair; his own was merely salt and pepper.

With a hand, Calder smoothed his hair from forehead

to collar, grinning. "And you look ugly," he retorted, indicating the deep scar on Gale's face.

Gale chuckled, his tension easing slightly. When they were boys, training under the same master, they were steadfast friends. After their journeys into the other realm they'd drifted apart and often didn't see eye to eye on matters concerning the humans. Gale had chosen to be more hands-on in the other realm, while Calder was more of a watcher, as the traditional Linkers were.

Calder invited him to sit by a large window, facing the bay that separated the island from the mainland. Gale waved refreshments away and sat down.

"I met the human, Finn, a few months back when he was here. He helped my great-great granddaughter, Harmony, before circumstances led him to take over the tribe. It was his idea to arrange this summit. He seems a steady young man. I assume that since he has taken over leadership your exile has been pardoned. It seems you were right, all those years ago, about there being something special about him," Calder affirmed.

"Yes. He is a born leader and has unique abilities… Calder, can you guess why he has special abilities?"

"He must be mixed blood. I've only ever seen extraordinary powers in Harmony," Calder stated calmly.

"Half-blooded—he is my son," Gale said.

Calder drew his bushy white brows together.

"I thought as much. What do you hope to gain by having your son here? The humans should stay in their own realm. Though Finn was largely raised among the tribe and could potentially be a great leader, what about the future when he is gone, when there is no one to adjust the weather? What will the people do then? That is your problem, Gale—you go too far. You only do what suits you."

Gale's jaw clenched. "I go too far? What about you?

67

You took a lover in the human realm, and now you have a great-great-granddaughter."

"I didn't try to bring them here!" Calder said in defense of his actions.

"Yet Harmony Parker found her way into our realm. You provided her the herbs."

Calder released a long breath. "I left them hidden in the walls of the Wentworth-by-the-Sea, but it was fate that she found them. Gale, you know the portal out there, our only link to the human realm, could be affected if this island is disturbed. Harmony is trying to help secure the island's stability."

"She is better served in our realm. She would make an optimal wife for Finn. Together they could make powerful changes, and their children's abilities will help future generations. Forget the human realm. We can sculpt a new age here. Make the Aquapopulean race magnificent." Gale stretched out his leg and adjusted his position in his seat.

"Harmony has gone back. Besides, she is married to an Aquapopulean named Kodiak Night, who went through with her. I do not know if he survived the crossing. He is a Diver, not a Linker. Anyway, it is done," Calder said, his face set.

"I want her for my son's bride." Gale narrowed his eyes. "I've brought her back to this realm."

Calder gripped the arms of the chair, sitting forward. "No!"

"Listen, Calder. Harmony *is* here, but she's sick. I need your help. Your herbal knowledge is more extensive than mine. Something is wrong. I think she is dying."

"Where is she?" Calder jumped up. "Why didn't you just take me to her right away?"

Gale ignored the latter question. "This way." He rose with a grimace; his leg had stiffened up after climbing two flights of stairs.

Leaving the private room in a rush, Gale noticed Morie, the keeper of the Wellness-by-the-Sea. She had obviously heard of his infamous return and had come to see with her own eyes, eyes set in a face void of expression. Their eyes locked briefly before he rushed past her.

Calder noticed Morie and gave her a *be cautious* look. He could tell by her facial expression that her instincts regarding Gale were already alerted.

Minutes later, Calder leaned over the bed, placing his hand on the damp brow of the girl before him. Gale had insisted he'd brought Harmony back, but this person was not his great-great-granddaughter, Harmony Parker. This poor human had been taken by mistake, and Gale was right; she was probably going to die. Calder, frustrated and troubled, thought again and again as he watched the girl's eyes move beneath her fevered lids that crossing was a Linker's business—and a sacred one at that.

Calder stood and faced Gale, who waited, appearing calm. But Calder was familiar with the anxious twitch he noticed in the man's left eye. Instinctively Calder decided not to let Gale in on the major mistake he'd made. If he thought this girl was Harmony and she were to die, which appeared likely, then Harmony would be safe in the other realm.

"You can help her," said Gale, his voice strong and steady.

Flattered Gale had such confidence in him, Calder simply grinned. "I'll do everything I can." He glanced again at the unconscious stranger, her pallor an indicator of death.

Calder understood he needed to downplay this unexpected situation. They were on the cusp of an unprecedented event, a summit, much like the peace

JENNIFER W. SMITH

summit he'd attended at the Wentworth in 1905, that was monumental to their future as a race. But Gale believed this person was his kin, and he had to play along. Turning to Gale, he asked. "Does Finn know of your plans concerning my granddaughter? He witnessed her marriage. You may have put her in danger for nothing." Calder suspected Gale had a hidden agenda and assumed his answers would be vague.

"I was planning to surprise him. Getting her here was the priority. I expected she would pass through without difficulties."

"And she agreed to come with you?" Calder indicated the sleeping woman.

"The choice was mine."

"I will keep you posted of her progress." Responding to Calder's dismissive tone, Gale and the two tribesmen who had followed him into the room left.

Calder, on their heels, peered into the hallway. He was relieved to see Morie in the hallway. He noticed Gale didn't bother to stop and speak with her; he entered the adjacent room and closed the door. The other men entered nearby rooms as well.

Calder waved the keeper of the Wellness temple into the room and shut the door behind her. Morie had met Harmony the night she'd crossed into their realm, and she and Calder had both questioned her then. Now, leading her into the girl's bedroom, he quietly confided in Morie. "Gale has meddled again! He brought over a human by mistake... He thinks she is Harmony!"

Morie's eyes widened when she saw the sickly girl in the bed. "I thought for a moment, because of her blond hair, that she was Harmony. Who is she?"

"I don't know, but she must be fully human. I suspect the result of the crossing will kill her. Stay with her while I get my bag and some attendants to help me nurse her. And as far as anyone is to know, she *is* Harmony.

Let's see how this plays out."

"Of course," Morie said with conviction. Calder's tight grin told her he appreciated her loyalty.

He quietly slipped from the room, heading to his room on the ground floor, all the while thinking about the past. When his great-great granddaughter had shown up at the Wellness, his lifelong secret had slowly been revealed. For almost one hundred years, he'd hidden from the community the fact that he'd procreated with a human. Such relationships across the realms were strictly forbidden, but he'd fallen in love. Worse than that were the years he'd spent secretly traveling to the human realm. He had regrets. He wished he'd stayed in the human realm long ago with the love of his life. Instead, he'd returned to marry someone else. But his wife knew she was his second choice and eventually figured out why he'd traveled in secret. He'd crossed time and again for another woman. When he was away she ended her own life because she couldn't cope with it. He'd suffered, her death on his conscience.

He'd told his story to Morie, a longtime friend and council member, the night she'd met Harmony. She had been shocked, but her forgiving nature allowed her to extend her support. Morie fulfilled the mandates of the Wellness Temple for both mental and spiritual care.

Calder followed the corridors until he stood outside one of the treatment rooms. He found who he was looking for and paused to have a word with her. The older woman gave instructions to several young girls. As the girls dashed off to attend their duties, it was his turn to give instruction. He wanted word sent to his daughter Nami and grandson Rio in the village. He needed people he could trust to help nurse the girl. With that settled, he continued on to his room.

As he reached for his doorknob, a messenger calling his name jogged down the hallway.

"Sir, Calder Sir! A message has arrived for you."

While he thanked the messenger, Calder was acutely aware of the official tribal seal on the letter. As he entered his room he read that Tribal Chief Finn, along with a substantial group of council members and hunters, were a day's ride away. Calder prayed he got the chance to speak with Finn about Gale's *surprise*— which was more importantly Gale's mistake.

10

Samantha heard the faint sound of ocean waves. She loved waking up to that sound. Her eyes still closed, she remembered her new life back in New Castle, her childhood seaside town. She groaned, still hurting over the loss of her employment. She'd quickly accepted the loss of her boyfriend, but her job—that had been her dream job!

Suddenly she heard something—someone was moving around in her room! Heart racing, she sharply remembered being abducted and then choking and waking in the ocean. That man with the scarred face had called her Harmony! Samantha's eyes flew open, and she scrambled to free herself from the tangled bed sheets.

"Whoa! Easy, easy." In response to the gentle male voice she stopped and focused on the unfamiliar room around her. She glanced out the window to see sunshine and ocean. She realized that time had passed.

Samantha turned her head sharply and saw a young man sitting in a chair by her bed.

"How are you feeling?" he asked gently.

When she tried to speak her voice croaked drily. He quickly reached for a glass of water on the nightstand and handed it to her.

She reached for the glass; her arm felt weak. Offering him a grateful smile, she took several sips. The water tasted refreshing. In fact, it was the best water she'd ever tasted, and she downed the whole glass. He lifted a pitcher to offer her more.

"I'm Rio," he said, refilling her glass.

Samantha couldn't help but notice his irises were slightly luminescent, like Kodiak's. She dropped her eyes to his hand. Yes, his fingers were webbed, like Kodiak's.

"Where am I?" She coughed.

"We're at the Wellness-by-the-Sea. You're safe, but you've been sick for a few days. Since our…umm…doctor gave you medicine you've responded well. You had us worried. What's your name?"

"My name's Samantha Finch. My friends call me Sam." She sipped the water, feeling a rush of healing energy surge through her. When she sat up the covers fell away and she noticed she was wearing strange clothing. Her fingers brushed the soft fabric. Her eyes returned to his.

"Rio…" She hesitated. "Am I in another…place? I mean another…?"

"Realm?" He filled in her uncompleted sentence.

She exhaled sharply as reality sunk in. Harmony had told her about this place. Kodiak was indisputably from another race, but she'd never suspected she would end up here—possibility and logic were colliding in her mind.

"I don't believe this," she whispered to herself.

"It's probably a good idea for me to get Calder. He's the doctor who helped you. And he's also my grandfather. I think he's the best one to answer your questions. I'll find an attendant to fetch him. I'll be right back." Rio stood. He instructed, "Stay in bed. You are very weak."

Samantha contemplated bolting, but she was indeed very weak. She could hardly hold the full glass of water steadily. And she had a lot of questions that needed answering.

Rio quickly returned and again sat beside her. "Someone is going to fetch you some broth. Are you hungry?" Pouring the last of the water into her glass, Rio glanced around the room, as if trying not to stare at her.

Samantha nodded. *Food will probably give me my strength back*, she thought. She noticed the way Rio nervously tapped his foot; it seemed like he was dying to ask her something. He'd said her doctor was his grandfather, so he must also be aware of what was going on.

"Rio, I was abducted—forced to come here."

She noted Rio's downcast gaze as he mumbled an apology. *So he knows about the foul play. What else does he know?*

"I think I was taken by mistake. I was in my friend's house. She wasn't home. He called me by her name."

"Yes, my grandfather told me about your unfortunate circumstance." He tapped his foot again. After a pause, he looked up at her and, a little too cheerfully, asked, "So you are friends with Harmony Parker?"

"Yes. Do you know her? She told me she was once here, at the Wellness-by-the-Sea."

"Indeed I know her—she is my cousin!" he responded with excitement.

"You are *the* cousin, Rio?" Samantha remembered. "But why would you force Harmony to come back here—well, force me?"

"It wasn't us. Calder will explain. How is Harmony? And Kodi?"

"I was just with Harmony and her husband, Kodiak. They told me about this place, but I have to admit it was hard to grasp."

"Kodi made it! He's okay. Really?"

"Yes, I promise he's fine. They are both fine." Samantha's aches were now easing considerably, and she took in a deep belly breath.

Slapping his hands on his thighs, Rio laughed out loud. "Wow, she told another human about our realm!" His doubtful voice made it clear that seemed like a dangerous idea to him.

"You don't have to worry. She only told me. We are very close. And Kodi, with his glowing irises and webbed fingers, made her story believable." Knowing he was related to Harmony helped her relax a bit, and Samantha leaned back against the headboard.

Rio smiled at her description of Kodiak. "Kodi and I grew up together."

Clearing the cobwebs from her mind, she tried to recall exactly what Harmony had said about her relatives here. She remembered the part about her great-great-grandmother Pearl shacking up with a man from this realm, but the rest eluded her.

"What did she tell you about us? About her family?"

She grinned at Rio's inquisitive expression. "Not much. I think she probably left a lot out. Why don't you tell me more about *you*?" She liked him. The fear and anxiety over the injustice that had been done to her subsided while she talked with him.

"I'm not very interesting." He seemed to search for something interesting to tell her. "I live with my mother in the village, not far from here. Her name is Nami, and she sat with you yesterday. My sister, Binda, recently passed away. Harmony got to know her while she was here. She was there when Binda was killed."

"Oh, I'm so sorry!" Samantha was stunned that Harmony had been there when his sister was killed. She'd never said anything about it. How could she watch someone be killed and not talk about it? It must have been especially hard for Harmony. Samantha had noticed changes in her friend since her return and now wondered what other things happened to her here, besides returning with a husband and a fantastic tale. She had seemed troubled. Samantha wondered whether if she hadn't had so much going on in her own life she might have been more receptive. Maybe Harmony might have shared more.

There was a knock at the door, and Rio jumped up. He trotted to the door and returned with a tray laden with bowls and dishes. "Is it okay to lay this on your lap? If you would prefer, there is a sitting room with a table?" He pointed his chin toward the hallway.

Samantha wondered how big this suite was. The private bedroom was a comfortable size. She indicated her lap was fine, and he gently set the tray there. He lifted the empty pitcher from her nightstand and offered to fetch more water. While he gone, she examined the bowl of broth. On the plate next to it was sliced fresh bread. Tentatively lifting the spoon to her nose, she sniffed the dark liquid. She took a hesitant sip of the broth.

Rio returned with a full jug of water. "It's root vegetable broth. It has excellent minerals and nutrients to revive you."

"It's good." Samantha dipped her spoon back into the bowl and lifted it to her mouth. *Delicious.* "You told me about your mom and your sister. What about you, Rio? What do you do, besides sit by sickbeds?"

He rattled off a description of his typical days, filled with fishing and repairs. "I like to play my flute. I don't have any special calling like Kodiak, who's a Diver, or my sister Binda, who was a Linker like our grandfather."

"What's a Linker?" She'd heard of divers and presumed the name meant what it sounded like, but the term *Linker* was foreign to her ears.

"Linkers are the only ones allowed to cross into your realm. They are born with a mark, and they start their training at an early age. They've traveled throughout your world since ancient times to gather knowledge and share it with us. Think of them as observers. It's said their interaction with humans should make very little impact in your world. Although that was not so in my grandfather's case."

"Harmony told me one of those men fell in love with her great-great-grandmother. She is a descendant from that affair." Harmony and Rio were cousins; Samantha figured out the math. "So you have the same great-great-grandfather."

"Not exactly. Calder is my grandfather, but he's Harmony's great-great-grandfather. In this realm our race lives longer, about fifty more years. Calder married my grandmother much later in life."

They sat in silence, pondering the strange dynamic. Soon a knock sounded at the door. This time it opened to reveal the very man they'd been discussing, Calder the Linker.

Rio made the introductions and offered his grandfather the chair next to the bed. Calder nodded his thanks to Rio and eased into the chair.

"I'm glad you have recovered," Calder said to the girl, whose coloring was now pink and glowing. "I understand you know my great-great-granddaughter, Harmony Parker."

"Yes, apparently I was taken instead of her. But why would someone force her back here?"

Calder answered, "A misguided Linker named Gale is causing trouble among our people. He hoped to bring Harmony here to marry his son." Calder held up his hand to stop Samantha's protest. "We know Harmony is already married. Gale's ambitions are clouding his judgment. And to make matters worse, we are presently preparing for a peace summit. Guests are arriving daily from the surrounding areas, primarily from the west. This will set quite a precedent—it's the first of its kind. It is crucial all goes smoothly to set the stage for future negotiations."

"What are you going to do about this Linker, Gale? He can't just get away with abducting me!" Samantha was sympathetic to diplomacy, but justice should be served.

"The Tribal chief will arrive soon. I must ask his counsel in this matter, because Gale is a subject in his tribe."

"All right," she said quietly. "What about me? How do I get home?" Samantha didn't like the subtle looks Calder and Rio exchanged. "What is it?"

Concentrating, Calder placed his fingers together in a steeple. Lines creased his forehead. "The problem is…humans were never supposed to cross into this realm. Throughout our history, though few know of this, some Linkers have attempted to bring humans through the portal. None have survived the crossing. However, it seems humans have evolved, because here you are. And it seems other changes have occurred—like a new mixed-race generation."

Samantha nodded, acknowledging she understood his words. *But what does that mean for me?* "I may not be able to go back?" Her face went pale.

"I will consult the old Linker journals. For now, Rio has agreed to assist you while you regain your strength."

"All right," she said, giving Rio a weak smile. At least she had found a friend to ride out this storm with. Besides, she discovered her curiosity about this place had spiked. While she'd traveled the globe reporting on a variety of weather conditions, adapting to foreign climates and cultures had become her specialty. She thought, *I can turn this misfortune into opportunity.*

Calder said, "You should continue to rest." He rose and added, "Let Rio know if there is anything you might need." Rio escorted Calder outside the room. They spoke in hushed tones; Samantha couldn't make out what they said. She remembered thinking her life couldn't get any worse right before she was abducted. Her life in the human realm had fallen apart. And although it was ludicrous that she was in another realm, she thought, *What the hell. I'll see what this place has to offer!*

11

Crowds had arrived daily over the last week, and now the summit meeting was just a day away. Extra food and provisions filled the jam-packed storage rooms, and the staff at the Wellness temple buzzed around achieving the tasks asked of them. Coastal clan council members and the few Linkers were claiming every available room in the building. Finn's large tribe, which had traveled for just over a week on elkback, filled almost an entire floor of rooms. Four months had passed since the earthquake, and Finn was glad to see repairs to the Wellness temple were just about complete.

Finn had watched the clan members greet his tribe with cautious politeness. He observed the tribesmen and women point at the ocean and look impressed. For many of them it was their first time seeing the ocean, and he knew they wanted to experience swimming in it. He itched to go in too, but more pressing matters meant he had to settle for using the shower in his room.

At the sound of knocking Finn answered his own door because he had left his attendant, Amadahy, back in the city. Having a room attendant felt extravagant, but it was expected of him in the city. He had always taken care of himself, and relying on others was not something he was comfortable with.

Calder, the clan Linker, stood in the hall and greeted him.

"Calder, it's good to see you are well. Come in." Finn stepped aside. "How are preparations coming for the summit?" Finn had suggested this united gathering, and Calder had assured him he could manage the event here at the Wellness temple, despite the damage suffered during the earthquake.

"All arrangements have been made, and everyone is here. We will begin tomorrow morning as scheduled." Calder entered and paused in the middle of the room, which was the same as every other room. None were more grand than the others. He held up a hand to Finn. "I have something of the utmost importance to talk over with you."

The men, both attentive and engaged, sat in the pair of comfortable chairs in the corner.

Finn braced himself. *What now?*

"I spoke with your father, Finn."

"Gale, the infamous, no longer exiled, Linker." Finn sniffed. "He suddenly seems eager to announce that I am his son. Especially now that I'm leading the tribe." Acknowledging Gale as his father tasted bitter in Finn's mouth. "He wants to be reinstated. Don't worry, I've decreed Gale must prove himself worthy before he can return to Linker status on our council. Although I hope it doesn't come to that."

"Finn, don't underestimate him. He has already done something undermining, and you are not going to like it."

Finn arched his neck this way and that, trying to ease the tension building there. *What has that man done now!* Finn gnashed his teeth at this recent thorn in his side. Gale had suggested that he go to the Wellness temple ahead of the tribe to reunite with his old friend Calder while Finn prepared his entourage to move east. Gale claimed that he and Calder had trained together when they were young boys. Finn had agreed and allowed Gale to leave early, if only to get him out of the way while he prepared for both the journey and the upcoming negotiations. Umiko and Taura had volunteered to escort Gale.

Calder continued. "When I met with Gale, he had decided that he wanted my great-great granddaughter,

Harmony, to be your bride. He thinks that our mixed-blooded families are the future of this realm."

"It's good Harmony left when she did. I'm sure he would have tried to stop her if he hadn't been in exile." Finn was not surprised about his father's insane plot, but why make a fuss about it now? Harmony was gone.

"Well, I hate to be the one to tell you this, but he crossed over to abduct her. The girl down the hall is…"

"He *what*?" Finn exploded. He rose from his chair, coiled to sprint to the door. "Where is she, Calder? What room?"

"Hold on, Finn." Calder's level voice only made Finn more impatient.

"What room?" he asked again from between clenched teeth, his temper barely controlled.

"It's not what you think."

Finn curled in fingers into fists, his face a mask of fury.

Calder sighed, pointed to the right, and said, "Last room on the left."

Finn shut the door behind him, making it clear he didn't want Calder to follow. He had to let Harmony know that he had no part in this. All too well, he remembered her commitment to Kodiak. She chose to marry Kodiak, despite Chief Nakoma's suggestion that Harmony marry him. Harmony's words still rang in his ears: "the heart wants what the heart wants." Instantly, from the moment they had met, Finn had felt a connection with Harmony. Now it all made sense; they were both of mixed races; they'd both struggled to find a home in the right realm.

During the time they had spent together, they had each believed Finn was a human brought over into the Aquapopulean realm. Harmony had been the only person who had understood his internal demons—demons he still struggled with. Despite his struggles, he had reached his ultimate goal and had risen to become chieftain of the Forest Tribe, and yet, he still felt something was missing. In dire need of her understanding, he hoped under the circumstances Harmony would believe and trust him. Despite his fury at his father's misguided interference, a part of him couldn't wait to see her again.

At the end of the hallway, Rio was leaving the last room on the left as Finn rapidly approached. Rio smiled. "Oh, hello, Finn...ah...Chief. I was just leaving, but she's—"

Finn gave Rio a curt nod and pushed past him to enter the room. Harmony's back was to him; she stood at the window, looking out. Her blond hair looked shorter, but he would recognize the color anywhere, especially in a realm full of brunettes. She obviously didn't hear him stride up behind her, and she squeaked in surprise when he spun her around to hug her fiercely and completely to him.

"Harmony!" he breathed into her hair, the locks caressing his cheek. He felt her slim hands press against his ribcage. His arms pinned her elbows and wrapped around her shoulders in a bear hug. Closing his eyes, he nestled his nose in the silky strands of her hair. He inhaled deeply, her scent pure, different from anything he'd ever smelled. But she was stiff in his arms. He abruptly realized she hadn't greeted him back. *She must be angry with me.* Still holding her, he drew his head back to look into her face. Then he saw the most beautiful woman he'd ever seen—and she wasn't Harmony Parker. The woman in his arms seemed just as stunned as he was. They both silently stared at each other for an awkward moment.

"Ah-hm." At the sound of a voice being cleared near the doorway, Finn released her arms and stepped back. He glanced over his shoulder at Rio, who seemed amused. Rio's chest vibrated with suppressed laughter.

"I thought Harmony was here. Calder said—" Finn's words died away as he remembered Calder trying to tell him more. But Finn had instead stubbornly insisted that he reveal which room she was in. His gazed returned to the pretty face.

She said, "Hi. I'm Samantha Finch." She extended her hand toward him.

Finn raised an eyebrow, his eyes on her small hand. His face went blank, disguising his confusion. *Who is this girl? She has to be human—she couldn't possibly be of mixed blood.* As he hesitantly reached his hand out, she closed the distance and clasped his to hers. She pumped his hand. When she tried to pull free, he continued to hold it. It was warm. A sudden pang of longing shuddered through him. He had gone so long without the warmth of human touch—until Harmony had reminded him that he missed it. Now this lovely, warm human was causing his own heat to stir.

Rio crossed the room and touched Finn's shoulder. "Finn, this is Harmony's friend. She was in Harmony's house, and Gale abducted her. He took the wrong girl." Rio shook his head, Finn surmised, at Gale's audacity. "And Samantha almost died crossing over."

"You have the same color hair, but it's not as wavy as Harmony's...and it's shorter." Finn gave her a thorough looking over. He realized his intense scrutiny was melting her confidence after her introduction moments ago. Her wide blue eyes looked pleadingly at Rio, and she swallowed hard.

Rio continued the introduction, since Finn's focus was elsewhere. "Samantha, this is Finn Falk, from the Forest Tribe. He's here representing his vast city of inland dwellers. He met Harmony when she was here, and he was vital in helping her return." Rio whispered quietly to Finn, "You can let her go now."

Finn released her hand. Samantha clutched her

elbows and retreated to a seating area.

"Would you care to sit down?" she asked politely, as if she had acclimated without difficulty.

"Has Gale discovered he's taken the wrong person?" Finn ignored the girl, turning to Rio for answers.

"No. Gale doesn't know. She was very sick, and he brought Calder in to care for her. Of course Calder knew right away. That's why he sent for my mother and I to look after Samantha—some of the staff saw Harmony before. We couldn't take the chance that someone would recognize that Samantha wasn't Harmony and announce it. Calder is keeping this a secret for now—at least until you came." Rio gave him a look.

Finn figured Rio was most likely wondering why Finn's conversation with Calder hadn't been more detailed. Finn snapped his eyes on Samantha, who was pouring herself a glass of water. *Damn it! Gale has been a thorn in my side since he returned from exile…and now he's complicated things even more. This summit is of the utmost importance.* Finn felt a great deal of pressure to unite the people and find a peaceful solution to their many issues. The last distractions he needed were an estranged father's interest and a bride forced on him.

Finn shook his head. Striding to the door, he said, "I'll go find Calder. This is a mess." Suddenly a thought occurred to him. He stopped and swiveled in Rio's direction. "Who is watching over her besides you? Who is protecting her?"

Rio shrugged his shoulders. "I don't know. Gale hasn't been back here. Calder sent him word that she was out of danger but wasn't to be disturbed. That's all I know."

Finn's gaze probed the girl, who seemed healthy enough. Though her features were delicate and she was petite compared to the huntresses, she exuded confidence. Still, what did a human woman know about protection?

"Stay with her, Rio," he ordered. Finn waited for him to nod in agreement. He said nothing more to the girl, and he left the room. He was off to create a plan with Calder—a plan that was already forming in his mind.

Finn found Calder waiting for him at the top of the stairs. He motioned for Finn to follow. "Let's take a stroll."

Finn hesitated, wondering if leaving the human was too risky. However, if Gale still thought she was Harmony she was probably safe for now, Finn reasoned. He nodded. They walked down the stairs in silence and left the building.

Finn's haste had put him at a disadvantage when he'd barged into Samantha's room. He scolded himself for his carelessness and shook off the strange emotion that seemed to linger in his body. Feelings buried long ago had been awakening, beginning with Harmony entering his life months ago. Then Gale's return had unsettled memories of Finn's human mother. Now he had held a human woman. Allowing his emotions to get the better of him wasn't on his agenda. He physically shook his unease off, rolling his shoulders as if preparing for a fight.

They walked toward the beach, away from the flurry of activity, and Finn asked, "What do you know? Tell me everything."

While Calder filled him in on his conversations with Gale and then with Samantha, Finn's mind found its way back to the human girl inside. Her lovely blue eyes flashed vividly before him. When he had first seen Harmony, he thought she was pretty and her blond hair outstanding, but compared to her friend Samantha Finch—well, he could hardly keep his thoughts of her exquisite face out of his mind. He pointedly thrust her image aside and concentrated on the task at hand.

"She seems to have recovered well enough with your potions. Can we send her back? Now that we are on to Gale's plan, surely he wouldn't travel through the portal again when he discovers his mistake. We won't let him—and he *will* be punished for his actions."

"Finn, we cannot send her back. It would kill her. It is a miracle she is alive."

"Can any of the other Linkers help?"

Calder looked back at the Wellness temple, recalling the architectural plans a previous Linker had brought back. The Linker had copied the Wentworth-by-the-Sea from the other realm, but the Aquapopuleans had constructed their version with an Asian-inspired flared roofline. "All the Linkers are here—there are only five. Gale and I are the oldest, and there are two children and a man named Deniz, who is twice your age. Deniz has been the acting master for the two children in training. I was training Binda before she passed. I could speak with Deniz if need be." Calder sighed. "Maybe we need to keep playing this charade until the summit is over. This summit is critical, and we need the peace talks to go smoothly."

"I agree this meeting must be our priority. But letting that man go unpunished..." The growl deep in Finn's throat made Calder stop walking and face him.

"It is only for a week or two. When Gale offers his plan to you, tell him that you are disappointed that he took action without seeking permission. Remind him that you had contemplated marrying her before when Nakoma was chief, but Nakoma allowed Harmony to marry Kodiak instead. Make him believe you will reconsider it now that Kodiak is out of the way in another realm, and tell him to stay away from Harmony while you try to convince her to stay."

"Your plan has merit. I planned to have him brought

back to the city, but I can't afford the loss of manpower or the scandal. All right, that is how we will proceed. But what of the girl, Samantha? Can we convince her to help us? And what will become of her when this is over—a human forced to remain here?" Finn knew how that felt.

"We tell her what she wants to hear. She helps us— we are her friend's family, after all—and we will do our best to send her home in a couple of weeks. I told her I'd consult the old Linker journals regarding returning her to her realm, but I know them well, and there is no hope there. I don't expect Deniz will have more to tell us." Calder continued walking, avoiding Finn's intense gaze. "She will adapt, just like you did. Humans and Aquapopuleans are not that different. We all share a common ancestor."

"We are different. I can't have children with the Aquapopuleans, though I'm half-blooded." Finn watched Calder pause in midstep, turning his head, his mouth open in surprise. Finn added, "It's not from lack of trying."

"I didn't know. I assumed if I could impregnate a human then anything was possible. Perhaps evolution hasn't made that leap yet." Calder's cackle made Finn scowl. Calder pondered aloud, "So we are uncertain about the procreation of half-bloods."

"I know for a fact Harmony and Kodiak consummated their marriage while in this realm, but whether she is pregnant or not..." Finn held up his hands.

"Gale is counting on his belief that two mixed-bloods can reproduce. He said he wanted a new, stronger bloodline for our future. Indeed, it's an interesting gamble."

12

Finn surveyed the Wellness-by-the-Sea. The temple sat on a bluff offering sweeping views of the ocean. He could hardly tell the building had been struck by a tidal wave four months ago. Finn had seen the paint stripped off, boards broken and stained by the flood of salt water. Now they were replaced and freshly painted.

The smashed glass, then looking like the jagged teeth of a sea serpent, had been refitted with panels that gleamed in the sunlight. The grounds, once covered in mud and debris, were again serene under manicured grass. The August day was brightened by yellow, red, and orange flowers. The felled trees had been put to good use for the needed repairs. Builders had broadened the expanse of the piers, and workers continued adding docks for larger ships. A new warehouse building and wharf area were included in the expansion. Finn recognized the needs of the coastal clans; the additions would move them into a new era. Like his own tribe, they were on the cusp of change. It was up to him as the leader of the upcoming summit to unite the tribes and the clans to build a better future for all the people of the realm.

Standing on the bluff, Finn quietly observed the industry around him. On the platform where the sailing vessels were docked, he saw the unmistakable profile of his father next to Umiko. Finn couldn't help but wonder what Gale was up to. He thought it was a waste and a shame that Gale couldn't use his knowledge to better serve the people. Finn supposed, in Gale's twisted mind, that he thought he *was* helping to shape the future, but his ways were selfish. There was no love lost between them. Finn recognized his own role through his father's eyes—merely a puppet. Finn strode down the grassy hill and crossed to the winding steps that took him closer to his enemy.

Umiko acknowledged Finn, his chief, respectfully. Gale greeted his son and asked how his journey had gone. After the basic pleasantries, Finn inquired, "What brings you to the docks?"

"It's been a long time since I've been to the Wellness temple, and I was interested in seeing the changes they've made to this area. Perhaps you and I can go somewhere private to talk about some ideas I have for the summit." Gale took the lead away from the busy docks, and Finn fell in next to Umiko; they followed Gale as if *he* were chief.

Finn quickly caught up with his father and walked shoulder to shoulder with him. He said with authority, "I will remind you that you are a guest. *I* will be representing the tribes."

"I have a lot of life experience in both realms, my son. I can only offer my wisdom and advice, but you are chieftain, and, naturally, you will decide what is right."

Gale's manipulative spin on who was in control was clear. Finn nearly flinched when Gale referred to him as *my son*. It took all his self-restraint not to rebuke the man. Forcing himself to fight this battle of wits, he calmly replied, "With that matter settled, we need to discuss why you've brought back Calder's great-great granddaughter."

"Splendid. Calder has ruined my surprise," Gale said sarcastically. "That man never could keep a secret—that is, until he fell in love with a human. It is funny how a human can change you."

His comment wasn't lost on Finn. Nor was the fact that when Gale reached the stairs, he paused to stretch his stiff leg. It was evident to Finn that Gale's old injury caused more pain than he let on. Umiko tried to engage

Finn in conversation and claim his attention away from Gale, but Finn was attuned to Gale's physical limitations. It surprised him that Gale had risked the trip to the other realm at his age.

Reaching the grassy hill, Gale paused to make a vague comment about the progress made, but Finn noticed the bead of sweat on his brow and the tightness around his mouth. The three of them moved to the veranda that circled the Wellness temple and sat in the chairs there. The area was semi-secluded, away from the other guests who were gathered in clusters, socializing.

"I have to say, I'm confused as to why you abducted Harmony. Tell me, Gale, what made you think she would want to stay in this realm? She is married, and her husband is in the other realm. She will just return."

"Her husband!" Gale's eyes flashed with anger. "I instructed Nakoma to have you marry Harmony when she was here before. She went against my wishes." Gale's eyelids slid closed, and he took a deep breath. Calmer, he added, "Her husband is of little concern to me. Harmony can be convinced to stay. Her family is here. She belongs in this realm. Finn, I'm sure you can appeal to her."

Finn pretended to consider Gale's suggestion. "I wanted that union as well. Harmony and I have a connection. Nakoma told me I would marry Harmony, but Kodiak announced they were already promised. Nakoma not only allowed them to marry, but she provided the speedy ceremony." He spoke the truth; at that time he had recognized that marrying Harmony would elevate his status, and he had connected with her. There were kindred spirits. Both understood what it was like to be human. Finn carefully chose his next words, knowing they would make Gale think he'd succeeded. "Could you imagine the two of us, with our abilities…" Finn saw the glimmer in Gale's eyes and decided to dial it back a bit. "But I'm not sure how to convince her to stay."

Gale began to rise from his chair and adjusted his knee. "You're a strapping young warrior, leader of the greatest city in this realm. Use your appeal, son." Standing, Gale leaned heavily on the railing.

Finn stood too, not allowing this man to stare down at him. Shoulders square, his stance powerful, he regarded his father eye to eye. "My first priority is this summit. Secondly, I will see what I can do to smooth over the discomfort you've caused Harmony. I strongly suggest you stay away from her and leave things to me."

"I have merely brought you a gift... Do with her what you will." The curve of Gales smile irritated Finn, but he turned away before he did something he'd regret, leaving the two men to ponder what he'd do next.

***

Samantha paced, restless. Although the two-room suite was spacious, she was itching to go outside. She had eaten her fill of everything served to her on trays and chatted for hours with her new friend, Rio, to pass the time. She'd enjoyed the sunset's pink sky, and though it was getting dark, she desperately wanted to take a walk. "Please, Rio, just a little walk around the building... Can't we?"

Suddenly a knock sounded. Rio sighed with relief as he crossed the room to answer it. Samantha knew Rio was weary of telling her no. She was irritated with him telling her that she was safer in her room and Finn would be furious if they left. True, the chieftain was intimidating. Her mind easily conjured his image. He was smoking hot. She had nearly lost the ability to stand when he had whipped her around and hugged her. If Finn hadn't been holding her so tightly she imagined her knees would have buckled. She recalled how hard his chest felt under her fingertips.

When Rio opened the door she tensed as she watched Finn stride in with Calder in tow.

Calder approached her. "How are you feeling?"

Samantha tried to keep her eyes on the older man, but her peripheral vision tracked Finn's movements. "I feel oddly fantastic. It must be something in the water," she joked.

"I'm pleased to hear that. Would you mind if we sit? We've come to discuss something with you."

The four of them settled in the chairs arranged in a circle for conversation. Finn sat across from her. His masked expression left her wondering about his role in all of this.

"As we've discussed before, Gale made the mistake of bringing you here instead of Harmony." She nodded; Calder had been clear about that in their earlier conversation. "His reasoning for the abduction is that he feels Harmony should marry his son."

"But Harmony's already married."

"Yes, but because she is of mixed blood, he feels she is *destined* to marry his son, who is also of mixed blood—half-blooded, to be exact. They are the only two such beings known. Gale feels that because Kodiak is in the human realm, he is out of the equation."

Samantha's eyebrows rose in question, not understanding how any of this mattered, because the real Harmony was still back home, and she was here.

"Years ago Gale abducted his son from the human realm. Gale was sent into exile for his unethical deed. However, circumstances have changed, and his son is now the chieftain of the tribe, so Gale has returned."

Calder's words jogged her memory. In the boat Gale had said something about his son that she couldn't quite remember.

"Make no mistake—he will be punished for your abduction!" Calder exclaimed passionately, though he softened his next words. "But right now, tomorrow in fact, we begin the first all-inclusive summit in our history and we can't afford a disruption as big as this. So we are asking you, Samantha, to help us."

Rio spoke up. "Harmony believed in our nations joining in peace."

Wide-eyed, Samantha looked from Rio to Finn, who kept his gaze on the floor, and back to Calder. "What do you want me to do?"

"This summit will last a week or two, and in that time we'd like you to be seen by Gale, and others, courting his son. Allow Gale to believe you are Harmony—we didn't tell him of his mistake. Convince him that you are considering the possibility of staying here," Calder emphasized, "with your family."

"Won't other people realize I'm not Harmony? She said she spent six weeks over here." Samantha figured people would recognize that she looked different from the other human.

Rio chuckled but received a reprimanding look from his grandfather.

Calder crossed his arms and leaned back, eyeing her critically, he said, "You look enough like Harmony to fool most people. I've taken the liberty of sending away the few attendants who interacted personally with her. I've spoken to the only others who knew her better— Morie, the keeper of the Wellness temple, and my daughter Nami. Of course, the people in this room knew her best."

Samantha couldn't deny his words; she and Harmony had often passed as sisters throughout the years. Rio had explained his race were brunettes, so her blond hair might sway folks.

"Of course I want to help you. I'd do anything for my

best friend, so helping Harmony's family is a no brainer. But after those couple weeks, how do I get back home?" The silence that followed was disconcerting. "Please, don't tell me that burning herbs and near drowning is the only way."

"I'm afraid so. You need to rest and recuperate, so while you're gaining strength you can help us at the same time. We will talk more about returning you home soon enough."

"All right," Samantha agreed. It wasn't as though she had a pressing job or anything waiting for her on the flip side. And it wasn't every day a human traveled to another realm. She had always had travel fever. She wanted to see the world. This could turn out to be the ultimate destination. She inquired intently, "But what about that man, the one who brought me here? He scares me."

Finn sat at the edge of his seat, leaning forward, his elbows resting on his knees. He looked up at her comment. "I told him to stay away from you. I will look after you from now on. I'll have your clothing moved into the suite adjoining mine."

"You? What for?" Samantha sputtered. This sexy but intense guy made her nervous in ways unfamiliar to her. She'd been around male models, swanky mega-rich industry men, and artsy schemers in the television business, but none of them held a candle to this guy. Being near him made her feel jittery.

Rio, chuckling again, said, "Finn, the tribe's chieftain, is Gale's half-blood son."

Samantha shook visibly. "Wait. I have to pretend *we* are courting?" She wiggled her finger between Finn and herself, seeking clarification in case she'd heard wrong. *Oh god, that scary guy who took me said something in the boat... His son was the leader of something. Shit!*

Finn drew his brows together at her reaction.

"Yes. And you will be safe with Finn, so you don't have to worry. And Rio will remain with you while Finn is attending the meetings," Calder said, seeming more relaxed. He even grinned.

Samantha swallowed the lump in her throat. "Okay, great." Her voice squeaked.

13

Samantha was escorted from the rooms near her abductor to identical rooms that adjoined her protector. Though she felt somewhat like a prisoner, she took comfort from her good-natured friend Rio, who lifted her spirits. After the evening meal, Rio bid her goodnight and promised to show her around tomorrow.

Not one to sit around by herself, Samantha knocked on the adjoining door and offered a friendly smile when Finn opened it.

"What is it, Samantha? Did you need something?"

"I'm okay. I just wondered if we could talk." Her eyes swept over his sleeveless tunic, and she couldn't help but notice the tattooed skin that was exposed by the deep V neck of the shirt. He wasn't wearing his thick belts. She knew he was settling in to relax for the night.

"Come in."

She entered and smiled when he offered her a seat. Before he could join her, a knock sounded. "Just a minute," he said before he strode across the room to open the door. In the hallway stood a man holding a tray with a large domed cover. Retrieving the tray, Finn said with authority, "That will be all." He used his foot to shut the door. Placing the tray on the low table between their seats, he sat before he lifted the lid. The smell of roasted meat filled her nostrils.

"My dinner," he explained. "I can't live on the usual vegetarian food. Would you care to join me?" He stabbed at the meat with the fork provided and dropped a slab onto his plate.

"No thanks, I already ate." She spied a pitcher of water on a console across the room. "Do you mind if I get us some water?"

"That would be fine."

She watched as he piled more meat on his plate. An elbow resting on his knee, he leaned forward to cut the meat and fill his mouth. She filled two glasses with water and stood before him to hand him his, forcing him to look up at her. Catching her breath, she was momentarily lost in the varied hues of green in his eyes. His hand brushed hers when he took the glass, sending tiny shivers up her arm. He nodded thanks and turned back to his meal. Samantha sat and sipped the water, trying to soothe the sudden dryness in her throat.

"I was wondering what you had in mind for us, as far as spending time together…in public. I don't know how well you knew Harmony—"

"I know her well enough. I know that she doesn't like deep water, nor would she want to go off into the forest alone again, especially after I had to rescue her from the wolves," Finn said nonchalantly before he took a long swallow of water.

"You rescued her from wolves?" Samantha repeated. He shrugged a shoulder, like it was no big deal. Samantha found it curious that Finn seemed to be staring her down, as if she'd offended him with her question about how well he knew Harmony. What exactly had happened between them? His next statement made her feel uncertain about which reality she was living in.

"Now that Harmony knows who she is and what she's done, no doubt she is struggling over where she truly belongs. That is why I think this plan can work. We are similar, Harmony and I, and I know she considered staying here. If Calder hadn't insisted she return to 'save us', well… Let's just say there were people here she connected with."

Wow, okay. Samantha hadn't expected Finn to speak so passionately about her best friend, and she couldn't help feeling a little miffed. Samantha had known

Harmony since they were kids, so in her mind she was more qualified to understand Harmony's feelings.

"Harmony is crazy in love with Kodi, and whatever connection you claim you have with her wouldn't alter her choice to live anywhere without him." If Finn had romantic feelings toward Harmony, Samantha wanted to make it clear Harmony didn't return his affection.

"Yes, I am aware of her feelings for Kodiak." He finished the last bite and rose to refill his glass. "But I'm speaking more about her duty to her people. Her ability to kill the god's creatures can alter our realm, the realm where the last of her family remains," he pointed out.

Watching him saunter away from her, Samantha rolled her eyes, silently asking how a man's behind could be sculpted to such masculine perfection. Keeping her eyes low, through her lashes she watched his thick, powerful thighs move past her. Her eyes lingered there until he returned to his seat. She took another sip. *Man, my throat is dry.* Swallowing the cool water, she pulled her thoughts together and asked, "I'm sorry, did you say 'ability to kill god's creatures'? I don't know what that means."

He perched on the edge of his seat again, set his glass down, and placed a rough hand on the soft skin of her knee, immediately getting Samantha's full attention. She momentarily regretted changing into a tunic dress. The dress was rather short. Under his intimate touch—his long fingers stretched up her thigh—she struggled to sit still. Looking into his eyes was like looking into a forest of evergreen trees, where dark flecks of pine met blue spruce.

"Harmony and I are connected. We're the only two people with mixed-blood ever known. We both have extraordinary abilities never before seen in either realm. Harmony didn't know she had them until she arrived here and was threatened. Her natural instincts took over, and she learned she was able to burn sirens with her touch, killing them when she needed to. Also, she used her unique ability to shield herself, and others, from a sea serpent's attack."

Samantha now understood why Harmony had left this part out of her story. Samantha never would have believed her.

"It took me a long time to control my ability. If she'd stayed here, she could learn to better control hers." He sat back, slipping his hand from her leg. "It's said the water god sends his sirens to lure the Aquapopuleans back into the sea. Many have been taken and drowned. She could protect them."

Samantha didn't know what to say. She was bewildered and a little repulsed by what he'd told her. Harmony had mentioned a water god but nothing about a special ability she had or about killing! Certainly this place—and the trauma of crossing into it—could change a person. The very idea of opening oneself to the endless possibilities in another realm couldn't be easy.

"I can see why Harmony left out this information when telling me where she had been and how she suddenly happened to be married to a nonhuman. But now that I'm here, I'd like to learn more about this place. I don't have anyone or anything waiting for me back home—except maybe Harmony. I'm sure she's wondering where I am."

"You were taken from *her* home, right?"

"Yes, I was dragged into a room, where Gale lit the herbs on fire." She shuddered at the memory.

"When Harmony sees the herbs, she will know where you are," he reasoned. At her silence he went on. "We will start our courtship tomorrow. After the commencement of the summit meetings, I will escort you to the banquet. You will sit by my side for dinner. That way, we'll be seen together. After the dinner, I will personally escort you back to your room." Finn spoke like a general laying out a strategic plan.

Samantha agreed it was a good start. She thought about how she could make their courtship look more convincing as the week went on. Her years of acting in drama club would come in handy.

"I need to prepare some notes for tomorrow's meetings." Finn's comment sent Samantha to her feet.

"Of course. I'm sure you're very busy. Thanks for explaining our plan." She walked to the threshold of her room and turned to bid Finn goodnight. She met his unflinching gaze and watched his eyes slowly move down her torso and back up again. His head cocked to the side, he seemed to be unabashedly enjoying what he saw. Feeling her cheeks flame red, Samantha murmured goodnight and shut the door behind her. Leaning against it, she let out a long breath and stifled the laugh that bubbled up. What was it about that half-blood, dangerous and alluring at the same time, that made her pulse dance to a different beat?

She padded barefoot down the hall and slipped into bed, thinking how crazy it was that *she* happened to know the only two mixed-blood people in existence— her best friend and the hottie in the next room.

The morning brought overcast skies and light rain. Looking out her window, Samantha noticed people going about their business as if oblivious to the weather, not one raincoat or umbrella anywhere. She showered and dressed, waiting impatiently for Rio to arrive. After the bell chimed to indicate the summit was in session, Rio tapped on her door.

"Good morning, Samantha!" Rio's smile was broad and his greeting enthusiastic.

"Hey!" she returned, gently pushing him into the hallway when he tried to enter her room. "No, no, no. I can't stay cooped up in this room for another second.

Let's go explore."

"Okay, where do you want to start?"

"I could use a cup of coffee," Samantha suggested hopefully. Without her daily Pepsi she was feeling the effects of caffeine withdrawal.

"We don't have that, but I can take you to the kitchens downstairs. Perhaps you can find something else you might like."

"Let's go!" She grabbed the sleeve of his tunic and dragged him down the hallway, grinning. She looked forward to her first adventure. The corridors and stairwells were empty. Rio explained the meetings were being held on the first floor in a large hall typically reserved for group worship.

Passing through the kitchens, Samantha noticed the staff gave Rio respectful nods, always followed by genuine smiles. It seemed Rio had clout in this place. Maybe his grandfather, being an influential figure, elevated his status. But Rio's demeanor was likable, and his smile was infectious.

After sampling several of his favorite culinary delights, they walked off with steaming mugs of tea. They stepped out onto the veranda at the back of the building, under a roof that protected them from the rain. They leaned against the railing and chatted until the rain stopped. The clouds eventually evaporated.

In those hours, one of the things Samantha asked about was the god the Aquapopuleans worshipped. She wondered why that god would send his creatures out to drown his subjects.

"No one knows why these drowning are happening. Some say because fewer people are worshipping him these days and he has become angry, taking out his revenge by drowning them. Harmony says Suijin drowned her family in the human realm. My poor cousin," Rio murmured.

Samantha thought Rio's concern for Harmony was sweet. She described the turmoil Harmony had gone through over losing her family. Then Samantha leaned out over the railing, stretching her neck to look up at the sky. "Looks like the rain is gone!" she announced, changing the subject. "So what do you do for fun around here?"

"I like to fish," Rio answered. Samantha wrinkled her nose. "Or it's fun to swim with the porpoise in the cove by my dwelling."

"No way! Can we?" Samantha cheeped excitedly.

"Sure, we can take a ride over. I'll introduce you to my mother."

They rode a bike that looked like a Fred Flintstone car down to Rio's dwelling. After dipping her toes into the freezing water off the shore, Samantha opted to watch Rio from the dock.

Before he jumped in, he said, "Sam, I don't want to alarm you if I don't resurface right away. We clansmen can hold our breath underwater for several minutes. I'll try not to stay under for more than five minutes."

She replied, "Okay. That's cool."

Rio dove in, leaving ripples in the water. He swam up after a few minutes accompanied by the playful porpoises, who splashed her and made clicking sounds that sounded like greetings. Samantha lived in the moment, enjoying the beautiful creatures, the warm afternoon sunshine, and her new-found friend. The crushing disaster in her life weeks ago was forgotten while she laughed so hard at Rio's antics with the porpoises that tears filled in her eyes.

She beamed at him while he climbed the ladder onto the dock. "Thank you for bringing me here. They are so cute."

While Rio was drying off on the dock, his mother returned from the trading market. Rio made introductions, and Nami wrapped Samantha in a warm hug.

"It's nice to finally meet you. I sat by your bed when you first arrived. I'm glad you've recovered," Nami said. She looked Samantha over.

"Thank you, I feel much better—revived, really."

"You look like Harmony. How is she?"

Samantha was suddenly overwhelmed by the fact Harmony had an aunt and cousin in this realm. Knowing how much family meant to her friend, she couldn't help but feel grieved for Harmony's sake. The water god had killed off her human family, yet these Aquapopulean relatives obviously cared for her—and they were realms apart.

Their conversation was brief. It was getting late, and Rio suggested they head back to the Wellness temple. When Nami lovingly hugged her good-bye it was just like the old times, when Harmony's grandmother had treated her like part of the family.

An hour later at the Wellness temple, Samantha walked in her suite to find that an attendant had set out an elegant dress and sandals for her to wear to dinner. She celebrated with a happy dance, whirling the dress around in a circle, glad that it wasn't the typical tunic style everyone seemed to wear. It was a wrap dress with capped sleeves and a thick belt that cinched around her slim waist. After she tried it on, satisfied with the fit, she wondered how to arrange her blond hair. Samantha swept some strands back from her face and secured them with a ribbon from a box of miscellaneous items she found in the closet. Next, she slipped her feet into sandals that offered a slightly wedged sole. Examining her reflection in the mirror, she thought, *All I need is my date.*

14

Finn approached Samantha's adjoining door feeling pleased with how the first day of the summit had wrapped up. In all, both the clans and tribes seemed of like minds. Finn had lingered downstairs, talking with others who were eager to continue the discussion on upcoming issues. He was late collecting Samantha. He knocked and then let himself in. "Ahh," he stuttered. "Samantha, did you lose something?"

Samantha was kneeling down, derriere in the air, looking under the bed. She turned awkwardly, giving him a surprised looked over her shoulder. Finn moved to help her up. He caught himself licking his lips when she wiggled to shimmy her dress back into place.

"I've lost my necklace. I don't remember if I had it on when I changed rooms. I was wondering if it slipped under the bed. I can't seem to find it anywhere," she said, and then nibbled on her bottom lip.

"I will ask an attendant to search the other room," he offered.

"Thanks. It's just a gold chain, but my brother gave it to me," she said, sounding sentimental.

She seemed to be waiting for him to say something, and choice comments on her appearance raced through his mind, so finally he said, "You look..." He held up a hand as if the right word were floating in the air. "Very beautiful."

She gave him the widest smile, and he felt his chest inflate with pride. It had been a while since he'd given a pretty girl a compliment. These last several months, after the murder of his lover, his escape with Harmony and Kodiak, and the earthquake that had killed his chief, had taken a toll on him. His easy manner was buried under the weight of his chiefly status. His new duties gave him little time for pleasure.

"Thank you. Now don't forget to look at me like that when we're downstairs performing our little show."

Her saucy statement made him fight back a wide grin. He cleared his throat. "Shall we?"

He kept the conversation formal while they walked down to the banquet. They could hear the noisy large crowd from the steps as they descended into the busy corridor. Finn firmly clasped her elbow, guiding Samantha through a side door to a long table. They sat down together. Immediately the ringing of a hand bell called all to gather. Morie, the keeper of the Wellness temple, welcomed everyone and offered a small prayer of thanks for their coming together.

Everyone took a seat at their respective tables, and Calder slid into the seat on the other side of Samantha. The men nodded to each other over her head. Finn glanced away, waiting for the brew to be served, half listening to Calder ask Samantha, "How was your day?"

"Great," she chirped. "I enjoyed spending time with your grandson, Rio. He is so funny, and sweet." Finn watched her out of the corner of his eye as she lifted the pitcher of water and offered to pour Calder a glass.

Calder nodded and grinned. "Oh? What have you been up to?"

"Rio took me to his dwelling, and I met your daughter, Nami, although only briefly. Also, I watched him swim with the porpoises. If the water wasn't so cold I'd have jumped right in."

Finn leaned forward and growled, "You left the building? I don't want you going off. I'll speak to Rio about it first thing tomorrow."

Finn wasn't prepared for her head to snap around, nor for the jaunty eyebrow she raised. He paused, in doubt over what kind of reaction he was going to get.

Before she spoke, her eyes left his and scanned the crowd. His too swept through the crowded tables, meeting several curious stares. She leaned over, nearly touching her cheek against his, the strands of her silky hair brushing his collarbone. Her mouth was so close to his ear that he could feel the heat from her breath. "I want to see this place, so either Rio shows me around or you can. But I will not stay a prisoner in this building."

She tilted away from his face, and their eyes locked. Before tonight, Finn had thought her quick smile and willingness to help meant she was a mild-tempered female. However, her earlier comment about his admiring look was bold. And now there was something in the way she looked at him. She was challenging him to contradict her in front of the crowd—it made him question his judgment about her.

"Very well, I will take you out tomorrow afternoon when our conferences are over." After the words tumbled out, he wondered at her easy manipulation of him. When she placed her slim hand on his shoulder, he tensed.

She gave him a bright smile. "Thank you. I'm looking forward to it," she purred, before turning back to Calder.

Finn was glad the pitcher of brew had finally arrived and motioned for the server to fill his glass. He cleared his throat several times and drank thirstily. *What was that Samantha just did?*

The meal couldn't pass quickly enough for Finn. Certainly eyes were always on them, the blond woman and the half-blood chieftain. Samantha revved up her charm for each brave person who approached their table. Her social skills were as diplomatic as Calder's. She easily introduced herself as Harmony, Calder's relative from the other realm. And she assured every single person that all was peaceful on the human side since the earthquake, as Calder had instructed her. Finn stayed quiet, observing her, hiding the fact that she unnerved him a little. With her sudden change in demeanor, he didn't know quite how to take her. Indeed, she intrigued him.

At one point, when his plate arrived laden with meats and vegetables, she leaned against him, peering at his entrée. "What are you eating?" she asked.

He noticed the server gave her the same vegetarian dinner the coastal clan ate.

Poking his fork at the meat drenched in a dark sauce, he said, "Looks like bison." He passed the fork into his mouth and nodded as he chewed. Bison.

"Wow. Have you eaten that before?"

"Yes, our tribe brought the meat." He stabbed a morsel, lifting it for her inspection. "We eat it all the time."

"Can I have a bite?" With her waiting mouth slightly open, inviting, something seemed to clench around his belly. Because he stalled, she opened her mouth wider, leaning even closer, her breasts pressing on his forearm. Giving her what she wanted, he watched her mouth close around the fork, where his had been moments before. He withdrew the utensil and paused, mesmerized. He watched her lick the sauce from her lips and then chew. She considered the flavor.

"Not bad. It tastes like steak," she said, reaching for her glass of water.

He blinked, quickly realizing he was the center of attention. He recovered by reaching for his own glass; that's when his eyes locked with Gale's. In the back corner of the dining room, the general seating for guests, Gale sat beside Taura and Umiko. Both Umiko and Taura were on the tribal council, earning them seats near Finn's table, yet they chose to sit with Gale.

Finn had warned Gale to stay away from Harmony.

So far he had, but Finn was sure that after watching his little exchange with Samantha, Gale would want to know how their courtship was progressing.

As soon as the fruit and cheese plates were taken away, signaling the end of the meal, Finn informed Samantha it was time to return to her room. She politely bid Calder a good evening and obediently followed Finn from the room.

"Could we step out onto the veranda for some fresh air? It was really stuffy in there," she asked, adjusting the rounded collar of her dress.

Finn felt uncomfortably warm and readily agreed; a moment or two was acceptable. They stepped out of a side door at the back of the building, where the wind wasn't blowing so strongly across the ocean. He watched her inhale the fresh night air.

She breathed in deeply. "The air smells so good and fresh here. Different from home."

Finn mimicked her inhale, and when he exhaled he said, "I don't remember."

"Oh." She frowned. "That's right—you're half-human. You must have lived in the human realm?"

Finn looked out at the bay, not really wanting to talk about his painful past, an unpalatable past altered by Gale, ironically the same man who had altered Samantha's path. She already knew what kind of man Gale was, so Finn obliged. "I lived in the human realm with my mother until I was twelve. I was forced to come over, same as you, by my father, Gale. Only I didn't know at the time who he was. I've only recently learned our history."

She stepped closer and rested her hand on his arm in sympathy and murmured, "I'm so sorry. How can you stand him being here?"

Finn recognized his unique connection with her for the first time —both had been abducted by his father and brought into this adaptable world. Regarding the lovely woman before him, he wondered what it would have been like to have met her in the human realm, just two ordinary people meeting and—

His thoughts were rudely interrupted.

"Well, well, it looks like you two have reunited."

At the sound of his father's voice, Finn instinctively stepped in front of Samantha. "It's not a good idea for you to be here. You've put her through a lot, and she doesn't need to be reminded—"

Finn felt her shove him aside, and he watched her, wide eyed, as she marched up to Gale.

"You have a lot of balls, mister!" At her show of outrage, both father and son stared at her. "It's one thing to snatch a grown woman and bring her back here—and you could have asked me instead of scaring the shit out of me—but to take a boy away from his mother!"

Finn reached for her arm, realizing she was going too far, that the contemptible history between his father and himself was a sensitive subject for both of them.

"Hmm. They said you could be a little spitfire when provoked." Gale's self-control seemed in place. He counseled his son, "They are always the best ones in bed."

Instead of taking Gale's intended words as an insult Samantha retorted, "What Finn and I do in bed is none of your concern."

"Let's go." Finn yanked her away from Gale, whose mirth rumbled in his chest.

He marched her up the stairs. Inside Samantha's room, he closed the door soundly behind him. Finn's stance, fists on his hips, was meant to intimidate her. Most people were overwhelmed by him. His height and muscle mass alone earned him respect among the other tribesmen. Tribal women wanted him but often feared his humanism. But instead being intimidated, Samantha just laughed.

"He's a trip!" Her strange comment which made light of a serious situation only confused Finn.

"What were you doing?" Finn demanded.

"After what you told me about him taking you away from your mother, I admit I was a little impulsive, but I won't let him scare me. Beside, you were there to protect me if anything went wrong. Finn, if you want to convince him that I'm Harmony and that I'd consider staying here to become your wife, than we need to up our acting—I mean mostly you. You're not very convincing."

"Why did you make that comment about us in bed?"

"It will keep him guessing," she said, lifting a shoulder.

"We will be seen together tomorrow," he stated while crossing the room to the adjoining door. "I'm certain he will be watching our every move, so I will be more attentive to you. I will act like I'm convincing you to stay." His hand rested on the knob, and he turned to bid her goodnight. She had released the hair tied back from her face and was running her fingers through it. He was caught like a rabbit in a snare. Never had any woman made him feel so…strange. Desire her he did, but there was something else… Whatever it was, he didn't like it. He flexed his shoulders, trying to ease the tension rooted in his core, creating tension throughout his body.

"Stay close to Rio tomorrow until I come for you," he said gruffly. Then he left to enter the sanctuary of his quiet room.

She is just a part in my plan for success. However, he allowed his thoughts to wander. He remembered his time alone with Harmony in the woods, when she'd hugged him, fierce as an ally. Yes, he could define his feelings for Harmony as…kin, related in the fact they were made from the same threads from two worlds, connecting them in understanding and compassion for what the other felt. This undefined connection he was experiencing with Samantha maddened him. Control was his motto. In the years of being ridiculed for being different, he'd learned to govern his emotions and rise above the oppression he'd felt growing up in this realm. This spunky beauty and the uncontainable emotions he was struggling to control had him spooked.

15

"I'll race you!" Samantha challenged Rio, and she dashed ahead of him up the steps. The library was on the floor above her suite, and it sprawled from one end of the building to the other.

Samantha felt fantastic. She had excess energy, and she was itching to burn it off. With his longer legs, Rio caught up to her, and she elbowed him as he passed her on the second-to-last step. The rapid beat of their footfalls rang in the air, and all heads turned when they reached the landing, huffing and puffing.

"You can't out run me with those stubby legs," Rio teased between breaths.

Samantha noticed the small audience of onlookers and shushed Rio. "Which way?" she whispered.

He led her into the library and through several large rooms that led to other smaller rooms until they reached an alcove of bookshelves. While he searched for a particular book, Samantha stepped away to study a globe perched on a carved wooden stand. When Rio appeared at her shoulder, she asked, "Is this your world or mine?"

"The land is mostly the same, but this is my world. The portal the Linker's pass through is just off our coast." He pointed to the spot and then added, "The water god also has access to the waters of both realms."

"This god of yours sounds more like a devil." Her comment was received by her companion with a grim look.

Rio thoughtfully stated, "I suspect all life has its challenges, whether divine or not."

"I suppose you're right." Samantha digested his kinder words, thinking his gentle soul was one of his most endearing qualities. "Did you find the book?"

He held up a thickly bound book and waved for her to follow him. They sat shoulder to shoulder at a nearby table as he flipped through the pages. "Here it is."

When Samantha had asked about his race and how they were different from humans, Rio suggested they go to the library so he could show her the books they used to teach the children about evolution.

"This book is the best one because it has great illustrations," he said, stopping at a page and pointing to apes in trees. The next drawings showed ape-like early Homo sapiens at the water's edge, and then a community of them wading up to their necks, eating floating seaweed, clams, or diving under to pull plants from the sandy ocean floor.

"These drawings depict how our early ancestors underwent an aquatic phase lasting for millions of years. Our Linkers estimate that this aquatic phase only lasted about four million years in your realm before your early ancestors returned to the African savannah. Since Homo sapiens stayed longer in the water here, our bodies began to change. We started to stand upright in order to keep our heads above water. Our bodies became adapted for better swimming."

Samantha read the captions, engrossed in this unbelievable history. Rio went on. "Being in water so much, the ancestors lost most of their body hair." Rio suddenly chuckled. "There are two kinds of habitats known to give rise to naked mammals, subterranean or wet ones. I'd rather live in the ocean than under the dirt."

"Me too," she agreed.

"We are so different from primates, though we share over ninety-eight percent of the same DNA. We don't have a twitch reflex, which keeps pesky bugs off skin. And we are born with ten times the number of fat cells, deposited under our skin like other aquatic mammals. And our babies are born with white fat, which is good for insulation in water as well as buoyancy."

"Wow, how do you know all this?" Samantha thumped her finger on the book.

"The Linkers provided us with this information from your realm. And every child learns evolution." Rio seemed to recall something before he continued. "When Harmony was here we talked about how our races were different. She had not heard the Aquatic Ape theory, which some human scientists have tried to explain. Calder suggested she look into it when she returned to your realm. Harmony never said anything to you about it?"

Shaking her head, she said grimly, "I think there was a lot she didn't tell me. I understand though." She held up her hands and looked around. "It's a lot to take in."

"I guess so." Rio rubbed his forehead. "Though our worlds started the same and we share a common ancestor, we evolved differently. Take our sacred island, for instance. Because our ancestors stayed longer in the water, they migrated away from the African continent and landed here on this island. That is why this place and this temple are sacred to us."

"What I find most impressive is how long you can hold your breath underwater."

"Yeah, we love the water. We swim every day. It's how most of us start our morning. No primate can hold their breath like us," Rio stated with pride.

"You're like those porpoises." Samantha cast her eyes around the vast bookshelves. "Let's go take a walk or something." Suddenly she wanted to be outside, to feel the breeze on skin.

"Finn said not to go far," Rio called to Samantha's retreating back. She flashed him a smile over her shoulder while he rushed to reshelf the book and then restrained himself from running in the library. She was already near the stairwell when he caught up with her.

Lovely lawns swept down to the docks. Samantha noticed fewer trees on the island in this realm, allowing more boat access to the land through grids of boardwalks. She was learning to discern the coastal clansmen from the tribespeople quite easily based on their variation in dress. It was like Native Americans and Puritans. She spied a group of tribal members off near some trees. They had drawn bows and were shooting at dyed cloth rags strung around the tree.

"Oh, let's go watch them." Samantha pointed to the group of three woman and four men talking among themselves.

"This is close enough. We can see from here." Rio tried to remain back. Ahead, the lawn rolled down into sparse scruffy grass and bushes. "There are pickers in there," Rio called after her.

Samantha sidestepped the bushes and trudged onward. She could hear Rio sigh as he followed her. Two of the shooters were retrieving their arrows from the tree trunk, and the others paused in silence as the blond human girl and the clan member approached.

"Hi! Nice shooting." Samantha's friendly smile seemed to put them at ease, but they still seemed hesitant about associating with her and Rio. Suddenly it occurred to her that she was from a different realm, a different race. *I may as well be from a different planet,* she thought as they stared at her.

"I have seen you before," said a tribesman, "in our city. I watched your marriage ceremony."

"Oh, right, when I married Kodiak. You were there?" Samantha regretted getting so close now. What if he realized she wasn't Harmony?

"I watched from a window above the city," he stated.

"Oh!" she smiled, relieved.

"We heard your husband returned with you to the human realm. He didn't come back with you?" asked a woman who eyed her suspiciously.

"No," she sighed sadly. Samantha's acting skills were coming in handy. "Actually, he stayed behind. After he learned there was sunken treasure beneath our oceans and lakes he chose to leave and pursue his other interests." Her face, a mask of regret during her comment, quickly flipped to a smile as she declared, "I came back because Finn wants me here. As I'm sure you've heard, Finn is my very good friend." She turned to Rio.

"Yes," he mumbled, crossing his arms and nodding.

Except for Rio, Samantha's performance was met with enthusiasm. They welcomed her, introduced themselves, and included her in their activity. She learned they traveled with the tribe as the council members' personal hunters, since the clans didn't provide meat. Now they were taking some time to practice their skills.

"May I try?" Samantha asked a female with a smaller bow, who wore several strands of shell necklaces.

"Do you know how to use this?" The woman's face was so thin her cheekbones jutted sharply.

"Yes. Although the bow I've used is different, but I know what to do." The tribesmen glanced at each other as Samantha took the bow and tested its weight and grip. She pulled her sleeve straight, securing it where she clasped the bow in her palm. Taking the arrow, she rested the point between her fingers and slid back the bowstring like an experienced hunter.

"Aim for the red tie," one of the men instructed.

With a *swish* of the arrow and a *twang* of the string, followed by the roar of the spectators, her target hit its mark. Samantha beamed.

"Whoohoo!" She jumped up and down. Her competitive nature kicked in and spurred several more rounds of target practice with the bow and arrows. Later the practice moved to knife throwing. Knives were definitely beyond her skill set, but she agreed when asked if she wanted to try. "Okay, I'll try it. How do I do this?" The expert tribesmen cheered her for her efforts. She asked Rio to join in, but he declined and hung back. Several times he suggested they move on to see other things. But no matter what he said, he couldn't get her to leave. She was having such fun.

Well over an hour later, the hunters reluctantly had to say good-bye and headed off to prepare the evening's meal. Each said they hoped to see her again, and perhaps soon in their city. "We are happy you came back to be with Finn. Our new chieftain could do well with you by his side," said the woman with the high cheekbones.

Samantha had encountered tribes in the human realm as she'd studied various climates, but none had been as friendly as this group. Touched by their kind words, she waved good-bye as she and Rio trailed up the grass toward the Wellness temple.

"How did you learn to shoot like that? Do you hunt?" Rio seemed hungry for answers.

"I don't hunt," Samantha stated right away. "I learned from my brother. He doesn't hunt either—he just does archery as a sport. He is really good at it and has won all kinds of awards. I couldn't let my big brother have all the fun, so I learned how. We had a target set up in our back yard, and when we were young we spent hours shooting."

"Oh, you didn't mention you had a brother."

Samantha, looking thoughtful, dropped her voice a notch. "I haven't seen him in a while. He lives on the west coast, and I've been traveling a lot."

Suddenly her stomach rumbled, and she was grateful for the distraction. "Hey, want to get something to eat?"

***

Finn stood at the window, his face a serious mask; inside he was raging. What was Samantha doing with the tribesmen? He was even more shocked to see her handling a bow. She spread her feet, locking into a solid stance, and drew back the bowstring. When she shot the bow and hit the target dead on, he blocked out the conversation in the room behind him, beyond surprised. He watched for a while as the tribe chatted with her in a jovial manner.

These particular hunters were fierce to look at, yet she'd walked unabashedly right up to them. Finn was astounded by her boldness.

"Finn!" Someone was nearly shouting his name, and he immediately returned his attention to the room.

"Sorry, can you repeat the question?" He glanced one last time out the window and carried the glass he had filled back to his seat. Normally, attendants walked around with refreshments, but he'd needed to stretch his legs and had gone to the side table for some water.

Now he tapped his foot, anxious for today's meeting to end.

16

Samantha watched Finn approach through the dissipating crowd. His stride wasn't a prowl of conceit; instead he walked with a confident, purposeful air. Sex appeal poured from him. She didn't notice the scowl on his face until he was close; his other attributes had captured her attention. She saw his eyes appraise her, penetrate her, until her cheeks grew pink.

He spoke directly to Rio. "Rio, I left you the responsibility for her welfare. Do you think interaction with my hunters a wise choice?"

Samantha frowned, her forehead creasing. She felt responsible for the scolding Rio was receiving, and she piped up on his behalf. "It was my idea." When Finn's eyes then focused intently on her face, she almost faltered. "I know how to shoot, and I was just having a little fun with them. They were very nice." She offered him a sheepish grin and watched one of his eyebrows lift. He seemed to consider her words. Her grin transformed into a wide smile, an antidote to his serious expression. "Really, it was fine! I needed to get out of this building and look around."

Finn suggested, after a long pause, "I could take you around the island by canoe, or we could walk along the beach."

"I know the island's layout. I live here—on the human side, remember? I want to see more of the town and meet the people. Isn't there a gathering place where young people hang out?"

"Keeping a low profile would be best. There's time now before our evening meal. We will head to the docks and take out a canoe," Finn said firmly, ignoring her question and her preference. Although irritated that apparently it was his way or no way, she thought spending time alone with him might be interesting. But weren't they supposed to be seen together?

Samantha hugged Rio and thanked him for his kindness. "I'll see you in the morning?"

Rio glanced at Finn and waited for his approval before he answered. "Yes, I'll see you in the morning."

Samantha watched Rio skirt the crowd gathering after the long day of negotiations. She turned to join Finn, and they walked down the path to the docks. Noticing the attention they were causing, Samantha slipped her hand into Finn's and smiled up at him. The smoldering look he gave her could melt an iceberg, and she suddenly wondered how far she could go with this pretend attraction. There was no pretending on her side. From the moment she'd clapped eyes on him, her hormonal instincts had kicked in, and her body responded. Finn, with his chiseled physique and wicked sexy, green eyes was ridiculously gorgeous. But she was in some strange world, and this guy wasn't even completely human! So she needed to be cautious. Her fantasies were her own, and they needed to remain that way.

As their tribal chieftain approached, tribesmen at the docks at once offered canoes. Finn selected one and held Samantha's hand steady while she stepped in and sat down. He took the paddle, stepped in with ease, and sat opposite her. She thought he looked comfortable as he began paddling, like he'd done it thousands of times. It had been awhile since she'd been in a canoe, all the kids who'd grown up on the island knew how to swim by the age of five and take a boat out on their own by the age of ten. *That's what kids did in those days,* she remembered.

While the shore regressed behind them, Samantha absorbed the bigger picture. The Wellness-by-the-Sea sat high on the bluff, looking remarkably like the Wentworth-by-the-Sea in her realm, except the roof line flared out and some details were altered. The blended Asian and Victorian styles gave the building in this realm a unique design. The roof tiles reminded Samantha of when she'd worked on the tsunami segments in Japan last year. Rio had told her about the earthquake, followed by the tidal wave, that had hammered the building. It was hard to image this place damaged; it was perfectly serene now.

Samantha had been fascinated with the weather since she was a child. The bigger and scarier the storm, the more excited she usually became. Strangely for a young kid, she sat glued for hours to the weather forecasts. Growing up in New England with its varying, changing-by-the-hour weather provided loads of experience in hands-on meteorology.

She remembered that Harmony had mentioned the architecture was different here. *How did Harmony accept and adjust to this altered realm? How did she feel when she found out she had living family here?* Harmony had said she was descended from Calder. At the time, part of Samantha couldn't completely believe Harmony's claim. Samantha now felt ashamed for doubting her friend, because here she sat, in the alternate realm! *I almost died crossing over. Will I survive crossing back to the human realm? Will I be able to go back?*

Dragging her gaze from the altered scenery, she rested her eyes on Finn, who paddled silently, watching her. "Thank you for bringing me out here. It looks different from my home in many ways."

He squinted, his gaze seeming to focus on the horizon. He said in a mystical voice, "I believe we have entered a new era. Gale and Calder are ultimately responsible. Both men have done an injustice to both realms. They both broke our laws."

"Yet only Gale was sent into exile when he brought

you over. What about Calder?" She asked rhetorically. Samantha had wondered why Calder had maintained his celebrated Linker status on the council. She repeated her newly acquired gossip. "Rio told me that after Calder's secret affair with Harmony's grandmother in the human realm, Calder returned here and married. He started a new family. Rio said Calder gave up his secret when Harmony showed up. Rio reasoned that of course the clans were upset, but there are few Linkers left, and Calder is near the end of his days. The clans realized they needed Calder's experience and help working out their differences with your tribe. Apparently, they voted to keep him on the council."

"It was the right decision," Finn agreed. He steered the canoe north along the tree line that now blocked the Wellness temple from view.

A tiny cove, a dimple in the land, with a sandy beach looked inviting. As the sun slanted low in the sky, the light reflected off the sand, making it shimmer.

"What *is* that?" Samantha pointed to the alcove.

"I don't know. This is my first time paddling around the island. My city is far from here in the forest."

"Can we go ashore? Let's check it out!"

"Okay, but we can't stay long. It will need to return for the evening meal."

As they got closer, the tiny rocks in the sand winked and glistened like diamonds in the light. Finn stepped into the shallow water and dragged the canoe onto the beach before Samantha jumped out.

Scooping up a handful of pearl-sized stones she gasped, "Wow, these look like diamonds! A whole beach of diamonds. Isn't it beautiful?" Scrutinizing her find, she crunched over to Finn, holding in her palm a larger pebble. "This one is huge!"

When she looked up into his face, all thoughts of gemstones turned to dust. The mossy green color of

Finn's eyes, absorbing the setting sun, immobilized her, and her tongue flicked out to lick her dry lips.

Finn lowered his eyes to the palm she held up. His finger rolled over the pebble and then dropped to her skin, drawing circles around the stone. The stirring motion of his touch reached all the way to her core. Slowly Samantha twisted her palm, and the stone slid to the ground while their fingers intertwined. With only their hands touching, gripping and relaxing, their breath came faster. Samantha licked her lips again. That seemed to get his attention. He scrutinized her face and shifted closer. She swallowed hard, watching a hunger cross his features.

Finn tilted his head, and a lock of hair fell across his forehead. Samantha's free hand brushed it off his handsome face. His dark hair was thick and soft. In a gentle motion he drew his arm back with their fingers still intertwined; she was forced to inch closer. Tiny stones scattered at her feet. She felt him grip the curve of her hip, bringing her closer still. Her hand riffled through his hair until it reached the thick column of his neck. Overwhelmed by his maleness, she stood, primed for him to kiss her. He was like a powerful wolf, his body poised for attack. His sexy eyes were focused and hungry for the kill, thrilling her. Just as her lashes fluttered closed, she felt something swoop by, scarcely touching the hairs on top of her head. Startled, she moved, and the couple broke apart.

Instinctively her hand grazed her hair as she asked, "What was that?"

"Bats." It was dusk, and she noticed several more flapping black bats dipping in the air above them. "The sun will be behind the trees soon. Time to go back and get ready for the evening meal."

Although Samantha wasn't a fan of bats, they didn't bother her. Half the houses on the island had a number of unwanted summer guests in their attics. Years ago during summer bike rides at dusk, she and the neighborhood kids challenged each other to spot the first bat. It was usually Samantha who did, since she was always looking up at the clouds.

Finn pushed the canoe into the ankle-deep water and turned to wait for her. Standing alone, Samantha inwardly grumbled because their kiss was foiled. She pocketed a stone before reluctantly sloshing into the waves. The water that covered her sandaled feet was cold, and she rushed to climb in. She noticed Finn didn't move to assist her into the canoe this time, instead almost deliberately keeping his distance. She took her seat, mulling over the fact that their near kiss had been ruined by a bat. Her first thought was to curse the creature, and her next was to curse Finn. He'd lured her so far…and then left her hanging. Her insides felt molten and volatile. She wanted to ask him why he'd dashed away at the interruption, but she was afraid she knew the answer. It was similar to her own. They were strangers—different races even—and their situation was beyond complicated.

Although Harmony and Kodiak… No! That's not the same. And obviously Finn is an important leader in this realm. It's unlikely he'd consider returning to the human realm, right? Dare I ask? Don't be an idiot—you will never ask that!

Finn paddled in silence. Since he seemed to be pretending nothing had *nearly* just happened between them, Samantha mused, "So what we were talking about earlier…the Linker's punishment, or lack thereof. What will happen with Gale this time? Is going to be punished for bringing me here?" Kidnapping was bad. But in a teensy way, she was okay with the outcome, because she'd met Finn and Rio and got to see this amazing world.

"Likely he'll return to banishment or be locked up. At the very least, he'll be denied a chair on my council if he's allowed to remain in the city," Finn said without compassion.

Samantha sensed Finn's animosity toward the father who'd lied, taken him from his mother, and now worked to manipulate him. Still, Gale was his father. Her heart ached for him, knowing his only family in this realm had treated him so badly.

"Will you return to your city when the summit is over?"

He slowed his strokes at the softening of her voice.

"Yes, I will return to the city." He stopped paddling and stared at her. His next words, probably meant as a gentle warning that she get a grip on reality, came with an underlying inquiry. "Calder has suggested another crossing for you is not advised."

"Would you be sad to see me go?" She tried to make light of her situation.

"What is it that you want, Samantha?"

That he answered her question with a question irritated her. He was avoiding the subject of his feelings toward her, leaving her to second-guess about them. Truthfully, she wanted to know why her entire life was now flipped upside down. Why she'd lost everything she'd worked so hard for. Why she'd ended up in another realm. It was as if she were having an odd dream. And to warp it even more, she'd met *him*! What she felt for Finn was beyond anything she had ever felt for anyone else. She was in trouble. What she ultimately wanted was for her life to settle. She answered, "I...want to be happy, no matter where I end up."

"I appreciate your helping me, my tribes, and the clans. This summit is crucial. I can't let Gale ruin it. Samantha, I will do whatever I can to help you. I will figure something out." His sincere declaration surprised her.

"Well, I'm here, so let's get to know each other better. Tell me more about you, about your city...this realm." She had a knack for being upbeat, looking on the positive side, and she asserted that skill now.

Finn nodded and resumed paddling. "All right." He thought a moment. "There are strange creatures in this realm. And vast differences from the human realm. For instance, this realm didn't have the last ice age your realm did, so we have different animals. The one I like best is the short-faced bear. Standing on their hind legs, they reach the height of two grown men. It's a huge challenge to hunt one of these killing machines. But I'm known for my skill and return to the city loaded with meat and hides."

"Your city is far away from here, right? Are there bears on this island? Should I not wander in the woods?" Her questions, meant only in jest, seemed to make him serious.

"My city is far away, as are the bears who travel in the northern regions above the great falls. But you should never wander around the island alone. You are under my protection. Heed my warning." His brows snapped together.

"I'm glad you're watching out for me, Finn. I like you watching me." After her bold statement their gazes locked again, until Samantha arched a teasing eyebrow.

She could tell Finn was fighting a grin. He swiftly glided the canoe toward the Wellness temple as it came into view. They soon rocked up to the dock, and clan members steadied the canoe while they climbed out. A tribal member stood with his arms crossed, waiting for Finn to acknowledge him.

"Good evening, Taura. Is there something that needs my attention?" Taura never looked at Samantha as he fell into step beside Finn.

Samantha skipped to keep up with Finn's long, purposeful strides and slipped her hand into his, momentarily catching his attention. He blinked at her before turning back to Taura.

"Chief, your father would like to speak with you, before dinner if possible." Taura's voice was curt but respectful. It wasn't lost on Samantha when Taura referred to Gale as Finn's father. Finn immediately tensed. She gave his hand an extra squeeze to relay her support.

"I'll escort Harmony to her room. Then I'll be available to speak with him. I will meet him in the library," Finn replied.

"I will let him know." Taura gave Samantha a once-over before he pivoted and walked away.

Finn rushed her up the hill, and they skipped up the stairs. He stopped outside her door and said, "I'll be right back to take you down to dinner. Wait for me."

His gruff command sent a shiver down her spine. She couldn't wait for him to come back, and she wished they didn't have to leave the room for dinner. He stood too close, making her blush. Their hands remained clasped. When he reached around her to open the door, she was momentarily sandwiched. She looked up at his mouth—this was her chance to stretch up and kiss him. She wanted him to keep Gale waiting and rekindle the earlier spark. But the door swung wide behind her, and he released her hand. She backed away from him, holding his gaze. For a moment, she thought he'd advance into the room and...

His hand on the doorknob, he released a low growl, his nostrils flaring. He sized her up again with that look. "Be ready for when I return." He stepped back and closed the door. Samantha bent over at the waist and took several deep breaths.

17

Finn chose to meet Gale in the library, where others were likely to see them together. Gale would get no favors from him. As Finn approached, he noticed that Taura and Umiko accompanied Gale. *They never seem to leave Gale's side.* These tribesmen were *his* council members, and they should be showing *him* this dedication and service, not his treacherous father.

Gale was making himself comfortable in an alcove with seating, a cozy nook meant to study journals in. He waited for Finn to sit before he commented, "Finn, I'm glad to see Harmony has missed you. She has readily succumbed to your charms. Has she tired of her clan husband so quickly?"

"Their marriage was a ploy to get away from Nakoma." Finn spoke the truth. Kodiak had announced that they were promised to be married right after Nakoma suggested Harmony and Finn wed. Kodiak had been protecting Harmony, but Kodiak was also in love with her.

Gale seemed to mull this over. Finn glanced beyond the alcove, down the vast room at the professors who gathered books and journals and then slipped from the room.

"Well, now that she's interested in you, we need to see if she is willing to use her abilities to further help the tribe. Her protection against Suijin and his creatures would be a tremendous asset. Don't you agree?"

"I think it's a little too soon to worry about that. It's enough to get through the summit. When she returns with me to the city—"

"Son, if she is on board, then the outcome of this summit could be vastly different. We need the clansmen to work the salt mines. Doubling the workforce in other areas too will advance our city."

Finn stood, pointing an angry finger at Gale. "You are overstepping. I want your word you will not interfere with the negotiations. Our advancement can be achieved by peaceful measures."

"I will leave the negotiations to you." Gale seemed to surrender.

Finn sensed Gale was biding his time. He had purposely avoided meeting with his father to discuss tribal affairs. He believed Gale's patience was running thin, and Finn hoped the man's focus would be on making amends and playing nicely to earn back his place on the council.

"However," Gale insisted, "I would like to see your girl in action. What abilities can we witness? I hear she can call the sirens with her singing."

Pushing his hair back from his face, Finn warned, "You shouldn't ask for what you don't understand. Harmony Parker can be quite deadly. She deliberately called upon the sirens to wipe out the tribe that threatened our escape. She left the siren that came for her burned and distorted—murdered. Remember, *that* deadly weapon isn't too thrilled with you right now. So stay away from her."

Finn conveyed this truth with a pointed look at his father's companions. After all, Umiko knew what Finn claimed was accurate. He had been up on the bridge with Finn and their chieftain the day Harmony burned two sirens right before their eyes. Harmony had been perched on the river's edge, talking with what she'd thought were young girls out for a swim. When the sirens tried to pull Harmony into the river, Harmony's touch had sizzled their skin. Ultimately Finn had picked them off with arrows; it seemed that Harmony was just as shocked as everyone watching had been.

"Yes, we saw what she is capable of," Umiko confirmed.

Umiko's corroboration seemed to vex Gale. Clearly Gale wanted to observe this phenomenon himself. Gale gave Finn a blank stare, but Finn knew he'd won this round. "Enjoy your meal," Finn concluded, and he strode away. Gale's words plagued him as he took the stairs. He wouldn't put it past the Linker to find a way to test Harmony's skills—only he wouldn't be testing Harmony. Samantha would be in grave danger.

Finn slipped into his room and changed his clothing before collecting Samantha for dinner. She gave him a bright smile when she answered his knock on the door, which took his mind off of his irksome relative and acutely reminded him he had almost kissed her earlier.

The lobby was crowded and noisy as the delegates made their way into the dining area. Samantha was the first to glimpse Rio down the hall.

"Rio!" Samantha called just loudly enough that Rio looked up from the group of people he was talking with. He waved. Both parties weaved through the throngs of socializers until they met. "What are you still doing here?" she asked.

"There's going to be a gathering in a bit, down the hill at the beach. I was just letting some friends know about it. It will be relaxed, a time for the tribes and the clans to socialize while the councilmen and women eat their fancy dinner." Rio beamed with enthusiasm. "You two should come."

Finn's forehead creased, his eyes narrowed, and he crossed his arms over his chest. He was chieftain, expected to attend the fancy dinner, no matter how much he would have preferred otherwise.

"I…um…meant after your dinner," Rio clarified, and he shuffled back a step at Finn's glare.

Finn took a breath, about to decline, but Samantha

squealed with delight. "Oooo, that sounds like fun! Can we go, Finn?"

Samantha gave her cutest pout—Finn knew no guy could resist it.

"Please?" she pleaded, her eyes beseeching, her voice soft. For emphasis, she placed her hand on his forearm, an intimate connection.

Rio bravely continued. "The beach is before the village. There's a shallow inlet for swimming and a fish-fry stand. Typically in the evenings, friends and couples bring blankets and gather after an evening swim. So it's the perfect place for the tribe to get to know us better. We're planning a bonfire, and I'll likely end up playing my flute."

Most of the crowd had funneled into the dining room; only a few people still lingered in the hall.

"Oh, I would love to hear—"

Tearing his eyes away from her pout, Finn cut in, "I'll take her to dinner, and we will join you afterward."

Samantha turned to Finn, her eyes bright. "Thanks for saying yes. It will be nice to meet the locals and more of your tribe."

"Okay," Rio said. "Just follow the road behind the temple and take a left. That path will lead you there. I'll look for you later." Rio waved as he turned and continued down the corridor.

"It will please the tribe members to see their chieftain among them," Finn remarked. But although it was good diplomacy, that wasn't why he'd agreed. "Also, people talk, and it's good for us to be seen together in public."

"Yes. We need to work on formulating a plan. If Gale is in the dining hall..."

"He will be," Finn affirmed.

"Then let's give him a little demonstration to convince him that his plan is working."

"Like what?"

She grinned and tugged at his crossed arms. He dropped them, and she held her hand out to him. When he reached for it, she drew his arm around her shoulder and cozied up next to him. "Make it look like you like me."

"Oh. All right, if you think this—"

Umiko called to Finn and approached. He greeted his chief and settled his eyes on Samantha.

Finn shifted, about to release Samantha, but she slid her arm around his waist, keeping them in physical contact. She gave him a sly grin when he stiffened at the awkward movement.

"Umiko, this is Harmony Parker. I don't think you were formally introduced when she was in our city before," said Finn, paying attention to his old friend's expression.

Finn didn't know that Umiko had waited in the boat for Gale to return with the girl. Yet he knew Umiko had helped Gale somehow. Finn disliked the intense way Umiko examined Samantha. As far as Finn remembered, Umiko had only seen Harmony from afar on the bridge when she was in the city months ago.

"It is my pleasure to finally meet you. I've heard much about you. I hope our chief realizes he is a lucky man to have your affections."

Although Umiko's voice was a monotone and lacked emotion, his words irritated Finn. How dare he speak so boldly? Umiko's loyalty was clearly drawn in the sand. Umiko was testing the boundaries, but Finn wouldn't let himself get riled. He set his jaw, speaking with authority to redirect Umiko's attention. "Umiko, thank you for your continued efforts with the negotiations today."

Umiko's stoic expression never changed, but he nodded at the praise.

Finn slid his hand down Samantha's back and possessively placed it on her hip.

"I would only do what is best for the tribe," Umiko replied in a deep, official voice, but he softened and stepped closer to Samantha. "I look forward to getting to know you. I'm pleased you are here." His dark eyes probed her, drinking her in, making Finn wild with jealousy. It seemed like Umiko was undressing her with his eyes. Samantha didn't rebuke him with stinging words—she only smiled politely.

Finn sniffed at Umiko's remark before he turned his head and said to her, "Let's get to our seats."

The look the two men exchanged was not unpleasant but challenging; their shoulders were squared and their chests expanded. Umiko had revealed his interest in Samantha with a few words and *that* look.

Finn spun her around and led her through the double doors. He didn't acknowledge it when she glanced backwards over her shoulder at Umiko. He knew Umiko stood there, watching them, while they took their seats.

As Finn took his seat she whispered, leaning close, "That was strange. So what's your relationship with that guy Umiko? He seems intense."

"Umiko and I have known each other a long time. We served as big game hunters for Nakoma, the chieftain before me, and we trained with weaponry side by side." He shrugged, but inside he felt raw with betrayal.

"I didn't get the impression you are very *good* friends," she commented, and she reached for a pitcher of water. He didn't answer, and she stopped pouring to look over at him. "What is it?"

He watched Umiko greet Gale and take the seat next to him. Her eyes followed his.

"Umiko seems close with the evil one," Samantha said out of the side of her mouth.

The corner of Finn's mouth turned up. She didn't refer to Gale as "your father" and he appreciated it. It seemed she understood that it pained him.

"Why do you call him evil?" Considering the obvious fact that Gale had altered Samantha's life, Finn wanted to hear that someone else despised this man.

"Are you kidding? After what he did to you? And what he tried to do to Harmony, attempting to take her away from Kodiak and her home? I feel nothing but contempt for him."

"Indeed."

Their food was set before them. Dinner proceeded pretty much the same way as the night before. Finn made an attempt to talk to her more, though many others solicited his attention. He offered her meat from his plate, and this time she used her own fork.

Under the weight of the summit negotiations, Finn felt Gale's presence as a distraction. He constantly needed to think and plot to stay one step ahead of everyone else. Resting his eyes on the beautiful woman next to him, he sighed. She was a distraction too—but at this moment a welcome one. Finn wanted to be outside, under the night sky with her. She was his feisty little ally. Dessert hadn't arrived, but he leaned across her and told Calder they were excusing themselves. Finn slid his chair back and overheard Samantha tell Calder where they were sneaking off to. Calder nodded when she told him his grandson, Rio, would be there.

"Enjoy yourselves." The wise old Linker grinned.

18

Samantha inhaled the fresh ocean air. She dropped her head back and slowed her steps so she could admire the trillions of stars in the velvet night sky. The sun had set almost two hours ago, and she pointed at the bright clouds in the distance. "Look! What a beautiful example of shining night clouds," she murmured softly.

"They look like they are glowing," Finn observed.

"Yes. They are called noctilucent clouds. We're nearing the end of their season. Here in the northern hemisphere, if you're above forty-five degrees latitude, you can see them from May until August. They are in the upper atmosphere, only visible at deep twilight," she said, contentment lacing her voice. "Perfect timing." She watched his eyes scan the view as they stood alone in the warm summer night.

He turned toward her. "Fortune is smiling upon you then, because we are at forty-four degrees latitude."

Her eyes widened, and a little chuckle escaped. "Okay, smarty pants."

Grinning, he replied, "If you are implying I'm intelligent—I am. And I'm impressed that you are an expert on *noc-til-ucent* clouds."

She liked his playful banter. "Yes, well, I'm an expert on *all* clouds. I'm a meteorologist. I report on the weather for my job." Samantha didn't expect such wonder to cross Finn's face. It seemed as though he was taken aback.

He shifted, hooked his thumbs in his belt, and shook his head. "Wow, we have a lot in common then."

"What do you mean?"

"My abilities. I told you that both Harmony and I have abilities. Well, mine is…I can control the weather."

Her mouth fell open. "No way!" He bobbed his head and looked away with a smile. For the first time, she noticed that he was uncomfortable. It was endearing. "So what can you do?"

He shrugged. "I can draw precipitation and make clouds, rain, hail, snow... I can summon hurricanes, or lightning."

"That is so amazing. Will you show me sometime?" she asked shyly. The tribal chieftain was already powerful enough, but this revelation put him in a different class of badass. *Damn, I am so hooked!*

"Yes, perhaps another time. We should go now. Rio is waiting."

As they followed the lamp-lit path to the cove, Finn's gaze seemed to constantly return to her. Watching his lips tuck into a smile sent her heart soaring. He was a tough nut to crack, but her reward, when he flashed his teeth in a wide smile, made her heart practically float away. *Wow, if only we'd met in the other realm!* She couldn't help but try to lighten his mood, to keep him smiling.

They reached the cove. Faces were lit by a raging bonfire. A group of tribesmen and woman greeted Finn.

"Chief, it is good to see you here." They gathered around, obviously enjoying the fact their chieftain had chosen to leave the lofty dining hall to hang outside with them.

"Yes, I'm thankful to my companion, Harmony, for suggesting it." She beamed at him for giving her the credit.

"I watched you with the bow and arrow this morning," a tribesman commented. "You are good. What did you hunt in the human realm?" Suddenly, their chieftain was forgotten. The group surrounded Samantha, waiting to hear her answer.

When she glanced at Finn, he seemed content to hang

back and listen to her. The cluster of both clan and tribe members around her grew, making it easy for Rio to spot and join them. Samantha enjoyed her time with these strangers, who quickly became friends. They hung on her every word, laughed at her stories, and tripped over themselves to impress her. Several tribesmen, testing their knife-throwing skills, preened in front of her. She looked at Finn every time they showed off.

Samantha noticed Finn's mood darken when one tribesman pulled her up from the blanket where she sat beside him. The man insisted that she show off her bow skills to the others hunters. Finn sat forward, elbows on his raised knees, ready to jump to action.

"Okay, just one shot," she said to the crowd. She accepted the bow given to her by a female dressed in animal skins. She set the arrow, raised the bow, and concentrated on the target the tribesman pointed out. Tossing her golden hair back, surely a magnificent display to the brunettes, Samantha turned her head slightly and winked at Finn. He didn't move a muscle. Turning away, she inhaled a steady breath. As she exhaled, she let the arrow fly. It hit its mark dead on.

The crowd cheered wildly. The human girl took a bow before she returned to Finn's side on the blanket.

"Nice shot," he said quietly. "If you are done entertaining your friends, we should head back."

Samantha wasn't sure how to take him. He'd returned to his solemn demeanor. She sighed. "Of course. I'm sure that you have a long day tomorrow. Thanks for bringing me. I had a really fun time. Your tribe cracks me up." She raised her eyebrows at his intense expression and laughed. She said, "Come on." They rose from the blanket a clan member had provided.

"Rio, we are heading back to the Wellness," Samantha called to him.

Rio approached and hugged her. "I'll see you

tomorrow."

A tribesman who notice they were leaving, shouted out, "I look forward to seeing you around." A few others raised their eyebrows and snickered at his audacity.

Finn paused at the hunter's words, his shoulders tense. But Samantha slipped her hand into his, waving to the crowd with her free hand. She tugged Finn along, and he allowed her to do so.

On the path, away from the gang of merrymakers, Samantha smiled. This gathering reminded her so much of her teenage years on the island. On summer nights just like this, she and Harmony walked down to the beach to meet friends, sip beers, and break curfew. "Your tribe is welcoming. Is everyone this friendly in your city?" she asked Finn, whose long legs set the pace. The hill steepened, and she had to scamper to keep up.

"I think some were a little too friendly," he said from the side of his mouth.

A giggle bubbled free, and she joked, "You sound jealous."

Finn stopped abruptly. Because he was still holding her hand, she was twisted and jerked against his chest. Trying to stay upright, she dropped her free hand against his bulging shoulder. Finn gripped her elbow to keep her steady as she settled against him. Her other hand was still vice-gripped in his. She stood on higher ground, so her gaze was level with his lips. Her amusement evaporated, and she stared at him with confusion.

"Let me be clear. I'm in charge of you...of your safety." His voice was a quiet snarl as he made his point.

"I feel safe with you, Finn," she whispered. There was no need to shout in the cool night; he was inches away. She watched his facial muscles relax. His hand also relaxed from her elbow and slid up the bare skin of her arm, skipping over the shoulder strap of her dress, continuing on to touch her collarbone. Her senses took over. His fingertip rested on the rapid pulse at her neck. *What are those powerful hands capable of,* she wondered, her heart hammering.

They mutually released their hands and allowed them to find other places to touch. Samantha's palm skimmed across his steely ribcage. Finn's floated up to cup her face. Suddenly, he dropped his forehead to hers, blowing out a frustrated breath. And with a low growl, he withdrew his touch from her body. His hands in midair, he drew his head back, his eyes screwed closed.

Samantha clung desperately to him. Their kiss couldn't be avoided a second time—she'd die! She was so turned on she had to chomp on her lip to stop from whimpering out loud.

Still biting her lip, she pleaded with her eyes. When he opened his, Finn wouldn't look at her. Instead, he gripped her arms and shifted her aside. She was wooden on the outside, glass on the inside. That glass shattered, and she twitched. Just then, she heard people coming up the path from the cove. Finn spun her decisively around, and they continued back to the Wellness temple in silence.

***

Finn felt barbaric for leading her down a path that had no future. At her door, he wanted to explain, but she slipped inside, mumbling a goodnight. He stood in the hallway a full minute, trying to decide if he should knock on her door. Finally, he gave up and entered his own room. The summit's crucial outcome was constantly on his mind. He didn't need the distraction of this human girl. Not only were the tribal members counting on him, but these decisions would affect the coastal clans just as strongly, bringing peace or perhaps war. This wasn't the time to fantasize about a girl with golden hair, her wide smile and lips that begged to be kissed. *How can she be merely human? She is more like an enchanting witch.* It was as if she'd cast a spell on him.

At night, his stirrings for her made him stroke the sheets. And his daydreams... Well, damn, he'd had to leave the room a couple times to get fresh air. Samantha was consuming his thoughts. He wanted to touch her, possess her, and he was slowly going mad knowing that he couldn't. What distracted him the most was that he knew she wanted it too.

He rubbed his hands on his face and then threaded his fingers through his hair. He felt exhausted. He sought his bed. His mind raced with all that had passed. Negotiations were going well; the last of the details were to be hammered out over the next couple of days. Soon he'd be on his way back to the city, leaving Samantha here to decide her fate. Gale would be confronted and punished yet again, but that was a tribal matter that would be dealt with upon their return to the city.

An hour ticked by. Then another. Finn tossed on the mattress, attempting to get comfortable, but sleep eluded him. He sat up and swung his feet to the floor. He rubbed the back of his neck, trying to ease his restlessness. Before he realized it, he rose from the bed and crossed to the adjoining door.

Wait, what am I doing? After a long deep breath he reasoned, *You are taking what you need! Have her already, and get her out of your mind.*

He'd been with many of the tribal women, but he'd never felt anything more than the need to slake his desire. Most of the tribal women wanted the same. This would be no different. Samantha was just a human woman; he didn't want anything more from her. He had enough pressure and responsibility as chief.

Finn tapped on the door. Nothing. He called her name. Nothing. *Could she already be asleep?* If she wasn't, she was obviously still angry with him. Finn returned to his bed. He forced the alluring smile that branded his mind from his consciousness and eventually managed a few hours of sleep.

19

The Human Realm

Harmony shifted the car into park and turned off the motor. Her head dropped back against the headrest, and she sighed. Fatigue was setting in. Glancing at her house, she felt an overwhelming sense of sadness. *I'm in a funk... Maybe I just need some lunch.* The day had started out rough...

Harmony couldn't sleep. She'd tossed and turned all night. It had been two weeks since Kodiak left for his expedition on Lake Superior. In the nights since he'd gone, her dreams were laced with apprehension and fear. The nightmares sent her into deep water, the god observing her struggles. Always, she looked for Kodiak to save her, but he was missing—just like when she was awake. He left a hole in her existence, and she felt like she was drowning without him.

Kodiak had called her faithfully, and she'd dutifully sat by the phone. The first day he went on about his experience on the airplane. The second day he told her about the other guys he'd met who were passionate about what they were trying to accomplish. He was clearly swept up in the excitement of what they were planning to achieve. Days after he boarded the boat that took him to the wreckage, he'd reported what the experience was like and what the ROV pictures had revealed.

"You wouldn't believe it!" he'd exclaimed. "The images were so clear we could detect minimal rust and sediment. We could see the damage done to the ship, but the reason for the sinking is still unexplained."

"I thought it sank in a storm." Harmony recalled the

popular song about the sinking of the *Edmund Fitzgerald.*

"Maybe not. They are still going over the footage. There's about five hours to review."

"It seems like they worked quickly," she said hopefully. Maybe Kodiak would come home now.

"Yeah, and the best part—we saw the ship's bell," he'd said, oblivious to her hint.

Over several days he relayed more facts about shipwrecks and how they pertained to this historic dive, and he mentioned that he'd be staying on for a while. "I miss you like crazy, Harmony. It's just for a few more weeks."

At least he sounded like he sincerely missed her, despite his need to remain a part of the expedition until the end. Of course this was exciting for him. All she could do was assure him she'd be waiting for him when he came back. Now she waited for the day he'd get to a landline and call to tell her he was coming home.

Harmony flung the sheets back and sat up. She thought it utterly unfair that now she had a husband he was off seeking adventure instead of building a life with her. Oh, she'd reassured him she was fine with him going, but deep inside her longing for him only grew sharper. He had pledged himself as her partner for life, and she took undeniable comfort in knowing she'd never be alone again.

Dressed in jeans and a Duran Duran tee shirt, she found her way into the kitchen in the predawn. The light over the sink came on with a snap. She swallowed instant coffee along with a Pop Tart and then reached for her hooded sweatshirt, which lay draped over a chair from the night before. There was only one destination in her mind when she was feeling melancholy—Wentworth-by-the-Sea.

Harmony rode her bike the short distance to the other

side of the island toward the hotel, considering her preservation group's efforts to save the abandoned, deteriorating structure. The nonprofit group Friends of the Wentworth was proposing to get the Victorian building on the list of Most Endangered Historic Properties in America. Harmony was all for the idea. Certainly the hotel would gain recognition, perhaps saving the piece of history that meant so much to her and the community she lived in.

She sighed as the mansard rooftops came into view above the trees. Stashing her bike in the usual place, behind a bush that hid it from the road, she trotted up the hill. Her timing was perfect; the sun was just rising, a fiery orb lifting out of the sea, making the surface of the ocean dance as if millions of diamonds floated on it. In the dawn of a new day, a lone seagull lifted on the breeze, silent for a little while longer while its groggy neighbors still huddled in their nests.

Harmony stood with her back to the hotel, staring at the horizon, distinguishing the many colors in the morning sky, and when she turned around to look past the gleam on the chain-link fence to the peeling paint, she smiled. The white façade of the hotel was cast in a rosy glow... *Lovely.*

In the other realm, she knew a similar building sat on this site, theirs full of life and activity while this one was full of ghosts and memories of bygone eras. She pictured the hotel years ago when her grandparents drove her past the hundreds of polished windows. Smartly dressed guests walked with an air of wealth while the help gathered at the bottom of the hill to smoke cigarettes, hidden behind the stately shrubs. Her grandparents had filled her head with stories of this hotspot, and Harmony could almost hear the music from within. It beckoned her.

The latest investment company had torn down eighty

percent of the building leaving only the original part intact. She surveyed the bare ground where the debris had been cleared with a sense of strangeness. The empty area where the huge extended structure once stood emitted a ghostly aura. She felt unsettled as she slipped through a section of fence waiting to be set in place and then climbed the fire escape to gain access to the inside from the upper window.

She entered the corridor and trotted down the stairs. She ran her hand along the wooden banister of the main staircase. Inhaling the musty scent, she took in the view as if she were watching a slow-motion film. When she was a child she remembered watching guests post letters at the lobby's mail booth. The fancy hotel had its own post office. Lost in her thoughts as she moved through the vacant space, Harmony unintentionally kicked an empty beer can. The loud noise echoed in the empty room. She nearly jumped out of her skin when she heard the distinct protest of a riled raccoon coming from the direction where the can landed. Startled, both she and the animal paused to stare at each other before the raccoon turned and scurried into an opening in the splintered floorboards.

"Humph. To think a president and a prince stayed here, and now it's home to raccoons."

Harmony saw a sedan pull over along the curb outside. She glanced at her watch and wondered who would be out so early. From a good vantage point, she peeked out the window as four men in suits stepped out of the car. One guy did most of the talking and pointing, while another guy jotted down notes in a fancy leather folder. She couldn't hear what was said. They looked like typical businessmen or, maybe, she thought, investors. For years this property had passed through various investment companies as it continued to decline. The townsfolk's hope was always high. Investors were optimistic until they estimated the costs of refurbishing. Each company inevitably proposed other options, usually tearing it down and building condos.

The chatty guy led the others away, undoubtedly to impress them with the killer view. Harmony slipped out the way she came in, unnoticed. Her ten-speed bike was safely hidden behind the bush, and she held back the branches to retrieve it. Glancing at her watch, Harmony estimated how long it would take to run some errands before she met up with Samantha later. She biked home and ditched two wheels for four; she motored over the tiny bridge onto the mainland. One of her errands included the library. It was time she read up on things she had briefly learned about in the other realm, like the aquatic ape theory and extinct giant American lions.

Home again, she dragged herself and her bag of books out of the car. On the back porch, she noticed the back door was open and assumed Samantha was inside waiting for her. She heaved the canvas book bag over her shoulder. The heavy science books on human evolution and the aquatic ape theory made a thud when she dropped them on the kitchen counter. That's when she noticed the refrigerator door was ajar.

What the hell? She rushed over and closed the door, jiggling it—nothing seemed loose. *Sam must have left it open.* Harmony knew sometimes her friend could be distracted or forgetful. She glanced at the counter, where Samantha had left her purse last night. It was still there.

"Sam! Sam, I'm back!" Harmony shouted. She listened for her friend. All was quiet. Crossing the kitchen, she heard a crunch under her shoe. Carefully lifting her foot, she saw the broken Pepsi bottle, its contents spilled all over the floor. Sidestepping the mess, she moved quickly down the hallway toward the living room, passing her grandfather's den. "Hello!" she called again. Nothing.

She realized she'd rushed past the den. The door was open—but she always made sure that door remained closed. Samantha knew that! Had Samantha carelessly left it open? The thoughtless act irritated her, because after her grandfather died, her grandmother kept the door closed to enshrine his scent of leather and pipe tobacco.

Half worried and half angry, Harmony stood at the doorway. The smell wasn't of leather and pipe tobacco—she smelled the distinct burnt smell of those herbs!

"Oh no!" She covered her nose and mouth with her palm, gasping in shock. Someone had lit the herbs! They were visible on the desk, partially back to their original state of dryness, charred around the edges.

Who? Who would light them? Harmony's first thought was Kodiak. Maybe he'd changed his mind and didn't want to live in the human realm any longer. Maybe he missed home? But that was impossible. He was far away on a boat, somewhere in Lake Superior. The only other person who knew about the herbs was Samantha. *But why would she light them?*

Taking one step forward, Harmony slowly removed her hand from her nose. A tentative sniff confirmed the smell from the burnt herbs was faint. *They weren't burned that recently.* She moved farther into the room and noticed stuff had been knocked from the desk onto the rug. Samantha had probably bumped them when she was choking. Harmony remembered the terrifying feeling all too well.

Why would you light them? She wracked her brain. One logical thought crossed her mind. *Samantha didn't believe me! She wanted to see for herself, so she lit them, thinking nothing would happen, proving my story was just a tall tale, a lie!*

Harmony panicked, and tears sprang to her eyes as she marched over to the desk where she'd stashed the satchel in a drawer. She yanked the drawer and lifted the bag, which she dropped on the desk. She was confused when she saw two tins were still inside the pouch. Had Sam dumped the herbs from the tin and then taken the time to put everything neatly away before lighting them? That seemed unlike her. Harmony lifted each tin and popped the lids. She stared at the full contents in each one.

"That's weird... Some of these should be missing." Looking again at the herbs on the desk, she realized they had to have come from somewhere else—someone else.

Someone came here. Calder? Maybe Calder came here looking for me? Maybe something terrible has happened in their realm. But why would he return without talking to me? This doesn't make any sense.

She wanted to clean up, not wanting that smell to further spoil the room's atmosphere. Crossing the room, she reached for an empty tea tin displayed on the bookshelf, one that her grandfather had brought back from the orient. Her grandparents had finished the tea long ago but kept the tin as a memento. It was the perfect size to contain the offensive pile on the desktop.

Her fingers trembled as she lifted it from the shelf, and she dropped the tin. It bounced on the thick carpet to land under the leg of a worn leather chair. Rolling her eyes, Harmony folded onto all fours and reached for the tin. From the corner of her eye, she caught a glint of gold under the chair. She reached toward a thin gold chain and snatched it, drawing it close for inspection. It was the chain Sam's brother gave her on her twenty-first birthday.

How did Sam's chain end up under a chair on the floor in the den? Fear started an ugly burn in her belly. Samantha Finch had been in this room—today! When her brother gave the chain to her, Samantha had confided that although she'd never been close to her brother, who lived on the west coast, his thoughtful gesture meant the world to her. She always wore the gold chain.

A wave of nausea pulsed through Harmony. This whole scene reeked of foul play: the open refrigerator door, the broken bottle, the additional herbs, perhaps signs of a struggle. Harmony's sense of foreboding began to escalate. Something was gravely wrong. She knew she had to return to find out what had happened. Samantha was gone… Taken! Harmony knew she had to help her friend—that is, *if* she'd made it! Samantha was only human, after all. She squeezed the chain in the palm of her hand. Finn was only human too, and yet he was able to survive the crossing. She was going to have to cross back to the other realm—through the deep, black, broken water that terrified her.

What about Kodiak? She must tell him! Climbing to her feet, she dashed into the kitchen, nearly wiping out when her sneakers hit the spilt soda. Hand on heart, she paused as adrenaline pulsed through her body. It was the middle of the afternoon, and Kodiak would be…well wherever they needed him to be. And she didn't have a direct number to reach him, except the hotel. He'd been the one who called her each night, often from the payphone at the local bar and grill the crew frequented. *Shit! I have to wait until he calls me! Or*, she thought, *I could leave him a message at the hotel. What will I say? I'm going to another realm? Think, idiot!* She smacked her palm against her forehead. Okay, she could leave a note here at their house in case he returned before she did. In a note she could tell him that she was visiting her relatives. That wouldn't make sense to anyone who knew her because she had no living relatives in this realm, but Kodiak would know where she'd gone. She'd be sure to warn him not to follow her. The crossing was too dangerous for him.

Harmony cleaned up the mess on the kitchen floor. In

the study she retrieved the tin off the floor and placed the herbs inside for safekeeping. Now she needed to prepare for her petrifying journey.

She did nothing that first night, telling herself she needed to talk to Kodiak first. But she never heard from him that night or the night after that. After two days she started writing the note; she couldn't keep stalling. Kodiak wasn't the only reason for her delay. She'd had to convince herself she could overcome her fear of deep water and cross again.

20

"Time to wake up."

Roused by the voice and the rolling beneath her, Samantha instantly became aware of her surroundings. She sensed she was no longer in her room but in a boat that gently rocked, surrounded by a cool breeze. The stern voice was unmistakably Umiko's. She kept her eyes closed.

She remembered that Umiko had come into her room just minutes after Finn left. She heard a discreet knock and thought it was Finn returning to talk about—or act on—what they had shared down by the cove. When she opened the door she said, surprised, "Oh, Umiko." Cautiously, she'd looked around him into the hallway to be sure Gale wasn't with him.

"Good evening. Sorry to disturb you so late, but there is something I want to tell you. May I come in? It will only take a minute," he assured her, and he attempted a tightlipped smile.

After glancing at the door that connected to Finn's room, Samantha agreed. All she had to do was scream and Finn would be there in a second.

"Come in." She was about to offer him a seat, but when the door closed behind him his demeanor seemed to change. The tall muscular man with a high forehead and flowing black hair stood magnified before her. Her senses kicked in, and the hairs on her neck stood up. The scent of leather from his belts and clothing permeated her panicky breath. The gleam of metal on the hilt of the knife he wore caught her widening eyes. She heard the distress in her voice when she asked, "What do you have to tell me?"

He started, "Serving the best interest of the tribe is

my compass."

She sensed a "but" coming. Her eyes swept the room for a potential weapon if necessary.

"I just want you to know that whatever happens, I will look out for you." As the last word left his lips he swiftly circled behind her and pressed a damp rag over her nose and mouth.

The smell of whatever was on the rag filled her lungs as she sucked in air to aid a hardy scream for Finn. The chemical produced inky spots before her eyes; quickly the blackness seeped into the far reaches of her mind. Before she dropped unconscious she felt her head loll and her knees buckle. Strong arms lifted her, but she was helpless to fight back. Her last thought was, *Not again!*

Samantha opened her eyes and confirmed the voice belonged to Umiko. Her intuition back in her room had been correct; Umiko's visit had been cause for concern. She could just make out his form standing above her in the rocking boat, surrounded by thick, dark fog. Umiko held out a hand to her; his other held a lantern. As she sat up she blinked away the fog in her mind that mimicked the fog around her. Determined to stand on her own, she ignored his hand and swung her legs inward in order to rise onto her knees and keep her balance. The vessel bumped and scraped the dock as the tide washed in. Startled by the sound of another voice coming from the dock, Samantha scrambled to her feet. Umiko's hand shot out to steady her elbow.

"Get her up here," commanded Gale.

Out of the glowing fog Gale's hand holding a lantern appeared first. Soon his face came into view as he stepped closer. Umiko urged her toward the bench she was forced to step on to climb out of the boat. This vessel was larger than the rowboat she'd traveled in with these two before. In the light cast by Umiko's lantern she saw its sails were tied into place. The masts disappeared upward into the darkness.

"What are you doing? Why have you taken me again?" Samantha's teeth were clenched in anger. This wooden pier wasn't the one down the hill from the Wellness temple. The Wellness's docks were new and still smelled of fresh lumber. This wood was brittle and splintered; she stumbled against broken boards. She couldn't guess where she was or how long she'd been unconscious.

"I have something I need you to do, Harmony," Gale said. He ordered Umiko, "This way."

The endless boardwalk was tedious to maneuver. "What do you want from me? Finn is not going to like this," she threatened. Gale led them through a tunnel of gray clouds, and Samantha noticed large boulders penetrating the gloom on one side of the boardwalk. *There must be land to my right*, she thought. *I could make a break for it. But where would I go? Into the dark fog? I'd be lost for sure.* "Where are we? Where are we going?"

Ignoring her questions, Gale posed one of his own. "I hear you like to sing, Harmony. Is this true?"

Samantha glanced at Umiko, hoping for some clue to the random inquiry. "Sure, I sing. What about it?" Umiko concentrated on illuminating the boardwalk, which worried her. He'd said something about looking after her, and she sensed his hesitation about doing so now.

After a few more steps Gale stopped and faced her. "Good. Let's hear you sing something. Loud and clear."

"Are you serious?"

"Dead serious." His words weren't spoken harshly, but nonetheless they sent a chill down her spine.

"Fine," she squeaked. Songs shuffled in her head, and one finally transferred to her lips. She belted out the chorus of a song popular back in her realm. Both men watched her for a moment until Gale nodded and indicated they should follow him.

"Keep singing," Gale called over his shoulder when he veered from the boardwalk onto a boulder.

The lanterns swung from their handles, casting creepy shadows while the men jumped from rock to rock, Samantha following as best she could. The surf rushed in around the boulders under their feet, and when it receded it revealed smaller rocks and beach sand.

"Right here will do." Gale stopped her on the largest, flattest ledge they'd encountered. "Sing to the sea. Loud and clear."

Her song faltered as she watched the two men climb to a higher boulder, holding the lanterns above her head. Umiko then set his on the ground, standing poised and ready—for what, she didn't know.

"Keep singing!" Gale barked.

Samantha flung her arms out wide. *What a crazy lunatic!* She turned as if facing a stage and dramatically bellowed out her song. She inwardly laughed at this nonsense. Suddenly something emerged from the foaming surf and clung to the rock's edge. Samantha cut off her song with a startled yelp. She leaned forward to see a young girl in the dim light. Strands of dark hair clung to her youthful, ivory cheeks, and her pink mouth grinned, as if she was happy to see Samantha. *What has Gale done? Is he responsible for leaving this poor girl here? Who is she?* She sent an accusing look over her shoulder, but both men were intently watching the scene below them.

The girl allowed the next wave to reposition her on a low end of the stone platform. Samantha moved in that direction to help the girl out of the waves. The water where the girl stood appeared to be waist deep. The milky whiteness of her skin glowed like the fog in the lantern's light. The water circled her slim waist, her arms and torso seeming to be wrapped in long hair and seaweed.

"Are you okay?" Samantha asked, reaching to take the girl's outstretched hand. Something in the way the girl's face contorted into an eerie smile and the icy touch of her fingers sent Samantha a spine-chilling urge to run. Instead she yanked her hand away. What she'd thought was a girl was clearly something different. She tried to dash as far away from this thing as possible, but Samantha's feet skated uselessly under her. The slick surface allowed the creature to pull herself swiftly along. She easily reached Samantha. She opened her mouth wide.

"What the hell is she!" Samantha screamed up at Gale and Umiko. "Help—get it away from me!" Samantha knew with a quick glance at Gale that he wasn't going to come to her aid. He just shifted the lantern to provide light for the best view. Umiko appeared ready to pounce, but Gale held up a palm to stop him.

Suddenly the siren gripped Samantha's ankle. She felt boney, icicle-like fingers against her bare skin. Frantic, she tried to shake free. She wobbled, upsetting her balance, and hit the boulder hard when she fell. The rock slanted slightly downward, the bottom corner disappearing into the abysmal water. With a long steady pull, the siren managed to drag Samantha's squirming body down to the end of the ledge, submerging her foot.

"She's a siren, Harmony! Use your ability—or she will drown you." Gale's voice echoed around her before the wind blew his warning out to sea.

Oh, shit! So that's what this is about! He wants to see Harmony fight off a siren. Oh shit—I'm in trouble!" Drawing on her inner strength, Samantha flipped on her back and drew up her free knee. With all the strength she could muster, she kicked out and struck the siren violently in the face. The siren twisted away in pain, releasing her ankle. In a moment Samantha was up and moving back the way she'd come. She sprinted off the platform and landed on the next boulder. She didn't have to look back to know that Gale and Umiko followed her because the lantern light behind her cast her shadow against the wall of fog. In maybe five feet of visibility, she hopped to the next landing. The boulder was slick from the constant batter of waves. This area reminded her of the tidal pools on the point not far from her family's home. She had climbed those jetty rocks a million times. She screamed to herself, *You are practically an expert at maneuvering on them. It doesn't matter that you are in near darkness with two dangerous men and a creature chasing you. Just get to the boat before them!*

A round boulder blocked her descent. She was forced to drop down to a smaller rock to get to the other side, where she hoped she would find better access to the boardwalk. She moved quickly; the incoming wave was likely to submerge the low-lying rock. But the wave brought not only cold, foamy water—it brought the siren.

The force of the siren's solid body slamming into her knocked Samantha's head against the boulder she was trying to get around. As the surf drew back, Samantha collapsed to the ground, the siren on top of her. Her hands clutched the siren's neck. She could feel the cords of neck muscles when the siren unhinged her jaw and opened her mouth impossibly wide. Light flashed over them, and Samantha saw the set of pointy teeth in an evil mouth that strained to bite her.

They know I'm not Harmony. I can't stop this thing! In just moments the surf would rush back and she would be trapped underwater by this thing. Suddenly she felt the siren's body jolt, and the attack ceased. As the siren's mouth went slack Samantha noticed a knife protruding from her skull.

A breath later, Umiko dragged the siren off Samantha by its hair, yanked the knife from its skull, and tossed the youthful body away. The waves broke and tumbled the body in the surf. Before Samantha realized it, she was standing, leaning against Umiko, watching the gruesome scene. Forcing herself to look away, she turned her attention to the man who had saved her life. She knew the knife belonged to Umiko. In a weak attempt to step away from him, she brought her hands up to push him away, but they shook violently.

Umiko clasped one of her hands and spoke quietly, "You are safe now."

Somehow, on shaky legs and with Umiko's support, she made it back to the boardwalk. Enlightened now about why Gale had brought her out here, she knew what was coming next—he would want to know why she'd pretended to be Harmony.

***

Gale stared blankly into the vast stone fireplace. It was cold; leaves and debris had collected in the hearth. Feeling the cool granite against his palm, Gale mused, *I should have known something was amiss.*

Early that evening during dinner, Umiko had commented there was something about Harmony that didn't seem right. His warning played into Gale's doubts. Umiko said he'd felt it from the moment Gale had crossed through with her. Umiko claimed he'd held his tongue this long because he wasn't sure what was different. Gale knew Umiko had seen Harmony when she was in the tribal city about five months ago. Although Umiko had said her size and blond hair seemed the same, his comment about her smile piqued Gale's interest. Umiko's unusually expressive statement that he didn't remember her having such a devastatingly alluring smile had set Gale to wondering.

Gale had sent Umiko to follow Finn and Harmony when the couple left the dining room early. When Umiko returned he assured Gale that Finn and the girl hadn't noticed him at the cove, confessing he'd observed from the shadows at first. Umiko had discreetly sought out several hunters who'd been in the city when Harmony was there before, asking if she was the same girl. During the bonfire, after the tribesmen had gotten a closer look at Harmony, they returned to the shadows. All agreed she might not be the same blond girl. After all, her bow skills hadn't been revealed before, and her personality seemed more outgoing. Umiko had left and returned to Gale to validate his suspicions. In hindsight it made sense to Gale. The girl had seemed confused after they'd crossed realms and become so sick that she'd almost died, which had baffled him. He'd seen no such effect in his mixed-race son when he'd crossed with Finn fifteen years ago.

After his little siren experiment, there was no question now—she was not Harmony Parker. So who was the stranger he'd captured?

Beyond the fact that Gale had grossly blundered, his own son Finn had tricked him—they'd all tried to deceive him! Calder's treachery didn't surprise him, but even the human girl had dared to defy him! She had no Aquapopulean blood—she was simply human. She *should* have died during the crossing. She was the first human to survive. Everyone had thought that Finn was fully human until Gale had revealed the truth. Gale tittered at his earlier efforts when he'd tried to save the little imposter. In the end, Calder had worked his magic. Gale would have let the siren kill her if Umiko hadn't intervened.

After the trio entered the fortress beyond the boardwalk, Umiko had surprised Gale when he'd pulled him aside to ask that he be granted authority to care for the human. Apparently Umiko was hoping to pursue his romantic interest in her.

Gale had replied, "When we are through with her."

The human wasn't the only dilemma. Although Gale was excluded from the meetings, Umiko and Taura sat on the council, giving him access to important information. This peace summit was futile in Gale's opinion, and he thought the leaders played at negotiating too long. Finn proved to be more independent and determined than he'd bargained on. Gale's face darkened. His son didn't accept him. It was Mary's fault that he and Finn had been estranged. He'd tried to explain that to Finn. Gale had loved Finn's mother once, and there had never been anyone like her since. But his lovely Mary couldn't accept him the way he was. Her rejection had mangled his heart. In the years after the loss of his family, his soul had blackened. Taking Finn for revenge wasn't a fatherly thing to do, but that had been long ago. Right now, there was a purpose to fulfill.

Gale heard Samantha suck air through her teeth as Umiko dabbed her injuries with salve.

"Gale?" Umiko called after he'd diligently attended the human.

Gale turned from the fireplace and watched Umiko tug the golden-haired beauty along. Umiko's entire hand enclosed her bare, slim bicep, his thumb easily resting on his fingertips.

"We know you are *not* Harmony Parker. What is your name?" He watched emotion cross her face. Of course she could lie, but there was no reason to. In the end he was convinced she'd tell the truth.

"I'm Harmony's best friend, Samantha Finch."

The statement made sense because Samantha had been in Harmony's house. Gale drew closer and lifted his hand to touch her hair.

"Don't touch me!" Samantha jerked away as far as she could until Umiko yanked on her arm and forced her even closer to Gale. But she announced feistily, "Finn will know you took me. He will come for me…and you will be sorry."

Gale chuckled at her threat and exchanged glances with Umiko. "You would have made Finn a lively partner. I've seen the way he looks at you. I do believe he will come for you. In fact, I'm counting on it." He watched her eyes widen with shock. "Yes, you are the bait. For now."

"Why 'for now'? What do you plan to do with me? You would have let that siren kill me!" Samantha shouted indignantly.

Nonchalant, Gale stepped back with a dismissive shrug of his shoulders. "Since you are only human and possess no unique ability, you are no longer suitable for my son, Finn. I have bigger plans for that boy. As for you…someone else has asked for you."

Gale indicated Umiko, the man who held her arm firmly, and he smirked when she shuffled uncomfortably. *That seemed to shut her up!* Gale thought.

Umiko's face remained unemotional and serious, but he gave her an affirmative nod and a onceover.

"There is an underground cell in this citadel. The last time I was out here the locking mechanism was functioning. Centuries ago, when they captured sirens and used them for sport, the residents could flood the area to contain them. Put Samantha Finch in there for now," Gale said to Umiko. "Take her downstairs and then come right back. We need to prepare for Finn's arrival. I'm done playing the bystander. If he won't listen, then he will have to deal with the consequences."

The fortress had both been built and abandoned centuries ago at a time in history when a large group of Aquapopuleans became hunters. Killing and eating animals didn't sit well with their fish-eating neighbors, so they became outcasts. They'd settled first on this strip of land that hooked out into the Atlantic Ocean. It was unpopulated because of the dangerous indigenous plants and wild creatures that inevitably prevented walkers from accessing the area from the land. The outcasts entered from the sea and built a fortress at its tip. It only took about a century for them to realize they'd isolated themselves not only from the costal clans but from the very animals they wanted to hunt. The year the great southern storm, lasting an entire moon cycle, tore up the east coast and caused abrupt climate change, the outcasts left the stone fortress behind and wandered west into the forests. The storm also brought a plague of alligators and eternal dense fog to the Cape. The group moved west beyond another swampy pocket and the Mahicantuck River, known in the human realm as the Hudson River. The group settled on the great falls. They became known as the Forest Tribes.

21

Finn didn't need to summon a fog for cover. An unnatural, ongoing stream of warm southern air flowed from the gulf to collide with the chilly northern currents at this very point.

Finished with playing diplomatic son in the face of Gale's schemes, Finn planned to take Gale back to the Wellness temple to stand immediate trial, again for bringing a human into their realm. The deception was over. People would know the truth once and for all.

When Finn had answered his door that morning before the council meeting, Taura entered and relayed the disturbing news that Gale had taken the girl. "Gale is determined to find out the truth about her. Umiko suspects she isn't Harmony Parker. Is she?"

A ferocious fear, as strong as the winds Finn could summon, twisted in his gut. Gale would test her abilities somehow. What was the Linker capable of?

"Where is she?" Finn's growl and menacing scowl made Taura regret his question.

"Last night, Umiko and Gale took her and sailed for the Cape, heading for the abandoned fortress. Gale wanted me to alert you at first light," Taura disclosed.

Finn charged out the door with Taura on his heels.

As the boat scraped against the Cape's decaying wooden dock Finn was glad he'd left in daylight; even so, they could hardly see through the dense fog.

Nearly seven hours had passed.

He took a moment to recall the crude map Calder had drawn for him. With no prior knowledge of ocean travel, especially over such a great distance, Finn, Taura, and two hunters did successfully complete the voyage, no thanks to the clan members who'd refused to travel with them to the dangerous peninsula. Finn had brought two hunters along to help apprehend Gale because he didn't trust where Taura's loyalties lay, and the highly skilled extra brawn was reassuring.

There had been little time to warn Calder about what was transpiring. Calder, like everyone who'd attended school, had learned the history of the fortress on the Cape. Calder mentioned that he and Gale had once visited the abandoned fortress with their master, who used it to educate them about the past, as well as about the poisonous plants that grew there. It was a secluded, dangerous swamp at the edge of the sea. That was why Calder was not surprised that Gale would take Samantha there. Not many would follow, he knew.

Finn's plan to avoid Gale until the summit negotiations were finished had backfired. Apparently his father demanded to be heard. This stunt irritated Finn; it was unnecessary to involve Samantha. Taking her had made the provocation very personal.

"He wants to talk to you on his terms. You must come to an agreement, Finn. Gale will help you and our nation become great," Taura asserted.

Finn mulled over Taura's words as the four men walked up the dock toward the soaring walls of stone. Finn felt the sense of betrayal by both Taura and Umiko. He'd known them as friends. To find out now they'd been consorting with his estranged father the whole time made him feel distrustful, angry, and disgusted. A chieftain's reign seemed a lonely one if he couldn't trust his closest friends.

When they located the door and entered without confrontation, Finn removed his blade from his scabbard.

"You won't need that, Finn. Gale is expecting you. He just wants to talk," Taura reassured him. Then Taura blew into a shiny whistle that hung on a string around his neck. The dark room was soon lit by the torch Umiko carried in.

"Hello, Finn," Umiko respectfully greeted the chieftain.

"What is this? You're my friends," Finn accused. "Why have you done this? Why follow Gale...a man who abducts children and women?"

"Come. Gale is waiting," was all Umiko offered. The group walked in silence to join father and son. Finn exchanged glances with the two hunters, both equipped for a fight. They followed, silent and watchful.

Within the grand room the smell of the sea drifted in from the glassless windows that overlooked patchy fog. An enormous wood trestle table, half rotted away, filled the chamber. Barrels were pulled up to provide seating. Gale lifted his face from his plate of food to smirk at his son.

"My boy, you've come at last. I see you've brought company." He indicated the two men armed with bows. "Finn, please join me for an evening meal. We have much to discuss—especially your betrayal."

"Where is she?" Finn quickly noticed that Samantha was nowhere in sight.

Gale glanced around the room, as if admiring the chipped walls and broken furniture. "Look at this place, Finn. This was built by the first tribe. Perhaps if not for the great storm we would have evolved differently. Maybe the tribesmen would still retain the ability to hold their breath underwater for as long as the clan people. Perhaps we wouldn't be at odds with the clans."

"How can you say that? They just want peace. You are the one trying to force their hand." Finn wondered about Gale's motives.

"Progress. I learned in the other realm that people need it—crave it," Gale stated simply.

Finn could not deny he wanted progress, wanted to

enhance the world around him for the good of the people, but at what cost? Gale's insistence that the clans people move to the salt mine village in the west would cause the ocean lovers considerable grief. The tribesmen and women had chosen to adapt to life in the forest and expand their skills. Still, it wasn't fair if the tribal workforce no longer wanted to work the mines after many generations.

Finn said, "We have negotiated to make things fair. The clans agree to set up a program for the young men and women coming out of school to try apprenticeships in the mines. They are working out the details for how long a work season might run, the pay, and the building of appropriate clan housing facilities.

"I don't see the tribal empire growing with that approach," Gale challenged.

"This is going to take time, but I think in the end the tribe will prosper. These negotiations include the expansion of roads and trade. All of this is bigger than you or me. You think my ability, or Harmony's ability, is the answer, but you are wrong. Because after I'm gone, the next leader, and the one after that, will have to figure out how the tribe is to go on and maintain a relationship with the clans. I'm trying to put multiple systems in place, like additional farming measures so the farmers don't rely on me to manipulate the weather. You've been to the other realm and learned so much. You could help us prepare and establish a future that is beneficial to everyone." Finn waited for Gale to respond. Finn raised his eyebrows at Umiko, as if to say, 'speak up at any time.' But no one spoke up.

Gale's laugh was fiendish. He asked, "How many in this program? And will they wait for their new dorms to be built before they step foot in the mines? Is the tribe responsible for building them? That would certainly be more labor for *our* people. And what of the conditions the mineworkers live in now? They will revolt if you continue to put the clans' welfare before their own."

"We've considered these concerns—look, this is pointless. I need to get back. We are concluding the summit. All is agreed. It's time to stop this foolishness. Tell me where she is," Finn demanded.

"Who? I know you don't mean Calder's mixed-breed great-great granddaughter, because I've come to realize it wasn't Harmony Parker who accompanied me when I returned from the human realm."

"No. It appears you've made a vital mistake." Finn's comment hit its target, and Gale lowered his eyes, his mouth pinched in frustration. "Her name is Samantha, and I want to see her now."

"Samantha is no use to us, Finn." Gale returned his gaze to Finn. Responding like hunters, both Umiko and Taura tensed as Finn closed the distance between him and his father. It wasn't Finn's intention to kill his father; he wanted justice. If that included shaking some sense into him, Finn would oblige.

"Take his weapons!" Gale barked.

At that moment, one of Finn's hunters drew an arrow into his bow. When Taura's knife landed in the man's forehead, he released the arrow, which ricocheted off the wall. Finn heard the man drop with a thud as the bow skidded and clattered across the stones.

The second of Finn's hunters accurately sank his arrow in Taura's chest, but not before Taura managed to take that bowman down with a second knife he launched; arrow fire and knife throw were simultaneous. Both men expertly hit their targets. Both men sprawled on the floor, blood seeping from their wounds, masks of death upon their faces.

Umiko launched himself at Finn. The old friends were no strangers to combat matches. Each struggled to overpower the other. Just as the two bodies crashed against the table, Gale sprang from his seat and then staggered back from the impact that knocked Gale's meal to the floor. Finn pinned Umiko on his back. The two powerful men gripped each other's throats, hands locked and squeezing, their muscles shaking with adrenaline. Umiko managed to wedge his heel against the edge of the table, gaining enough leverage to flip Finn over his head. They both rolled off the other side of the table. Umiko had the upper hand when he landed on top of Finn. The crack of Gale's cane against Finn's temple knocked Finn unconscious.

Finn woke sometime later. His head throbbed, and pain stabbed behind his eyes. Instinctively before he opened his eyes, his body tensed, ready to continue the fight. But his shoulder had gone numb against the hard surface of the stone floor. He realized that his arms were drawn tightly behind his back and his wrists were bound. Finn painfully opened his eyes. An arm's length away, he saw Taura's lifeless, tattooed hand, as if it reached for him. Despite the brutal pain in his head, he remembered why he was here. Finn managed to sit up, wincing. His eyes sliced to the fireplace, where Gale and Umiko spoke in hushed tones.

Both men turned to stare at the tribal chieftain now glowering at them.

Finn growled in disgust. "Look what you've done." He turned his head and swept his gaze over the three fallen tribesmen. He had expected anything from Gale, but Umiko...

The pair crossed the room, surveying the dead men.

"You've enabled him," Finn accused Umiko, sniffing in repugnance at his actions. "Don't you see that he only causes harm? Taura was our friend...these men were our tribal family. He doesn't care about the tribes' welfare. He only cares about himself." Finn swore he saw doubt in Umiko's eyes, but still Umiko forced him to his feet.

Umiko unlatched the thick belts Finn wore and removed them from his torso. Finn knew his friend was wise to the hidden blades concealed within the leather panels because he was the one who'd taught Finn to hide them.

Gale's eyes lingered a moment on Taura. Finn could only guess at the Linker's feelings. Did he even care these men were dead because of him? Gale's chin dropped to his chest, and he pinched the bridge of his nose. *Clearly, things didn't go as he'd planned*, thought Finn. He'd underestimated Finn's backup. Allowing Finn to bring the others had been Taura's fatal flaw.

"What have you done with Samantha? If you hurt her…" Finn's threat was cut off by Gale's unexpected laughter.

"Oh, son, we do have a thing for the fair-haired human girls." Gale's eyes twinkled with mirth.

How can anyone laugh when dead tribesmen lay at their feet? Truly Gale must be insane. Finn wasn't going to deny what he felt for Samantha, but he kept his cool.

"Yes, Father, like my human mother, so innocent before you used her." Calling Gale "Father" was bitter on his tongue, but it roused the response he had hoped for. Gale's mistake was telling Finn that he'd loved his mother, and Finn could easily see now that she still had some hold over him.

Gale rushed forward a little too enthusiastically and stopped to clutch his bad leg. Finn could see his father's clipped rage in the set of his mouth.

Gale growled, "You don't know what you are talking about. Leave that woman out of this. You are an ungrateful child—*ungrateful,* just like she was." Gale swirled away, walking in a circle, as though he were trying to get feeling back into his rigid leg. When he faced Finn again he confessed, "I offered her the world—this world. I offered to bring her to this realm

170

with you. We could have been together here, but she didn't want to come. She thought I'd gone crazy. I tried to protect you, but she left me and stole you away. And now I offer you a kingdom—and you refuse!"

"You are blinded by greed. You don't have to give me a kingdom. Respect and honesty would have done nicely. There is still time to stop this and make amends. Now, where is Samantha?"

"I've worked diligently to get to this point. I brought you to this realm. Had the tribe look after you, train you and groom you to one day become tribal leader."

When Gale indicated Umiko and Taura, it all became crystal clear to Finn. They had befriended him for Gale, as spies.

Gale continued, "With my help you have achieved this. Now it is time to expand the kingdom. To do so you must utilize the clans. They will become the workforce you need to forge a new era. This realm could become great—like the human realm. I have so much knowledge to share with you."

"Enough. I will not comply," Finn responded, and then he turned to his old companion. Finn recognized Umiko's alliance to his father, but he was giving him a chance to make the right choice now. "This radical idea is dead, and it won't come to pass. As chief, I command you to untie me and take Gale into custody. He will stand trial before the council for his recent crimes."

Finn heard Gale chuckle before he ordered, "Put him in the siren's cell. Apparently he needs a little time to reconsider my offer. When you return, we will give our fallen water burials."

Umiko led Finn down dozens of staircases to the bowels of the underground; torches lit the way. Once they were out of Gale's range, Finn urged, "The least you can do is tell me what he has done with Samantha. Did he hurt her? Umiko!"

Behind Finn's shoulder, knife in hand, Umiko finally answered. "She is fine. You will see her soon."

Before Gale had made his return, Finn would have sworn Umiko was honest and righteous, but Finn didn't know what to believe anymore. He had never seen Umiko treat anyone badly and hoped his old friend now told the truth. Finn was wildly invested in Samantha's whereabouts and safety; he probed for answers.

"So you've been in on Gale's plan since he brought me into this realm? What about the last chieftain, Nakoma—was she influenced by Gale as well?" Finn's questions rang against the hollow stone stairwell.

Umiko answered. "Yes, Chief Nakoma knew, and she agreed it was time to evolve. After the discovery of the mixed-race girl and her abilities, Nakoma promised Gale that Harmony would be your mate. But Nakoma lied. She allowed Harmony to marry that Diver from the clan. The chieftain strayed from Gale's plan. It is no matter now. You are chieftain, and you can make things right if you allow Gale to guide you."

"I'm trying to make things right. Our people can make changes and coexist. I'm for expanding our city, but there are better ways, peaceful ways, we can do so. What has that man promised you that I have not?" Finn couldn't figure out what had made his companions so loyal to a kidnapper and menace.

Lifting his chin a few inches, Umiko said, "I will be the head councilmen of my own outlying tribal city. I will rule under you, with Gale as your wise adviser."

Finn considered this news, surprised Umiko wanted this. Did Umiko feel he was owed such a privilege, or was it something else? Finn thought the latter. They trudged down another staircase, and Finn prodded his oldest friend. "What more has he offered you, Umiko?"

After several silent steps, Umiko sighed. "It's not what he's offered, it's what I promised my father. When my father died that day we rode onto the sacred island, during the earthquake, I made him a promise when we left to hunt you down. He asked that I help Gale forge a better future. He said Gale had told him many stories from the other realm, about war, industry, empires... He wants that for us, and Gale knows how to get it. So I promised my father, and I keep my promises."

The stairwell became noticeably darker. They had finally reached the base level. It was damp, cold, and miserable. Finn cursed the thought that Samantha might be down here.

"Over here." Umiko maneuvered Finn toward a wall of bars. Umiko worked the mechanism to open the barred cell. He nudged Finn through the opening and began to close the cell. Umiko pointed with his chin. "She's in there."

Finn paused to listen. He heard something.

"Finn? Finn, is that you?" Samantha's voice was laced with apprehension and fear.

"Yes, Samantha!" Finn called to her. He turned to Umiko and said with disgust, "She's human, for god's sake. She must be freezing down here."

Samantha appeared in the dim light, her face pale, her lovely eyes dilated with fear. Finn rushed to her.

Surprised, she flung her arms around him, expelling a breath. In a fraction of a second, she noticed his hands were tied. She released her arms from his neck and moved behind him to untie his bonds.

Free, he turned and pulled her into his arms. He stroked the silky skin of her arms before he leaned back to look her over in the semidarkness.

Umiko locked the cell and stood watching them. Finn noticed the anxious look that passed between Samantha and Umiko. Umiko dropped his gaze and said, "I'll bring more blankets and some food." Umiko's practicality, if nothing else, moved him to light several more torches that gave off heat as well as light. The imprisoned pair listened to Umiko's heavy footfalls as he climbed the stairs.

"Why did they lock you in? How are we going to get out of here?" Samantha asked frantically.

"Are you hurt?" Finn ignored her questions. He noticed the red scratch near her temple.

"I'm fine, but they know I'm not Harmony. There was a siren, and they made me sing." Samantha gagged at the memory, but she recovered and said in a rush, "Umiko killed it before it killed me. I hit my head in the process." She brushed her fingertips over the scratch. "And then Gale said he was using me as bait to get you here. What is going on?"

"I should kill him—forget a trial." Finn's nostrils flared.

"Don't say that. Even after everything he's done he's still your father. We just need to figure this out, find common ground." She ran her hand over his arm, soothing him.

He knew she hoped she could quell his worry and anger. Maybe that was one of the qualities that drew him to her. She made him feel...special. In the time it took for Finn to fill Samantha in on all that had happened, Umiko returned carrying a bowl brimming with stew, and a pile of blankets slung over his shoulder. He slid the items through a slot on the floor and watched Finn wrap Samantha in a blanket. Finn didn't miss the look between them before Umiko's features darkened and he strutted away with a heavy sigh.

"What was that about?" Finn had been so gripped by their exchanged he hadn't said one word more to Umiko about why he should release them.

Samantha dismissed his question. "Nothing. I'm really hungry."

Finn quickly bent to retrieve their meal and handed

her the bowl and the single spoon. "Have as much as you want." He picked up a blanket and spread it on the floor for them to sit on.

She gave him a grateful smile and settled on the soft fabric. "Here, have some. It's not bad."

He sat with his back against the wall and accepted the dish, taking a few spoonfuls. "You finish the rest."

Samantha finished up the last spoonful and stood. "So sirens were kept down here? What did the early tribes do with them? Never mind—I don't think I want to know." She crossed the cell and placed the bowl as far as she could away from where they would likely sleep. Making conversation, she asked, "How far are we from the Wellness temple?"

"We are on the Cape, about five hours away by boat." Finn shrugged. "It depends on the wind."

"Cape Cod?" She half laughed. "Sure looks different on the flipside. I used to vacation there when I was a kid."

When she grew quiet, Finn cleared his throat. "Samantha, we are going to get out of this cell. I'm going to make Gale listen to me. And when we get back, if you want to, I mean, I'd like you to come back to my city. That is, of course, if you don't return to the human realm."

Her eyes grew round. She faced him. "I know Calder thinks there is no hope of me going home. It's nice of you to offer that I go to your city, but what would I do there?"

"There could be worse fates than being stuck with me all your life."

"All my life?"

"You have knowledge of a diverse world, great bow skills, and, my personal favorite, understanding of the weather." He was rewarded with her wide smile. His heart beat faster. "I saw how my tribe accepted you at the beach. I don't think they'd object to you becoming their chieftain's wife."

"Wow. I don't know what to say."

"You would remain under my protection. It is a solid offer."

"Oh."

A marriage proposal from a tribal chieftain was a great honor, and he didn't comprehend her hesitation.

The evening stretched on; two of the three torches fizzled out. Finn paced while Samantha attempted to make them a cozy bed with the blankets. Finished, she stood at the bars and said, "I think they are going to leave us in here all night."

"I'm sorry you got caught up in this insane mess. From the moment Gale returned to the city, I knew he couldn't be trusted, but Umiko and Taura...they were my friends." Finn, conflicted and frustrated, reached for comfort—Samantha. She came to him willingly and placed her slim hands on his chest. She touched the V-neck of his sleeveless tunic, tracing the V. He suspected she felt his pulse racing. Her eyes followed her finger, her gaze level.

He slid his hands down her back, slipping his fingers under the fabric at her waist. When his fingertips came into contact with her warm soft skin, he sighed. He had never been with a human woman before. He'd come to this realm as a boy. Although the tribe offered a ready supply of lovers, they only offered him rough animalistic pleasures. Somehow, this delicate flower before him made him want to savor every part of her. But first he couldn't deny what he wanted most at this moment—to kiss her. Should he cross that line? If he did, there was no turning back.

"Finn, kiss me," she urged breathlessly.

How could he resist? His head dropped and his mouth hungrily captured hers. She responded by winding her arms around his neck and pressing against him. His body jerked to life, and his hands went on to explore. Soon she swept his shirt over his head and he eagerly rid Samantha of hers.

Threading his fingers through her hair he gently tugged her head back, and she gasped for air when his mouth left hers to taste other areas she had to offer. Kissing the length of her jaw, he slid his tongue up and down the column of her throat, slowly tipping her head backwards. She arched her back and clutched his biceps to keep from tipping over. Her eyes were closed, and her mouth, plump and pink from his kisses, was slightly open, drawing in shallow breaths.

Finn's free palm skimmed over her exposed chest until he got the desired response. His hot, wet mouth left a trail to her breast. He licked and teased her until she sagged against him. He eased her onto the blankets and returned his mouth to hers.

"You are so beautiful," he breathed into her mouth. "I want you."

He slowed his invasion of her lovely body to make sure she wanted him. He was a chieftain who wanted the respect worthy of him, and taking advantage of her wasn't his plan. He knew she'd been lost in ecstasy before now.

She opened her eyes and regarded him. "I'm ready for you."

22

Suijin knew where every fish, mammal, siren, and creature swam because his senses, far beyond any other being in either realm, were in tune with aquatic life. When Aquapopulean Linkers passed through the portal, a distinct ringing throbbed in his ears. When humans passed the vibration was a different frequency. And when it came to the mixed-race human Harmony Parker, the pulse was low and long lasting, a vibration that left him tingling. Suijin could feel it now as he swam toward her. The portal in the depth of broken waters that linked their worlds had delivered her. She drifted, unconscious, an exquisite vision.

Harmony Parker has returned!

He couldn't help but smile at his good fortune. Though he was the god of two realms, he felt this realm was his home, the sirens his family. At one time he coexisted with the Aquapopuleans. But over the many long centuries, the people had separated themselves from him, choosing to idolize him for the god he was.

During his long imprisonment in the earthly realms, Suijin had never seen or experienced anyone with Harmony's ability—the remarkable ability to physically wound him. Of course, there was the young chieftain with the ability to command the weather, but Suijin had encountered Finn when he was a small child in the human realm and at the time found his abilities unremarkable. Suijin had chosen not to take the child's life. However, after Finn had grown and crossed realms, he became powerful. Suijin was hesitant to test the chieftain now.

Harmony was a different creature entirely. She had burned him! She couldn't kill him, of course. He was immortal, like the other gods beyond the realms, but she was able to project a force that was hard for him to break. When she'd used her force to deflect a sea serpent, Suijin was astonished when he sensed the beast's fury. And when she had burned the sirens, he heard their tormented screams in his head.

Harmony Parker was an anomaly.

Since the moment he'd discovered her, a child who fell in the river, she had never left his thoughts. He should have killed her that day, along with her mother, but something made him hesitate. Though he had never killed a child, that wasn't what stopped him. He wanted to know more about her, and so he'd watched over her ever since.

Suijin was keeper of the dual earthly realms. His unique connection began with early life forms in the oceans. As plant and animal species, and eventually Homo sapiens, evolved, he'd observed the progression of the modern races. Human evolution had surged through the centuries with peaks and plummets of progress and devastation. The Aquapopuleans were closer to Suijin's underwater families, until a small group broke away, heading into the forest to seek more than the great oceans could offer them. They were now known as the Forest Tribe.

Still, he preferred this realm above the human one; he only interfered with humans when necessary. Deeming it necessary, he'd hunted Brook, Harmony's mother, because the mixed-blood girl shouldn't have existed, nor the women before her. The realms were meant to remain separate—that was the deal he'd made with the Linkers of ancient times after the Linkers discovered the powerful herbs that afforded them unique travel benefits.

Pearl had been the first human to become impregnated by an Aquapopulean. Suijin eliminated the Linker Calder's mate, but remarkably she'd raised a daughter before he did so. Pearl and Calder's daughter managed to elude Suijin for half her life, long enough to conceive a girl child and create another generation. That child was Margaret Parker, who was Harmony's grandmother. Margaret had survived the longest. Last year, he'd sent a sea serpent to capsize a small boat and drown her and two of her friends. He didn't enjoy killing. Perhaps because of his delays their offspring continued. It irked him that these women were capable of pregnancy. He would rather they just die off and extinguish their line naturally.

Life always finds a way.

The day he'd gone after Margaret Parker's daughter he felt differently, though. His weariness over cleansing the human realm became a renewed interest in what was now offered. Encountering another of their line— Harmony Parker—had changed him forever.

Stealthily, he'd assassinated her mother, grandmother, great-grandmother, and the first woman to start the line, Harmony's great-great-grandmother Pearl. Now Harmony was alone in the world, the last mixed-race female, a grown woman.

Suijin was finished with watching and waiting. He wanted Harmony for himself. The time was right. And here she was, in the water for him to take. He hoped that with careful planning he'd get her to come with him willingly. His chance to get her in a vulnerable position was at a pinnacle. He wanted to win her trust to start with, so he set out to do so. In a moment she'd awaken and swim up for air.

In the blink of an eye, he captured her hand, and they vanished.

***

Harmony's eyelids fluttered. She focused on the cloudy

vapor around her. It was daytime, but the fog was thick and she could only make out tree trunks, the branches erased. Her nose wrinkled at the pungent smell coming from the stagnant water all around her. Wiggling her fingers, she felt dry grass beneath her; her feet were at the water's edge. Hearing distant ocean waves, she adjusted her focus slightly. She blinked again to be sure she wasn't hallucinating.

In knee-deep water stood an almost naked man, his only clothing a narrow strip of leather that hung across his square hips. He stood in profile, abdominal muscles rippling with each slight movement. Her eyes scanned upward to his broad chest and lingered there. The definition of his muscles led her to believe he was strong and powerful. The sweeping upward motion of his arms made her blink. His face tilted skyward, his fingers combed back his black hair and worked to secure some strands in a knot at his crown. He stood, surely a figment of her imagination, surrounded by swirling white smoke, his jet-black hair contrasting against it, flowing like wet silk between his thick shoulder blades. The outline of his straight nose, full lips, and perfectly chiseled chin couldn't be real.

Wow, some dream!

After he secured his hair, he dropped his arms to hook his hands at his waist. He swiveled his head to look right at her.

This is no dream! She recognized him—it was a face she'd never forget!

She shot to her feet, slipping on the wet grass. She quickly glanced around—it looked like she was in a swamp. And it smelled like one too. Her wild eyes searched for an escape route. She was standing on one of many raised hills of grass that supported tree trunks; surely she could run through the water. He was only knee deep...

181

Sloshing water drew her attention back to the man approaching her.

"That's far enough!" she yelled, holding her hands up to emphasize her warning. Suddenly she felt a warming sensation in the palms of her hands. Her ability was being activated somehow. She was certain he was none other than Suijin, the water god.

"P-p-pleease, don't come any closer." Her desperate pleading stopped him, mere feet from her. Standing in ankle deep water, he was regarding her with his intense eyes. She had only seen him underwater before, once when she was a child and then again before she had left this realm nearly four months ago. But all too often he invaded her dreams, leaving her quaking in terror.

"Please, don't kill me." Whispering her greatest fear, she watched him closely. She swore she saw shock on his face, but whatever it was, his expression changed when his eyes lifted upward. The light penetrated the fog and filtered through. His eyes, now free from shadows, looked like mirrors reflecting the white sky.

Harmony was caught off guard, and she felt the heat leave her hands—her ability was receding!

His eyes came to rest on her face again. "Harmony, I would never hurt you."

"You tried to drown me!" Strength returned to her voice, and the tingling resumed, traveling down her arms.

"No, I wasn't trying to drown you. You misunderstand what it is that I want."

"What do you want?"

"I have watched you since you were young, since the day you revealed your power to resist me, and I've never stopped thinking about you. I have waited an eternity for someone like you, Harmony. Someone who could be my equal. I want you to come with me and get to know me—it's all that I ask."

"I know who you are! You're Suijin, the water god."

"Yes. That is what the Aquapopuleans call me." Shifting, he crossed his bulging arms over his chest. Flashing silvery scales ran the length of his outer arms.

At this closer proximity, Harmony noticed the scales ran down his thick outer thighs and tight calves as well. She cursed herself when her eyes yo-yoed down his torso once more—verifying only a god could have a physique so devastatingly *divine*. He was sexy in a beastly way! She shook her head to dislodge her runaway thoughts. Tossing her damp hair over her shoulder, she stood her ground.

What is wrong with me?

Swallowing hard to get control of her unbelievable reaction to this man-god she explained, "Look, I'm not going anywhere with you. I came here to help a friend of mine. I need to get back to the sacred island, to the temple."

"I have seen this woman you speak of with you many times in the past. I saw this human woman pass through several days ago. However, she is not at the temple; she is here. We are just down the coast from the sacred island, on the Cape."

Harmony felt her uneasiness decrease, and she stepped closer to him. "So Samantha is alive?" She stopped and looked around. "Where are we? The Cape? Do you mean Cape Cod?"

He nodded. She rationalized that because he was a god who passed between the realms, he must know Cape Cod. But then again, she was standing in a swamp. The dual realms were the same, yet so different.

"Your friend is alive, but perhaps not for long. She was taken against her will to an abandoned outpost by an exiled Linker. The fortress lies just there, a stone's throw away."

"An exiled Linker," she repeated. There was a Linker

who'd brought Finn here as a child... How many exiled Linkers were there? Could it be the same one? Harmony followed Suijin's gaze, scarcely making out a structure through the fog.

"I've brought you here so you can help her, but I want something in return."

As she waited for him to continue, Harmony heard movement behind her. Looking over her shoulder to see what other dangers lurked there, she staggered between the two threats—Suijin and the giant alligator. The alligator's upper body now occupied the same small grass patch she did.

"Harmony, do not fear him. The alligators won't touch you. I've commanded them to allow you safe passage from this place. I've staked my claim on you."

Whimpering in fear, she inched closer to Suijin, who looked a hell of a lot friendlier than the alligator at this point, not that she would trust the water god. Whatever claim he'd staked on her could prove useful for protecting her, for now at least. Besides, if he could take her closer to Samantha, she could get back to her realm sooner. "Can you get me inside?"

"This way." His smile, warm and hopeful, gave her a sense of dread. What was she going to owe this guy—this man-god?

Her sneakers sank in the mud as she followed him through the knee-deep water, past several pairs of eyes peeking just above the murky surface. In a matter of minutes a stone wall became clearly visible, within arm's reach.

"Follow this wall until you reach the steps. They will lead you into the fortress. After you find your friend, leave by the sea. Don't come back into the swamp. There are other dangers here."

"Okay." Harmony's heart was hammering double-time. She'd done the hardest part—crossing into the realm from deep water. *Wait!* she thought. *I woke up on the grass. Suijin must have carried me out of the water.*

"Hey, thank you," she offered cautiously.

He stepped closer.

Again she held up a hand, and heat pulsed. "I mean for helping me out of the ocean…before. And for helping me with my friend now."

"I will find you again, Harmony Parker. Remember, I want something in return."

Before she could tell him that she'd never go anywhere with him, that she was in a relationship and planned to return to the human realm, Suijin had turned and sauntered away, disappearing in the fog. She almost called to him. She wondered again why he wanted to spend time with her, why he thought she was his equal. He was a god; how could she be his equal?

But now she needed to focus on the task at hand. She held onto the rough stone wall as she trudged forward to help her friend, Samantha Finch.

As promised, the wall led her to the fortress, a looming stone behemoth. Finding her way inside through an obscure doorway, Harmony exhaled to slow her heart rate. She stopped to allow her eyes to adjust to the dim corridor. All she could hear was the surf outside. There was no indication which direction she should take. The place was mammoth. *Where should I start? Where are you, Samantha?*

Her wet sneakers echoed against the stone floor. When she heard distant voices, she stopped and flattened herself against the wall of an alcove.

"I don't know how long this will take—that depends on Finn," a deep, dry voice said.

"He has to agree with you. He's a fool not to—and he's wasting time," said another masculine voice.

"Yes, I'll likely be dead within a year."

"We don't know how much longer you have. You

shouldn't have crossed again. The risk to your health was too great. Besides, now we have the wrong girl." The scolding seemed to irritate the other man.

He ordered gruffly, "Just get down there with that food. Finn can be very persuasive, so don't talk to him unless he's ready to listen to what I have to say."

Harmony held her breath. As one of the men jogged down the steps, the other's heavy footfall was audible on the upper staircase. She thought, *Wow, that was lucky! So Finn is here too. How is Finn involved in this?* When she'd left this realm, Finn had been preparing to take leadership of the tribe. Had he been successful?

Harmony digested the fact that the Linker who took Samantha, who had apparently meant to take her, was here. Harmony squeezed her eyes closed. She pressed her knuckles to her forehead, trying to ease the tension and questions swirling in her mind. It wasn't long before she heard the man return, passing by her hiding place and continuing up the next stairwell. The footsteps faded, and she dashed down into the darkness.

23

Samantha felt a cool draft on her backside, which made her snuggled closer to the heat source her arm was wrapped around. Finn. He was lying on his back with her shoulder tucked under his arm. When he stirred, her eyelids fluttered open to gaze at his handsome face. Again she shivered in the chilly cell and adjusted the blanket around her naked body.

She allowed her mind to wander. What kind of a life could she make here—assuming she ever got out of this cell? The passionate night they'd shared and the bond that grew between them might be worth the obstacles she'd encountered in this realm. When she asked herself if she could return to her realm and leave Finn, a kind of grief overtook her. What they'd shared was beyond her wildest imagination, and she had to admit her imagination could be pretty wild. Untamed, rugged, and domineering were not the qualities that usually attracted her, but there was something more about Finn. Aside from his animal magnetism, he reacted to her in a way that made her heart flutter. Last night he'd offered her protection and devotion. Could they make a compatible and happy life together?

She watched the rise and fall of his chest, noticing where the skin was scarred from old wounds that crossed and contrasted with the artful tattoos. What did she know of him? He was a hunter and a warrior, the chieftain of a tribe. He claimed he knew Harmony, yet Harmony had never spoken of him when she talked about this place. Her thoughts were crowded out by her rising desire as her eyes roved over the beautiful landscape of his body. She stretched her tongue to taste the salty skin at the hollow of his neck. The stirrings in her belly begged her to tame him once again.

Completely surprised, Samantha found herself on her back in an instant, her arms pinned overhead, Finn's crushing weight pressing her against the hard floor. Her startled cry was a mixture of complete shock and erotic excitement.

"You shouldn't wake a sleeping bear like that." His voice was groggy from sleep, low and sexy. Her mind screamed for him to kiss her, but she said nothing. Skin against skin, their breath mingled, the pause escalating her anticipation.

"Someone's coming!" Finn said quickly. In an instant he rolled off her, dropping the blanket to cover her nakedness before he scrambled to dress.

Now hearing the distant footsteps echoing against the stones, Samantha reached for her clothes. By the time Umiko came into view they were both dressed and standing at the cell's bars.

"Step back, Finn," Umiko ordered. He held up a flask and a small basket containing apples and bread. Finn retreated while Umiko bent to slide their breakfast under the bar. After he stood, he gave Samantha a curious once-over. She wondered if Umiko could guess what had passed between her and Finn last night. She contemplated reaching out to him but decided to let Finn handle the situation.

Finn gradually came forward spreading his bare hands to emphasize his vulnerable, defenseless position. He spoke with a gentle tenderness, but Umiko backed away. Even locked behind iron bars, Finn could be dangerous, she surmised from Umiko's movements.

Finn said, "Umiko, my friend, it is time to end this. You and I could certainly come to an agreement. You of all people know of my god-given ability. Without it or my support, how can the tribe advance? Don't let an old exiled Linker guide you in this."

"It doesn't sound like a night down here has cleared your head. Why do you want to protect the clans anyway? Gale is one of us—a true tribal Linker. He says this could be a battle easily won, and the advancement to our civilization would improve our lives tenfold."

Samantha thought Umiko sounded radical, welcoming war. She admired Finn's compassion for the coastal clan and his strong resolve to keep the peace. His own father used him as a pawn and, worse, forced his closest friends to betray him.

"Look, I'll talk to him. Just let us out of this damp cage. Umiko, she's human, she needs to stay warm." Finn tried to stall Umiko's exit, if only for a moment.

"I'll let Gale know you are ready to talk," Umiko responded.

When Umiko rested his gaze on her once again, Samantha braced herself, just knowing he was going to say something to further complicate their situation.

"Samantha, soon you will be under my protection."

And there it was.

She could almost feel the testosterone rising between the two men. Her gaze swept back and forth between them.

"No! She stays with me!" Finn insisted as his shrewd eyes probed his lifelong friend. Perhaps he was looking for a clue to the mystery between Umiko and Samantha.

Preoccupied by the blonde behind the bars, Umiko ignored Finn's outburst. Umiko gave her a long, lingering glance before he turned and walked away.

Finn gripped the bars, barking Umiko's name. His voice echoed off the empty walls. His head swiveled, and his eyes bore into hers. "What did he mean by that? What's happened between you and Umiko?"

"Nothing happened between us. Apparently he's inquired about me. They know I'm not Harmony and I have no ability. I'm a useless human. Well, I guess not

189

completely useless." Being with Umiko in a romantic way, Samantha imagined, would be void of passion, like his no-nonsense demeanor.

Finn released his white-knuckled grip on the bars and moved to pull her into his arms. "That is never going to happen." He slipped his hand into her hair above the nape of her neck and tightened his fist, gently drawing her head back. His dominating hold roused her. His swooping mouth caught her lips, coaxing them to part. She gave him access, sighing when he plunged his tongue inside. If he weren't holding her up by her hair, caveman-style, she was sure she'd sink. Eventually, his grip loosened. His hand moved downward, rubbing and squeezing whatever he desired to explore. She did the same to him. Suddenly he paused, tense and alert. This time she also heard someone coming.

Soft footsteps stepped from the shadows, and their visitor was revealed.

"Oh my god! It can't be!" Samantha whispered in disbelief. "In here, Harmony, in here!" She attempted not to scream as relief washed over her.

"Sam!" Harmony cried as she ran to the bars. "Finn! Finn, I can't believe you are here. I can't believe I found you two. How do I get you out?"

Finn, reaching through the bars, clasped one of her hands; Samantha grabbed the other. "You crossed back!" he said with astonishment. After a second he released her hand and pointed. "There! Slide the rod and turn the wheel." Samantha watched Harmony find the locking mechanism in the semidark, windowless chamber. Only one torch remained burning, somewhere in the stairwell.

The metal scraped loudly as the cell door rolled open. Finn and Harmony rushed to embrace. Samantha hurried from her prison and stood awkwardly, watching them. After her night of passion and promises with Finn, she found this emotional reunion between her new lover and best friend somewhat disheartening. Harmony had returned to the human realm married to Kodiak, but Finn had told her he'd spent time with Harmony. Again, she wondered why Harmony hadn't mentioned Finn. She strained to listen to their hushed words.

"I didn't think I'd ever see you again. I know it must have been terrifying for you to come back," Finn said. Finally, after a very long embrace he let her go, but he paused to look into her face. "I can't believe you're here." Almost as if an afterthought, Finn glanced around. "Is Kodi with you?"

Harmony shook her head, "No, Kodi doesn't even know I'm here. It was urgent that I come right away. Finn, I came home to evidence that Sam had crossed—that someone had taken her across." Harmony reached for Samantha for a hug. "Thank god you are all right. I found the open refrigerator, the broken bottle, and your gold necklace." Harmony pulled free and reached behind her neck to unfasten her friend's necklace. "I brought it." She held up the gold chain for inspection before she reached around Samantha's neck to fasten it where it belonged.

In the moment after her best friend returned her sentimental necklace, Samantha remembered all the times Harmony had been there for her. And now she had crossed a realm to help her. Tears filled her eyes.

"What happened at my house?" Harmony asked.

"First," Samantha sniffed, "thanks for coming back for me. And second, Gale followed me into your house and dragged me into your grandfather's den. After he lit the herbs I coughed until I passed out. I woke up in the ocean, just like you told me had happened to you." Samantha glanced at Finn for a moment and added, "Finn is here because Gale the Linker is his father." Samantha looked into Harmony's shocked eyes and noticed for the first time they had a slight glow, similar to the other Aquapopuleans. Strange she'd never noticed it before.

"What do you mean? *Gale the Linker* is Finn's father?"

"It's true," Finn stated grimly. "I've recently learned this news myself when Gale resurfaced from exile. There is much to tell you, but right now we must leave!" Finn retrieved and fastened his belt, which Umiko dropped on the other side of the chamber, out of reach of the cell. He motioned the girls toward the stairs.

"Have you brought others from the clan and a boat?" Finn asked Harmony in hushed tones.

"I'm alone. It's a long story. I don't have a boat."

"Okay. Not to worry, I came in one. Let's head out to the dock. I need to alert my tribal council about what is happening, and we need to contain Gale. Let's hurry. I've been away from the summit for two days." They mounted a second staircase and continued upward.

"Summit? What's happened since I left?" Harmony asked, taking the steps by his side. Samantha listened to their exchange while she trailed close behind.

"As chieftain, I'm here for a summit with leaders and Linkers from outlying areas to work out trade and other issues. The summit is coming to its conclusion, but when Gale kidnapped Samantha and took her here, I followed. Two of my council members, *my friends*, have been helping Gale all along. He has more ambitious plans for the clans, the same ambitions that drove Chief Nakoma."

They reached a landing where windows allowed daylight in, defused by gray mist. Immediately they stopped talking. Finn slowed and listened, and then he spoke quietly. "I came in this way." He tipped his head toward a passageway. They resumed their escape.

Samantha allowed Finn to lead her to safety. Her shoulders relaxed when they exited through a wooden door. She felt the moist air hit her skin, instantly misting her in its pungent smell. She stumbled on the loose and broken stones as they made their way down the sloping road toward the sound of the surf. Although she couldn't see more than a few feet in front of her, she followed at a rapid speed. Suddenly she skidded to a halt. Umiko stood between them and the invisible phantom boat that rested in the fog somewhere nearby.

Finn reached for his blade. "Umiko, I don't want to fight you. Let us go."

Another voice answered from somewhere in the mist; Samantha twirled around. Gale stood behind them.

"Well, look who's here! It must be fate that Harmony Parker has returned." Gale glanced at Umiko, who gave an affirmative nod. Gale ventured closer.

Samantha shouldered closer to Harmony. Fear that Finn would fight sent a cold sweat trickling down Samantha's spine.

"Now that you two blonds are together, I can see how similar you look." Gale's smile was shallow. "Son, now that Harmony is here, we can move forward with my original plans. It's time you had a wife with abilities that equal your own."

"I will marry, but it won't be Harmony Parker. It's time you pay for your crimes," Finn declared.

Samantha watched Gale snap his fingers, signaling Umiko. Gale snarled, "Get his blade!"

As Umiko closed in on Finn, Harmony grabbed Samantha's wrist. "This way!"

Tearing her wide, terrified eyes away from Finn, Samantha peered down at the broken stone ledge of the elevated bridge. Over the edge, large boulders disappeared into the patchy fog along the swampy grasses below.

"Finn, this way!" Harmony called, pulling Samantha down onto the boulders.

"You don't want to go that way!" Gale's voice

boomed. "There are nasty creatures in that swamp."

Samantha paused, but Harmony yanked her over the slippery surfaces. Hastily, Samantha squatted down, using her hands to guide her to the ground so she wouldn't fall. When she reached the tall, sharp grass she turn back to look for Finn. Last time she saw him, he had his knife drawn against Umiko.

"Come on!" Harmony urged.

"Wait, where's Finn?" Samantha's voice shook with concern. *He came to rescue me. If anything happens to him...* Samantha felt a rising hysteria. She couldn't see anything—she heard grunts and shouts. Suddenly the sound came closer. Rapidly, she dashed out of the way as Finn's dark form crashed through the wall of fog. He landed on his haunches and then stood, nodding at Harmony.

The trio zigzagged through the brush until they were forced to slow down; the swamp gave way to large puddles and small waterways. Samantha wondered why they weren't being followed. She remembered Gale's warning not to go into the swamp. The creepy place was oddly silent.

Both girls leaned against a tree trunk to catch their breath. Finn, who didn't seem winded at all, surveyed their surroundings. He said, "What is your plan? Gale is correct about this swamp. There are evil creatures in here. The great storm that caused this eternal fog also brought the giant alligators, among other things that live here. The Aquapopuleans have forsaken this place. Please tell me you have a plan."

"Yeah. Yeah, well, you don't have to worry about the alligators. At least I hope not." At Harmony's wishy-washy answer, Samantha threw up her hands.

"What are you talking about!" she squeaked.

"I don't know why exactly, but Suijin helped me—he brought me here. He saw Gale with Sam and knew I had come to help her. And he said he told the alligators not to harm me. So just stay close. We'll get to the bay and make a swim for it…or something."

"Who the hell is Suijin?" Samantha shouted, distressed that this rescue seemed to have left them lost in a deadly swamp. As if on cue, there was movement in the grass. Finn thrust Samantha behind him, his knife poised for attack. She whispered, "We're going to die here!" An alligator, the length of a train car, shimmied away into the water, and Samantha stared open-mouthed at Harmony.

"Suijin said the gators would stay away. See, the gator didn't eat us."

With the immediate danger out of the way, Finn unlatched a pouch on his belt and pulled out a compass. "The bay is that way. Watch where you step."

24

The trio was tense while they detoured around slow-moving waterways and dodged alligators. They covered several miles; at least that's how it felt to Harmony. Harmony rested her arm against a tree trunk as sweat dripped down her clammy torso. When she was last in this realm it had been March, and although the weather was different between the realms, it had certainly been cooler then. Now it was August in New England, and it felt like August here.

"We must be getting close to the bay by now. The trees are thinning out," Harmony said, squinting into the gloom. "Finn, can't you do something about this fog?"

"Yeah. Finn, if you can control the weather, why are we still blindly trying to find our way?" Samantha added, sounding irritated.

"I've tried to dissipate it, but this area is vast. Maybe I'll try a strong wind." Finn twirled his wrists and concentrated on the sky. Soon a clean breeze washed over Harmony, and she sighed over the freshness it brought. It strengthened her resolve to reach the tree line.

As the mist lifted, the light became brighter, revealing a field of green plants, their vines supporting one another in a strange web. At shoulder height, large botanicals bloomed. Beyond the field was the beach—and the bay.

They each exhaled with relief.

"You did it!" Samantha laughed. She sent Finn a wide smile before she turned to trudge ahead. Lifting her damp hair off her shoulders and letting the wind take it, Samantha began to hum.

Harmony grinned, recognizing the typical liveliness of Samantha Finch.

Finn fell into step beside Harmony. "She's pretty amazing."

Harmony cast him a sideways glance, curious. "Yeah, Sam's great."

Finn didn't look at her; his eyes followed the blond skipping ahead. "I want to warn you, Calder said she would never make the return trip. She almost died crossing."

Harmony made an unladylike sound and grumbled, "She's trapped here because of me."

"*Trapped* is a strong word."

"Oh?" Suddenly the pitch of her voice changed. "You think maybe she wants to stay here? Are you the reason?" Harmony elbowed him hard enough to get him to finally look at her.

"We've mated," he confessed.

"Okie dokie, that was blunt. All right. Well, have you two talked about the future?" Her eyes cut back to Samantha, who'd stopped to admire the exotic flowers.

"I will take her as my wife. The tribe will understand my choice for taking a human mate, as I am half-human. I will make them understand that with her vast knowledge of the other realm she is an asset. Certainly she is a better choice than Gale when it comes to otherworldly topics."

"So you're marrying her for political reasons?"

"No, there are other reasons." He couldn't keep the satisfaction out of his voice.

Harmony shook her head, and they both smirked at each other. She wondered what her best friend thought about this remarkable news. "So you asked her to marry you and she said yes? Just like that?"

"Her actions last night confirmed her answer." Finn grinned wolfishly.

Before Harmony could comment, a sudden cry pierced the air. Harmony recognized Samantha's scream.

Finn was already leaping through the tall plants, ripping at the vines to reach her. The lovely exotic flowers, clustered at shoulder height, looked like birds of paradise but acted like Venus flytraps. Samantha's entire hand was enclosed in one. Finn reached her first. He yanked her arm and pried at the clamped mouth of the bloom, but it wouldn't open.

"It's crushing my hand! It's burning!" Samantha franticly cried.

By the time Harmony reached them, Finn was hacking away at the thick stem of the flower. "Oh my god, Finn, hurry!" Harmony noticed as the other blooms deliberately stretched in their direction. The vines snaked rapidly around their ankles, curling up their legs.

We didn't make it all this way to be eaten by plants! Harmony unbuttoned her back pocket and took out her pocketknife. She flipped it open and slashed the stem that circled her waist. She slashed again when another plant sucked at her sleeve.

"Finn!" Harmony screamed for help, but when she darted her gaze at him, she saw to her horror that Finn's arms were being dragged by vines. They were forcing him to bend forward; the knife he held was being consumed by layers of thin, looping vines. Samantha, on her knees, struggled to free her hand, to no avail. Harmony's knife slipped from her fingers when her wrist was captured.

She couldn't give up! Harmony twisted and strained as hard as she could. She screamed in rage when she felt her hip hit the ground. Her ability had no application here. She couldn't help her friends; she couldn't help herself. She had come all this way…and she was going to die.

Above the sound of her rapid breathing came the sound of rushing water. It filled her ears before the actual seawater rushed in. The water flooded everything around her and dunked her under. She knew her friends suffered the same fate. While she floated in the current of the rushing surge she was jerked against the vines that held fast, but only for several moments.

The vines were flattened by the far-reaching wave, forcing them to release their victims.

Harmony untangled herself from the lifeless vines. She stood among the sodden plants, looking toward the calm bay as the water receded. *The water is calm. Where did the sudden rogue wave come from?*

Harmony saw Suijin riding in on another strangely contained wave. His godly posture directed the water beneath his feet, as if he were surfing without a board. He lowered his body in the surf and stared intently at her.

He has rescued me twice today. It was an effort to tear her eyes away from him, but she turned and watched Finn help Samantha up. Finn trained his guarded gaze on the man in the water until he was distracted by Samantha's moan. The bloom had released its grip on Samantha's hand. Finn pulled her hand free and whipped the saturated bloom to the ground. Her hand was blistered and covered in a glistening gel.

"Let's rinse this off," he asserted as he wrapped a supportive arm around Samantha's waist. Finn guided Samantha toward where Suijin floated in the water.

Harmony figured Finn would guess the man was none other than the water god. As the colorful flowers shifted beneath her feet, Harmony managed to stay upright as she slipped over the vines on her way to the beach.

Reaching the sand, Finn and Samantha rushed straight into the sea, which had returned to its former tranquil version. Samantha dunked her hand, attempting to wash away the poison. She screamed in pain. Harmony looked around, trying to figure out what to do.

They had no boat, and it was too far to swim or walk back to the temple. Surely Gale and Umiko would sail around to the bay to recapture them. Relieved her friends were out of apparent danger for the moment, Harmony turned and noticed that the god waited.

"Suijin!" she called.

"Harmony! Stop!" Finn protested. "We can't trust the water god. He's dangerous."

"It's okay. He saved us, Finn." Although Harmony reassured her friends, she wasn't sure why Suijin had saved their lives. How had he known she was in danger again? Harmony didn't turn back or wait for her friends; she jogged down the beach, her focus on Suijin.

"What are you doing? Stop!" Finn warned. He held Samantha, who sobbed and hoarsely pleaded for her friend to come back.

But Harmony was desperate to help her friends and get them away from there—especially with Samantha's injury. Waves foamed at her feet as she took a hesitant step into the water. Suijin, yards away, observed her. He stood upright, water pooling around his calves even though he was probably five feet above the sandy bottom. *A god who walks on water.* The scales on the outer half of his legs appeared dark and oily. His large hands hooked over his square hipbones; the outline of his muscles gleamed in the hazy yellow light. Harmony waded in, calling out.

"You came. You saved us. Why are you helping me?"

"I sense when you are in life-threatening danger, Harmony. I will never let anything happen to you," he answered, drifting farther away.

She waded out to her chest. "I'm still... I mean, we, my friends and I, are still in danger." She swam, closing the distance between them. "Could you help us...again? Please."

Slowly his body sank beneath the surface to his shoulders. He and Harmony floated face to face. She held her breath, anticipating his answer. But a moment later he slipped under the water, disappearing all together.

Her heart sank. *He's not going to help!* She was well over her head now. The waves were soft swells. Swallowing her fear, she called for Suijin again. His dark head broke the surface, and though she was thankful he'd returned, she was concerned she'd owe him more than she could give.

"What do you require?" His voice was calm and conversational; his irises appeared eerily black and unnatural.

"A way to return to the temple. A boat, maybe?" Harmony treaded water and glanced over her shoulder. Finn had returned Samantha to the sand and was wrapping her hand with his torn shirt. She looked at Suijin again, pleading, "Please! I will spend time with you later, after my friends are safe. That's what you want, right?" His black irises swirled, and the color changed to sapphire. A chill shivered down her spine. Suijin might resemble a man, but he was a powerful deity.

"All right, Harmony." The corners of his mouth turned up. "I'll return with a boat," he said before he slipped under the water.

Harmony tried to catch her breath. Seeing him again was intense. She swam toward the shore, his handsome face lingering in her mind.

"He'll bring us a boat." She waded out from the water near her friends.

"What's going on? Last I knew you hated the water god for taking your family. What's changed?" Finn demanded. "I can't even believe he was here. Why has he shown himself after so long?"

Samantha chimed in. "Harmony, that *thing* in the water...he drowned your family! He could have killed you. What were you thinking?"

Rapidly shifting her gaze from one friend to the other, Harmony considered their questions. The truth was that she didn't know how she felt about Suijin now. She dropped to her knees beside Samantha. "It's crazy, because I thought he was trying to drown me before...but he wasn't. In fact, he's got this crazy idea that he wants me to...umm, to get to know him. Spend time with him..." She shrugged one shoulder.

"What is that supposed to mean?" Finn sounded angry.

Harmony told her friends about her earlier encounter with the god. Just as she finished the brief version, an explosion erupted in the sea just offshore. A large rowboat burst upward, piercing the sky, before dropping to settle on the surface.

The threesome sprang to their feet at the commotion and stared at each other in shock. Finn was the first to sprint forward. He plunged in and swam to their escape boat. He dragged it to shore and lifted Samantha into it. Harmony jumped in and earnestly scanned the waters for any sign of Suijin.

He didn't appear.

25

Samantha smiled when she glanced at Finn, who hovered nearby while Calder applied ointment to her wounded hand. She rested comfortably on her bed back in the Wellness temple. Calder closed his eyes, waving his hands over hers, using his healer's gift. His daughter Nami and her son Rio stood behind him.

Though the clan members wouldn't travel to the foggy Cape, they had sent several sailing vessels into the surrounding waters to aid the chieftain in any way they could—from a safe distance. Their foresight paid off. The rowboat provided by the water god was spotted scarcely an hour after the trio had made their way out of the bay. The clan sailors swiftly escorted them back to the Wellness temple.

Samantha witnessed the tearful reunion between Harmony and her new family. When Nami and Rio moved to embrace her as well, Samantha felt grateful. She still found it remarkable that Harmony had family in this realm.

During the return voyage to the Wellness temple, Harmony confided that she felt torn. If the choice were solely hers, Harmony would stay here where her family lived. But she feared Kodiak was stuck in the human realm, just as Samantha was stuck in the Aquapopulean realm. Samantha completely understood. She too had someone of profound importance here.

Samantha's eyes locked with Finn's, and she knew from his look of intense concern that he had feelings for her. There was no denying what she felt for him. Their night together had been the beginning of something wonderful.

"There. You should feel immediate relief," Calder

said.

Samantha returned her attention to the clan Linker and healer. "Yes, it's much better. Thank you."

Calder redirected his gaze to the hovering chieftain. "Finn, we should talk about Gale. Now that his plan is botched and you've told him you'll never agree to his demands, he's most likely going to call upon his warriors and pick up where your old chieftain Nakoma left off. If it's true that Harmony has a friend in Suijin, then perhaps she can help?"

"I don't think involving the water god is a good plan. It's too risky. Besides, I don't trust his intentions. He told Harmony he wanted to spend time with her—why?" Samantha heard the protectiveness in Finn's voice. "We can handle this."

Samantha swung her feet over the bed and stood. Finn rushed to her side. "I'm fine now," she reassured him. "So where do you think Gale went? Back to your city?"

No one knew. No one answered.

Harmony, who'd been staring out the window for some time, silent and deep in thought, turned when Samantha got up. Samantha took the opportunity to include her in the conversation.

"Harmony and I can talk to your council. I will tell them that Gale kidnapped me—twice—and threatened me. I will give testimony that he is misguided and must be stopped. At least then the truth will be out there. We can prepare everyone so Gale can't sneak-attack us." Samantha skirted the bed, heading for the window and Harmony. "We could talk to them, right?" she asked her friend.

Harmony shrugged, looking uncertain.

Calder responded, "Someone needs to talk to the council. This summit has been put on hold. The council was told the tribal chieftain had to step away to take care of an urgent matter."

"Yes, I will speak with them," Finn clarified as he reached Samantha's side.

She nodded, believing he agreed with her. "I will come with you."

"Hold on. You should rest." He lifted his hand as if he were about to smooth her hair. Under Calder's watchful eye, instead he dropped his palm along her arm. "You've been through a lot. It's been a long day for us all. I think we should assemble the council first thing in the morning. Both of you girls should get some rest."

"What about you?" Samantha asked. She sensed he was prepared to exit.

"I'm going to gather some hunters to look for Gale and Umiko. I want them to cover the roads to the west in case they come ashore and head back to the city."

"I have several boats patrolling the harbor," Calder said.

Samantha sent a pleading look in Harmony's direction, hoping she would make these men see that they wanted to do more to help right now. Samantha frowned when Harmony spoke.

"It's all right, Sam. We are safe here. Gale is probably miles away by now." Her weary voice surprised Samantha. Clearly her friend was exhausted. Just this morning she'd passed through the realms, was almost eaten by a plant, negotiated with a god, and took an eight-hour journey to reach the Wellness temple.

"Yeah." Samantha eyeballed Rio and Nami across the room. "Maybe we could get something to eat and turn in early."

Finn seemed to sag with relief, and he leaned forward to kiss her mouth tenderly despite everyone in the room. "I'll return later," he said quietly to her and then turned and beckoned to Calder to follow him out the door. It was almost sunset.

Nami and Rio left right behind them, promising to return with some dinner.

***

They remained at the Wellness temple for a few days, with no sign of Gale. The summit resumed and had finished yesterday, peace achieved. Today, they would plan their trip back to the tribal city.

Harmony smirked at Finn. "So you're not human after all."

"Half human—my mother was human. Gale claims he loved her," he added.

"That's messed up." They nodded at each other. "Do you think that is why we have abilities?" Harmony wasn't the only one caught between two worlds. She'd bonded with Finn, and this news seemed to strengthen that bond.

"Maybe." Finn's eyes drifted over her shoulder to where Samantha peeked around the corner into the sitting room as she finished braiding her hair.

Turning to verify what was distracting Finn, Harmony smiled at Samantha, who smiled back. *These two certainly have a thing for each other*, Harmony thought. Samantha disappeared into the hallway. Waiting for her to finish getting ready, Harmony questioned Finn. "So have you talked more about a wedding? Did you get a real answer from Sam?"

Finn's mouth twitched; he nodded. "She said yes last night with her words—as well as her actions."

Harmony raised her eyebrows. Apparently Samantha had relinquished the hope of returning to the human realm.

"She wants to tell you herself—if she ever finishes getting ready. What's taking so long?"

"She always takes forever." Harmony waved a

dismissive hand, pondering what this revelation meant. If the couple returned to the city and married right away, then she could be there for her best friend's wedding and still have enough time to return to the coast to cross back over. She figured she still had the rest of the month before Kodiak returned from his expedition. No sense sitting at home alone; she might never see her best friend again.

It was settled. She'd travel with them to the tribal city. The journey was long and tedious, but she'd cherish the little time she had left with her friends.

Finn tapped an impatient finger, and Harmony commented, "She's a weathergirl, you know." Harmony found the coincidence comical.

That got a big smile. "I know."

Harmony believed in her heart that Finn would make Samantha happy, but she'd lose her friend after she crossed. "It's a good thing that she has you. You'll look out for her?"

"Of course." His smile disappeared, and he seemed to study her face. She could only guess what he was thinking. Finally he said, "I wish you and Kodiak could return someday. How is he adjusting?"

Toying with a lock of her blond hair, she sighed. "Truth is, I'm not sure how Kodi feels about the human realm." Harmony shook her head. "I should have come sooner, but I tried to reach Kodi at first. Finn, he left a while ago. He's gone on an expedition. I know I owe him time to find his way in a new realm, but I'm feeling so confused. Maybe I don't truly know him. What if he doesn't want to come back to me?"

"He would be a fool. And anyway, I know he loves you. Your feelings haven't changed about him?"

"Of course not." She shook her head. "It's just harder than I thought it would be. I still feel...lost." She knew no one could understand that better than Finn. "And

Finn..." she paused, her expression grave, "it took me five days to gather up enough courage to light the herbs and cross again. The water terrifies me! I don't think I'll ever come back."

"It's okay. I know. It was brave of you to come for Samantha. But I'm here, and I promise you I will look after her."

"Right, I know you will." Tears sparkled in her eyes. "I'm struggling. I want to go back to Kodi, but I'm truly dreading the crossing."

"I'm sorry, kitten." Finn placed his hand on hers. Hearing the pet name he'd used when they met months ago brought a lopsided smile to her mouth.

Samantha breezed around the corner. Harmony sensed her curiosity about their conversation. She slipped her hand from Finn's and said to them both, "I'm glad you've found each other in this crazy mess."

"Yeah, and you two got to see each other again," Samantha nonchalantly observed. "Although you never mentioned Finn when you told me about this place..."

"I'm hurt by that, Harmony!" he jested. "I thought we had a strong bond. After all, I did save your life from those wolves, and I helped you escape from the city."

Harmony chuckled. "We are bonded, Finn—you are a brother to me."

"I'm a lucky man. I have a new sister and a soon-to-be new wife."

Samantha blushed prettily, and Finn captured her waist and pulled her onto his lap. "Gale may have broken the law by bringing you here, yet you are exactly the woman I want. How can I punish him for that?"

Finn and Samantha were caught up in the moment, locked in an embrace and kissing. To give them some privacy, Harmony wandered to the window, mindlessly fingering her lavender pearl ring. Looking out at the ocean, her thoughts drifted. She wondered where Suijin was. She'd promised she would spend time with him. What did a god want with her? Before she could think more about it, she froze. Her gaze dropped to the sudden commotion below.

"Finn!" She swirled around. "Gale is here…and he's not alone."

26

Finn fought his way through the crowded lobby. Linker Gale and his legion of warriors had been shown into the banquet room, the only space large enough to house the group. Finn had recognized the southern tribes from the window. He'd trained with them over the years when Nakoma was chieftain. Clearly Gale's influence ran deep in the tribal community. Finn spotted Calder and moved to his side.

"What is happening?" Finn growled.

"Gale has requested—more like insisted on—an audience with the council. This is bad, Finn. He may try to take over your position as chief. And he has an army to back him up," Calder whispered in outrage.

As the council members rushed to join the impromptu session, tables were rearranged in the banquet hall. Many warriors stood shoulder to shoulder around the room's perimeter. Finn and Calder joined the other prominent members gathered around a conference table. Gale occupied a strategic seat, casually leaning back in his chair.

Calder prompted, "What is it that you want to say, Gale?"

Finn endured Gale's easy leadership as he spoke of his demands. The clans' council members were outraged at his insistence that it was time for their people to work the salt mines, as well as pay larger taxes on salt. He laid out the future plans to expand the city, saying the clans were a vital part. Finn understood, of course, that the clans wanted no part in that. He had underestimated his father. Gale had been smart to keep warriors nearby, at the ready. Finn only wished he and his father could take a different path, but Gale was too far gone.

When the clan turned to Finn to control his tribal Linker, Finn leaned in. "This man, a Linker who's seen firsthand the workings of a realm vastly different from ours, should know this attempt will fail." The room quieted as Finn continued. "Calder can confirm that devastating changes like this can poison our nations, just like in the human realm. We can work together on each issue. We don't have to end up like the humans. Their wrong choices and advances came with wars, death, famine, and disease."

"Finn is right," Calder asserted. "Our lives in this realm are simple and good. We should learn from the humans' mistakes—from my mistakes—and join together to avoid war at all cost."

Gale's voice easily commanded the room. "We need an army if we are to be free from the god. Our expansion would include more hunters—hunters who will eradicate the sirens."

Murmurs rose. The problem of the sirens taking people was a genuine threat.

Suddenly, the double doors swung open. The room became quiet as two blond girls waltzed into the banquet room.

The dynamics in the room changed. Every person stared, whether because of the girls' unusual human hair color or the fact that there were two of them in this realm. It didn't matter. Finn watched his father. The man seemed to calculate the outcome in his dark eyes.

Samantha spoke, loud and clear, her voice laced with a slight human accent. "This is Harmony Parker, the mixed-blood soldier who has befriended your water god. And I am her closest friend, Samantha Finch."

Finn was impressed with Samantha's opening but wondered where she would go from there. Harmony spoke next, more confident than he'd ever heard her.

"I have recently spoken with the water god, Suijin,

and I plan to do so again soon. I will ask him to stop the sirens' attacks."

"What if he doesn't listen?" asked a man from the southern tribe, who seemed determined to shake up the crowd.

Finn was glad to see Harmony wasn't deterred.

"I will do what I can to help, but only if you respect and follow your rightful chieftain, Finn Falk." Harmony turned to face Gale. Gale raised his chin a notch, ready to challenge her. She said quietly, "You should take what little time you have left and make amends with your son."

When Gale's eyes narrowed on Harmony, Finn sensed she knew something. He was stunned by her next words. "I know you are dying, Gale."

Finn's gasp was echoed by others in the room, including the southern warriors, who now eyed Gale furiously. Surely no one could follow a dead man.

"I understand that you may not live out the year." Murmurs broke out, and Harmony's gaze landed on Finn, as if to say *I'm sorry I didn't tell you sooner.*

"How could you know that?" Umiko questioned, a deep crease in his brow. "I'm the only one who knows about this…" He glanced down at the Linker he served and said, "I've never spoken of it."

"I overheard you two talking in the fortress hallway. I figured it out."

"Well, I think this changes things, Gale," said Calder, who sent his oldest acquaintance a pessimistic nod.

Gale stood immediately. "I have given you the greatest possible future, Finn. You have warriors to carry out what needs to be done. And Harmony Parker is here to help you. Don't let this setback dissuade you from your destiny."

Finn also stood, watching as Umiko stepped behind Gale. Umiko's eyes swept the disheartened faces of the southern tribesmen and landed on the lovely blond Finn knew he'd inquired about. Finally he locked eyes with Finn. They had been inseparable friends once. Finn had thought he knew Umiko well. In fact, the look he was giving him now seemed to say *I've made a mistake.* Finn tensed, ready to grab his blade, unwilling to underestimate Gale again. But it was Umiko who surprised him.

Umiko said, "Gale, it is over."

His words seemed to shake Gale, who instantly became annoyed. Gale turned to Umiko and said with conviction, "We can convince them, Umiko. We are the powerful Forest Tribe, and my son is leader. The clans are powerless."

His rant did not go over well.

"I have allowed this to go on too long," Umiko said to Finn, who stood ready for any action from the southern tribes, but they hung back and seemed to await instructions from their chieftain. Umiko continued forlornly, "Gale said a summit would never come to pass, never mind be successful, but you have proven it can be done, Finn. I see now that you have proven yourself an asset and a capable leader, while Gale has continued to stoop to his old tricks of abduction and force." Umiko stepped over to Finn and held out his hand. "I renounce any oath I made to Gale the Linker. I pledge my loyalty to you, my chieftain and friend, knowing my father would agree."

"I've known you almost my entire life, Umiko, and I know you to be an honorable man. We've all had lapses in judgment. That said, I welcome your pledge. But you must prove yourself not only to me but to the tribe and clan." Umiko swore to do so, and the men clasped wrists in a sign of union.

"Bind the prisoner," Finn ordered a hunter poised to do his bidding.

The Linker glared at Umiko and then flicked his gaze at his son. He didn't resist when the hunter bound his wrists.

Gale was sentenced to remain under guard at the Wellness temple and on the journey back to the tribal city. After the wedding he would stand trial for abduction and treason.

27

Harmony thought this realm, with all its serene beauty and spiritual karma, seemed to host just as much drama as her own. Yet she wasn't ready to return home. Two weeks had passed since Samantha had crossed the realms. It had taken Harmony five days to build up enough courage to follow her. Now the girls would make the five-hundred-mile trek over the hills to the tribal city—Samantha's new home. Harmony vowed not to miss her best friend's wedding, especially since Samantha had been unable to witness hers. With the summit successfully behind them, Harmony and the couple prepared to leave the coast.

Harmony hugged Nami, Rio, and Calder farewell. She promised to visit them when she returned for the crossing. It was always better to cross closest to the portal, Calder had advised. When he asked her about the Wentworth-by-the-Sea, she sighed.

"All is well for now. But the earthquake must have been caused by the razing of the building. More than half of the hotel was destroyed."

"It has been a very long time since I last saw that place," Calder said nostalgically.

Harmony noticed a far-off look in his eyes. She understood the Wentworth held sentimental value to him too. After all, he'd met her great-great grandmother, Pearl, there in 1905. They shared that connection to the building.

"Good-bye, Calder."

Harmony crossed paths with Umiko when she headed to her mount. She didn't remember seeing him the last time she was here, although Finn had mentioned it was Umiko who'd suspected Samantha was not the same

JENNIFER W. SMITH

human girl. Umiko had proved vital in helping convince the clan that Gale's meddling was over and that the Linker was dying. Calder's examination confirmed that fact. While Umiko and the southern tribesmen were not punished, they were placed under watch until otherwise noted. Sullen after their reprimand, the southern tribesmen had left immediately for their villages.

Harmony stroked the nose of her elk, estimating that it would probably take about eight days to reach the Great Falls. Next to her, Finn mounted his elk and helped Samantha up behind him.

"I think you should improve transportation between your city and the coast. Maybe a high speed train?" Harmony joked with Finn after settling into her elk's saddle. She decided to give riding solo a try; she had clocked uncountable hours in the saddle when she'd made this trip before. Stopping each evening at the posts and resting in a bed for the night would help ease the soreness from the saddle.

Finn chuckled. "That may not be a bad idea. I always did like trains when I was a kid."

Harmony watched Samantha snuggle up behind Finn on the elk. Adoration lit her face as she chirped, "Oh, I bet you were such a cute little boy." Samantha rested her cheek against his shoulder and looked meaningfully at Harmony.

The days stretched by, but Harmony thought this trip was immensely more enjoyable than the last one. On the fourth night, when the entourage reached the Hudson River trading village, the girls had finally had a chance to talk privately. While Finn and his tribal escort met to discuss how they would proceed with Gale's trial and all that it entailed, the girls stayed behind in Harmony's room.

Harmony smiled at her best friend. They'd grown up together, cried over breakups, laughed at movies, and confided their deepest secrets to each other. It was no secret how happy Samantha was. It was strange how something good had come from something so...odd. This realm had given her Kodiak, and now it gave her friend Finn. Samantha had confessed she was madly in love with Finn, and she suspected that she carried his child.

Samantha badgered Harmony. "Tell me everything you know about the Aquapopulean race, since my baby will be a part of it."

"What baby?" Harmony doubted it could be true, but Calder said life finds a way to survive—even if it has to evolve.

"When Finn and I were Gale's prisoners, we—"

"Yeah. Well..." Harmony eyes focused into space while she calculated the weeks. "It's early yet."

"I know...but I'm never late. Still, let's keep it between us for now."

Harmony agreed, though she remained skeptical. She answered Samantha's question. "After leaving this realm, I wanted to know more about this race and how closely related they are to our ancestors, so I read up on it at the Portsmouth library." Harmony paused; her library books were going to be way overdue. "Calder told me both realms started off the same and that early ancestors of Homo sapiens came down from the trees and waded at the water's edge. He called it the Aquatic Ape theory. Those ape-like ancestors transitioned in the water instead of on the African savannah, as most of our scientists suggest."

"Right. Rio took me to the library at the Wellness and showed me a book on evolution," Samantha mentioned. "But remind me again."

Harmony remembered that her friend's interest in science was strictly weather related. Besides, church girls where taught to dismiss evolution theory in favor of

Genesis.

Harmony explained, "Yeah. For example, the apes lost most of their hair because it wasn't needed in the water. The hair remaining flows down because of the water pushing it when they swam. Swimming allowed their bodies to become more streamlined, and they became bipedal—walking upright out of the water or wading to keep their heads above water to breath. These changes made early humans slow and exposed and allowed them to evolve against gravity."

"Why did they go into the water?"

"Probably for food, or to avoid predators."

"Hey, remember Mr. Macy's science class in middle school when he told us about some fossilized skeleton found in Ethiopia?"

"Right, that was Lucy. Mr. Macy was pretty excited about it. I read that there are no fossils to prove the Aquatic Ape theory, but then again anthropologists suggest the bones are buried under the sea." Harmony added thoughtfully, "I wonder if scientists will ever find them."

"So why don't we have the ability to hold our breath like the Aquapopulean clans? Finn said the tribe lost their ability to do so too. Do you think our ancestors could hold their breath like the clans?"

"Not according the Aquatic Ape theory. They say something drove us back onto land, so we can't hold our breath to that extent. But we can hold our breath for a bit, something no ape or other terrestrial animal can do. Also we developed extended lyrics to speak—kind of like dolphins. Again we are more like whales and dolphins in that regard I guess."

"So weird—all of this!" Samantha said, shaking her head. She looked beseechingly at Harmony. "I wish you didn't have to go back. Is there any way you and Kodi might return?"

Harmony rubbed her fingers on her forehead. "I've wracked my brains, trying to think of a way to make sure the Wentworth and the land is safe, but even if that happens, I don't know if Kodi could survive another crossing." She stretched her palm in Samantha's direction. "You know how powerful those herbs are."

"Calder said I almost died—that I wasn't expected to make it." Quivering, Samantha placed her hand over her stomach. Her expression changed to wonder as she added, "But now I feel fantastic."

"I guess miracles can happen." Harmony half-shrugged, thinking about how mysterious things can be.

Samantha smiled and said, "Maybe it will happen for you and Kodi too." Harmony averted her eyes at Samantha's comment. "Hey, what is it? Is everything all right with you two?"

"We're okay. It's just that Kodi told me he lost his ability to breathe underwater after we crossed into the human realm. And he kept it a secret from me for a while. I knew something was going on with him... I feel responsible. He says it's not my fault, but gosh, Sam, he was a legendary Aquapopulean Diver!" She threw up her hands in frustration. "He wasn't even supposed to pass through—he did it on impulse."

"I don't believe that for a second! He wanted to be with you," Samantha reassured her, but Harmony twisted her lips.

"Maybe. But he left me to search the mysteries of the human underwater realm." Her voice was sullen, her eyes bright with tears.

"Be fair. I told you before that he needs to find his place in our world. We all do. And besides, it's not like you're home waiting for him—"

"Yeahhh," Harmony interrupted. She wiped away a fallen tear with her sleeve. "Because I'm here saving your ass."

Laughter bubbled from Harmony lips at their bizarre predicament, and both girls laughed until Samantha had tears in her eyes too.

28

A light rain misted over the stone city. The farmer's son stuck to the shadows, but not to avoid getting wet. He'd never been to the tribal city, and despite his bravado he was feeling somewhat out of his element. Colossal stone cats flanked the entrance, but it was the living, breathing, taller-than-his-eight-year-old-shoulder lions that he watched with apprehension. He'd come a long way on foot from the outlying fields. His father refused to allow him to take one of the elk, insisting the animals were needed on the farm.

"There's nothing wrong with your legs, boy. You be respectful to our chieftain, and don't dally along the way. I would not send you, but the chieftain himself asked for you. You remember that, boy."

So the boy had left at dawn carrying a large satchel across his body, bringing a gift to their chieftain for his good service for the farmer and his crops. Despite his father's warning not to dally, Bo was curious about the falls. He climbed to an open balcony to experience its magnificent force of sound and spray.

Then he wandered, trying to find the chieftain's residence. The city dwellers bustled around, silly grins plastered to their faces. Bo stopped to watch a young girl about his age who handed bundled flowers up to a woman standing on a chair. Bo wondered why the shop owners in this lane were hanging garlands of greens and flowers. There was no special occasion he knew of.

The sheer size and grandeur of the city filled his eyes with astonishment. Not even the thickest, tallest forests compared to this. Bo felt the strain in the back of his neck from looking up at the stone walls and arches, balconies and spires. He looked up, blinking as the misty rain clung to his lashes. When he dropped his chin he saw the girl across the street looking at him. Their eyes locked. Bo suddenly felt awkward. With his chin to his chest he strode down the lane, away from the city's entrance gate.

At the end of the street, he slowed and glanced over his shoulder. The woman was stepping down from her chair, and the girl was nowhere in sight. Glancing around, he figured she'd gone inside the shop, as the woman carrying the chair now did. Bo kept moving and turned the corner to the left. He nearly collided with the girl from the store.

"Hey, watch it!" He sidestepped away from her and shuffled to a stop. Again their eyes locked. "You're the girl from the store."

She nodded, looking him over. "Where are you from?"

"I live on a farm in the outlying fields," he said, his eyes downcast. He lifted them and stated in a stronger voice, "I'm here to see the chieftain—he asked me to come and report on the crops."

"He did not!"

"He did so!"

"Well, he's not even here!" The girl propped her fists on her narrow hips just below her wide leather belt carved with intricate flowers. At his disheartened expression she laughed. "But he's due back any moment now—along with his new *human* lady! Several of the hunters have already returned."

Bo swept his eyes down the street, noticing the crowds making efforts to spruce up the retail part of the city. "My mother says they'll pass by our flower shop. You could wait outside with me if you like."

Her softer words brought Bo's attention back to her belt. "All right, flower girl," he said. "I'll stick around for a little while."

"Have you ever been here before? You looked kind of lost."

"Naa, this is my first time." He fell into step next to her, and they turned back the way he'd come. "What did you mean by a *human* lady? When did she get here?" Like everyone else, Bo knew the legend that their chieftain was human. But in recent weeks he'd heard differently. He'd overheard his mother telling his father that a Linker had returned to the city who claimed to be their chieftain's father. Bo had never heard his mother's voice so high. According to a chain of several other ladies his mother knew, Finn was a half-blood human.

"All I know is, he found her at the sacred Wellness temple on the coast while he was there at some big gathering."

The crowd grew, and welcoming calls could be heard down the lane. "Here they come!" she said excitedly before she dashed away, dodging the expanding crowds that poured out of the surrounding shops.

Bo tried to keep up but was effectively blocked by the shop owners and their families. A tall wooden display unit provided vertical access, and he scaled its shelves. The ropes that held the neighbor's awning were in reach and Bo swung himself over the heads of the well-wishers. Stealthily, he landed. He stepped up behind his new friend, who held a bouquet of yellow flowers in her hands.

"What are those for?" he whispered in her ear. She was startled but didn't look over her shoulder at him. Her eyes were focused down the lane at a group of hunters walking in a procession.

"They are for the lady. I picked them myself this morn— Ahhh, here she comes!" The girl began jumping up and down on her toes, frantically waving her arm. After an astonished breath, she squealed, "Isn't she lovely?"

Bo had taken a step back to avoid being battered by the girl's erratic movements, but he stepped up again when the chieftain came into view. He was relieved that he hadn't come all this way to find the chief was not here. But mostly he was in awe of their powerful leader. Then he noticed the reason why the girl was reacting jubilantly and thrusting her fist clutching the flowers into the street. When the chieftain paused to talk to someone, the blond woman waving politely to the crowd stopped directly in front of the girl.

"What pretty flowers!" the woman said kindly to the girl, who looked up at her mother. The mother had rushed up behind her daughter, placing protective hands on her shoulders.

"They are for you," said the girl.

"Aww, that is so sweet. What is your name?"

Bo heard her say, "Ren." Then he heard her mother explain her name meant water lily. His nickname for her, flower girl, had been appropriate. While the lady with yellow hair blazing in the noon sun continued her conversation with the girl and her mother, Bo watched Finn come closer to see what his lady was doing. After he said hello to the flower vendors, his eyes scanned the area until they landed on him. Bo saw recognition.

"You. You're the farmer's boy." The chieftain stepped past the tribesmen waiting to greet him. Finn leaned his forearm on a column in the shade of the vestibule where the row of shops began. "Have you come to report on the farm?" he asked the boy, much to the surprise of the bystanders.

"Yes." Bo cursed his small voice. He cleared his throat and squared his slender shoulders. "Yes, and I bring you a gift from my parents."

"You've come alone?" The chieftain glanced around, looking for anyone to claim the young child, but he didn't seem surprised that no one stepped forward.

Bo nodded.

"Come with us. I'll receive your gift in my council chamber. Then you can have a meal. I'll have someone give you a ride home before nightfall." Finn called to a woman in the procession, "Look after this one. He's coming with us."

Bo was chaperoned by a woman with a toothy smile. He waved to the girl, Ren, who waved back joyfully.

***

Samantha felt like a princess in a fairytale during their parade through the city. The tribal custom left her elated but exhausted. She dropped on the bed in her new room and allowed her eyes to drift shut. The bed sagged, and Finn's warm, hard body leaned against hers. When he slipped his hand under her shirt the corners of her mouth turned up. Next she felt his lips brush hers. She was too tired to even open her eyes but focused her remaining energy on kissing him back. He stretched his body against hers and pulled her close to nuzzle her neck.

She rested her hands on the square of his hips. "This would really relax me. Then we can take a nap," she whispered seductively into his hair.

"I can't stay," he said curtly.

She felt the scratch of stubble against her neck before he lifted his head. Her eyes opened, and she looked at him, confused.

"A chieftain is always in demand. You get some rest. I'll send word to Harmony that you'll see her later."

"Oh yeah, I should get up." Samantha felt guilty; she'd forgotten about her friend.

"No. I'll send an old friend to keep her company," Finn assured her as he moved off the bed. He gave her a quick smile and left the room with a purposeful stride.

As the group approached the city, Harmony had

become melancholy. She had insisted she be escorted directly into the city with her hair hidden under a hood. Harmony said the honor of the parade should concentrate on Samantha since she was the bride. Harmony had admitted this city had left her with bittersweet feelings, but it would always be special because she'd married Kodiak here. Nevertheless she'd been held prisoner here. And worse than that, she'd witnessed her cousin Binda's murder within these walls.

Samantha hadn't realized how deeply this place would affect Harmony. Samantha felt guilty that she'd gone directly to her room. Exhausted in a way she had never experienced before, Samantha knew for certain she was pregnant.

29

Hood low over her brow, Harmony rode with a band of hunters through the city gate and veered off toward the elk paddock. Arrangements had been made for someone to meet her there and escort her to her room. She was glad for the misty day. Although it was warm, at least the sun wasn't beating down on her hood. The host maneuvered her through the hallways and courtyards, and Harmony absorbed the views that brought back memories. One new feature in one of the larger courtyards was an enormous steel cage. Sure that the sleeping brown mound was the infamous short-faced bear, she wondered what Kodiak would think of it. When Binda, Rio, and Kodiak had to outmaneuver two of them in order to obtain the last ingredient for sending Harmony home, they told tales about how ferocious the twelve-foot bears were. That was when she was last in this city, where she married a man she'd sworn to *dislike*.

The lavender pearl ring on her finger shifted, and she ran her thumb over it. She missed Kodiak acutely. It was just a matter of time before they would be together again, and she knew she would do whatever it took to make their life together work for both of them. She loved him, truly, deeply loved him.

They skirted the cage and mounted the steps to the chieftain's tower, where the most esteemed were housed. Harmony entered her guestroom, recognizing it had been Finn's old suite. Finn would have Chief Nakoma's quarters now. She flashed back, watching Catori snarl with both her voice and her fingers as Harmony had passed the lovers in the hallway outside this door. She shuddered, thinking of the girl's fate.

Inside, Harmony stood alone at the window. The view from this height revealed the distant gate entrance, the bridges that arched over the river, and the great waterfall. The parade of fifty hunters that escorted Finn and Samantha crossed the bridge with ceremony. Harmony imagined she could hear the crowd roaring, but she was too far up to hear anything but the rumble of the falls. Alone, haunted by too many memories, Harmony was relieved when someone eventually knocked on her door.

"Amadahy!" Harmony cried, overjoyed to see Chief Nakoma's young room attendant. Harmony wondered what had become of her after Amadahy had helped her, Kodiak, and Finn escape the city. Had Nakoma discovered she had been drugged by Amadahy? She suspected not; Amadahy now stood before her, smiling. "Come in!"

"It is good to see you again, Harmony, though I never expected you to return here," she said honestly.

Nodding, Harmony agreed. "Yes, these are strange circumstances. After all, Finn is leader now. *And* he is marrying my best friend Samantha. I came to witness the special event. But I will be going back right after—return to Kodiak who's in the human realm."

"So much has changed." Amadahy sighed and added, "For the good. I'm glad our chieftain has found a suitable wife."

"Oh?" Harmony continued casually. "Your good-bye kiss with Finn suggests otherwise." Finn and Catori had been lovers. Perhaps he had been romantic with Amadahy after Catori was gone.

The girl shook her head. "It may have been my wish, but I am only a room attendant to him."

"And a friend—if I know Finn."

"Yes, a friend," Amadahy concluded.

"You will be Sam's friend as well. How about I

introduce you—if you haven't met her yet?"

"I haven't. Finn said she was resting."

Harmony guessed why her usually energetic pal was napping. Indeed, evolution seemed to have found its way. "Let's let her rest. Can you sit with me awhile?" At her nod and grin, Harmony offered her a seat. When Amadahy sat and placed her slim hand on the armrest, Harmony noticed the shell bracelet on her wrist. "You still have it." She pointed.

"I've worn it since the day you gave it to me in the woods," Amadahy confessed, holding up her wrist to admire the bracelet.

"My aunt Nami made it. She is talented, isn't she?" Harmony relaxed and caught up with her old friend. Amadahy gave her a sense of how much the tribe liked Finn as their leader. She said that they were hopeful about the results of the summit. In turn, Harmony eased the girl's apprehension about attending to the chieftain's soon-to-be wife. She wanted Samantha to have a friend here after she was gone for good. Amadahy might be that person.

***

That evening, while he socialized with two beautiful blonds at his elbows, Finn was recharged by the energy and excitement in the room. The elite group consisted of the council members and their families, several overseers of outlying villages, tradesmen, and hunters. Finn saw to it the hunters who'd befriended Samantha at the coast where in attendance, hoping to make her feel at ease. Although Finn noticed that while Harmony hung back quietly, and listened politely, Samantha was just the opposite, chatting and smiling like she'd known these people all their lives. She truly amazed him, and often his eyes drifted in her direction.

Finn and the girls eventually moved to a larger gallery so a broader spectrum of folk could interact with their chief one on one. Finn saw to it that subtle changes were made in the gallery, like an informal seating area arranged for private conversation, where a person or family seeking to speak with the chieftain could do so with his full attention. At the close of the hour after seeing more than a dozen people, Finn's last guest was the farmer's son Bo. The boy was led over; he sat in the chair indicated, perched at its edge.

"It's good to see you, my young friend. How are things on the farm?" Finn asked. While he watched the boy he remembered the day he'd gone to the farm. The crops had suffered from a drought, and he had summoned a torrential rain. Finn conjured memories of his own childhood, believing this child was as neglected by his father as Finn had been by his.

The boy's eyes drifted toward the blond girls who sat together and then snapped back to the chieftain. "We've yielded a good crop, thanks to you—to the rain you brought us." As if suddenly remembering something important, he said, "My parents have sent along a gift for your help." Bo opened the satchel and drew out a paper package, which he handed to the chieftain.

Finn accepted the floppy package tied with string and a sprig of rosemary. He glanced at the girls, who leaned in with interest. With one tug he unraveled the string, and the wrapper unfolded. Inside was a square of fine cloth embroidered with a field of lavender flowers.

"That's beautiful! May I see it?" Samantha requested.

Finn handed the cloth to his bride, happy she liked it, and discarded the paper on a nearby table heaped with gifts.

"It's for your table," Bo offered. "My mother made it."

Finn heard Harmony whispered to Samantha, "This is

like a bridal shower."

"These people are so generous." Samantha raised her eyes to Finn, her expression thoughtful and serene.

"Be sure to thank your mother for her fine craftsmanship and let her know she has pleased my lady. I'm glad to hear the crops recovered. Tell your father I will come during the sowing season." Finn couldn't help but smile at the boy's tooth-challenged grin. This little boy with the soft curve of his cheek, perhaps eight years old, set Finn's mind wondering if he'd ever have a son. Would it be possible with Samantha? If not, Bo wasn't the only child in his tribe who needed extra looking after. Finn didn't approve that this child had been sent on the long trek to the city with no chaperon. Perhaps Samantha could advise him what was done for orphans or overlooked youth in the human realm.

For now, he dismissed the boy into the hands of an attendant who would see he was fed, given provisions and new boots, and returned home safely.

30

Within five days, all the wedding preparations came together. Forest Tribe weddings, while certainly affairs to celebrate, especially a chieftain's, were much less elaborate than church and country club weddings in the human realm. Samantha was feeling the queasy effects of pregnancy and apprehension blended with the excitement over her upcoming life. Her father and brother would never know the truth about what had become of her. The girls discussed it and agreed that Harmony would tell them for now that Samantha had taken a job in a remote place. Later, she would spin a story about Samantha finding someone to share her life with. It wouldn't be a lie.

The other situation that nagged at Samantha was Finn's relationship with Gale...and her own relationship with Gale, for that matter. Samantha wanted to face the man who had abducted her and tell him once and for all how she felt. It was easy to find his holding room, and she ordered the guard to let her in. Persuasiveness was her dominant quality.

Gale looked up from his desk, pen in hand, when she entered the room. He seemed to pause, waiting for someone else to enter behind her. But the guard just closed the door, leaving them alone.

"What an honor." He rose from the chair and leaned against the heavy desk. "What brings you here, away from your wedding plans?"

Samantha walked up to him and crossed her arms over her chest, studying him. She could see the family resemblance. Gale had been a looker in his youth, she was sure.

"The wedding details are taken care of. But I came

here for two reasons. One, I want you to know that despite the fact you abducted me—and terrified me—it has made me stronger. In the past weeks trying to adapt to this world, I've learned to embrace it. I've been to the far corners of the human realm. I'm a true adventurer at heart. All my life I've been seeking something...someone. You may have forced my course to change, but it put me on the right path. I know you wanted your son to marry Harmony and have babies, but I can give him that as well."

A glimmer reflected in his eye; he seemed struck by her insinuation. The silence stretched.

"Anyway, the second thing is I think you should make amends with Finn. You are dying, and after all you've put him through I think he deserves to hear a sincere apology. I know you think you were helping him become chieftain in your own way, but you have to admit it was underhanded and cruelly done."

"Does my son know that you are here?" Gale asked skeptically.

"No. I'm here because I love him, and I want to make him happy. You've brought us together—inadvertently—but still, this wedding is your doing. *And* it was a good thing. Start with that."

"Well." He ran his palm on his thigh and shifted position. "I don't think 'sorry, kid, that things didn't work out with your mom' will set aside his hatred for me. Even if I did find him his match in a wife."

Samantha felt a smidge relieved that she was getting through to him; she appreciated his appraisal of her. Still, small words like "I'm sorry" have patched numerous relationships. If only these two stubborn men could get there.

"Look, Gale, you've been around a long time, and I'm sure you've seen a lot. Every family has its drama. And nobody's perfect. All kids want to know their parents care about them and are proud of them." She rolled her eyes. "Finn is an amazing man. It's a shame you missed out on his life all those years."

"I knew he would be great. With his ability, he has afforded the tribe such potential."

"It is a miracle that Finn has an incredible ability, but you can't take credit for that—nor the fact that the people have long respected him," Samantha pointed out.

Gale dropped his chin to his chest and laughed. The sound irritated her. She snapped, "What's so funny?"

He cocked his head, returning his gaze to her. "I do believe you are the better choice for him. However, only your friend Harmony has the ability to ward off the water god and his sirens. Will she stay?"

"No, she will go home after the wedding. Since she is eager to return, we've rushed the ceremony. It's tomorrow. As for the sirens, they are a threat like any other animal. The tribes and clans will deal with them as we see fit."

Gale sat at his desk once more, and Samantha figured that was a hint to leave. However she placed her hands on the desk and leaned over. "Please think about what I said." She placed one slim hand against her abdomen and implored, "I want to tell my child something admirable about you—the grandfather who in the end understood the importance of family."

His eyes rose slowly from her belly to her face. Gale had a way of masking feelings from his expression, just like Finn did. But she could tell her words had resonated. She stood and dropped her hands to her sides. With a heavy inhale she turned and walked to the door. She knocked, and the door soon opened. She let out a long sigh. She had done it. She'd made her peace, and she hoped for the sake of her future husband that his father would do the same.

***

There wouldn't be inclement weather on his son's wedding day—Finn would command it to change if necessary. Gale sensed his son would please the woman he loved. It was the way Finn looked at her, like he'd die for her or kill for her. Finn reminded him of himself when he'd first met Mary Falk. *Damn, how I've missed her all these years.*

Gale couldn't get Samantha Finch's words out of his mind all night. *I want to tell my child something admirable about you—the grandfather who in the end understood the importance of family.* When Mary had become pregnant he couldn't believe it. Until the day he held Finn in his arms he had wondered if the baby belonged to another man. His doubt fled the moment he held Finn. His Mary was true to him, and the tiny infant looked just like him.

Somehow, after thousands of years, his DNA had aided this evolution. Later, when he found out that Calder had also successfully procreated with a human, the fact didn't diminish his ego. The two Linkers had started a new race. Surely their offspring would be the ones to empower the future race in this realm.

Gale stared out his window, down at the couple standing at the altar. His handsome, strong son and the feisty but levelheaded blond who carried his grandchild were exchanging vows. His legacy was already living on.

His thoughts turned to what Calder had said to him in confidence during his medical examination. Calder had been a friend in their youth and tried to be one in the final phase of Gale's life.

Calder had said, "It is true you are dying. It can only be the result of you crossing too many times. I know. I suffered for many years when I went back to see Pearl. I regret not staying with her."

Only a Linker could truly understand what motivated other Linkers.

Calder had added, "Linkers sacrifice for the greater good of knowledge and healing, but we don't take regrets to the grave, Gale."

The couple came into focus again. They walked hand in hand into the secluded garden where the ceremonial pool was hidden, like a Garden of Eden. He watched the miniature guests from his bird's eye view as they filed away, giving the couple privacy. He recognized Harmony even from this distance, her yellow hair waving like a flag in the afternoon breeze. Though he was unwanted, Gale believed that a father should be at his son's side on his wedding day, not locked in a tower serving out his punishment under house arrest until his passing.

Gale turned from the window and sat at his desk. He reached for a blank piece of paper and stared at it thoughtfully. It was time to make amends. He began his note to his son.

Finn,

I realize that you know what it feels like when you lose the person you love most in these realms. I should not have taken you away from your mother. I've suffered every day from the decisions I made in the past regarding the two of you. My ambitions clouded my judgment. I apologize for taking out my anger at your mother on you, son. Taking you and abandoning you in a foreign realm was unforgiveable. My only hope is that because my interference brought Samantha into your life you hate me a little less. Ironically, the human girl *is* a good match for you.

In the time that I have left, I've returned to the human realm to find your mother. Don't send anyone to follow me. I will do her no harm. My dying wish is to just lay eyes on her one last time. I don't deserve her forgiveness."

Tell my grandchildren I am proud of their father. I know you will love and raise them as should be.

This is my last Linker log, August 1989.
Gale the Linker

Satisfied, Gale reached inside his vest. A hidden pocket contained two pouches. One was filled with herbs, the other with matches.

31

Samantha adapted efficiently to foreign environments and customs. Her career traveling the globe and integrating in foreigner's lives had proved she was a model student. Still, Harmony's guidance on what her new home would be like in the Forest Tribe's city had been hugely convenient. While the stone city felt somewhat like she imagined ancient Pompeii would have felt like, it offered modern conveniences and technologies the Linkers had brought back from the human realm. Hydro-powered turbines used the falls to generate electricity and plumbing. She toured the shopping district where true artisans peddled their wares, from furniture to tattoos to pottery. Harmony mentioned the tribe was known for its fine fabric and took Samantha to the vast rooms where ladies and their daughters spun their magic on looms.

Mystified by the fact that this world had evolved without horses or any kind of birds, Samantha's reaction to the lions that roamed beside their huntresses intrigued her. She'd ridden on the back of an elk from the coast, which wasn't completely unheard of in her world; she knew elks were used for transportation in remote places in the human realm. Gale had provided the city with a live short-faced bear, now kept in the square like a zoo animal. Samantha heard that her fiancé was known for hunting these animals; she hoped his chieftain role would keep him out of the northern forests.

Samantha immersed herself in tribal city life over the next few days and quickly realized being married to a chieftain would be like being married to a rock star. Finn was a celebrity in demand. Every day was filled to capacity. However, his nights were hers. Although he showed her infinite passion and held her though the night as though he would never let her go, he had never said the words she longed to hear. *I love you.*

Many times those words were on the tip of her tongue, but she didn't say them. She thought back to her previous relationship with David. He'd used the word *love* loosely. Had she said it back because he'd said it first?

After the ceremony, Samantha followed Finn into the pool. Harmony let her in on the secret that it was meant for mating—a good luck ritual to boost fertility.

Finn swam to the middle. Samantha sighed and allowed the refreshing waters to sooth way the tension and anxiety of the wedding preparations, not to mention a vast audience staring at her during the ceremony. Usually she was fine being a media hog, but this union finalized the reality that she was in this realm to stay. Like when she'd been on camera, she had to hold her emotions in check.

Now they were alone. Finn stood submerged to his shoulders in the pool and pulled her tightly against him. She wrapped her arms around his neck and her legs around his waist.

"So are you ready to start your life with me, chief?" She expected her question would bring a lighthearted answer, but he became serious.

"Samantha, the moment I laid eyes on you I knew you would change me."

"Change you…?"

"Yes, you've changed me." His finger brushed across her cheek while his eyes implored hers to understand. "After Gale took me from my family I had to make a life for myself here in this realm. I grew accustomed to the reality that I'd likely not fall in love. You have changed that for me. You've opened my heart. I have indeed fallen in love with you, and I am thrilled to start our life together. My greatest hope is that in these circumstances I can make you as happy as you make me."

His declaration of love elated her. She felt the prick of tears as she said, "Our circumstances, however insanely orchestrated, are truly destiny's plan." He seemed to hang on her every word as his eyes caressed her face. She stated simply. "I love you too, Finn." His broad smile confirmed her suspicion that he had been waiting to hear her say it. Before he could kiss her, she untangled her arms from around his neck and gently placed a palm on his chest, "One more thing." Jittery with nerves, she expelled a sudden, excited breath. "I know why we are in this pool, but we don't need the help of spiritual water to create our child—life has already found its way. I'm pregnant."

Awe transformed his face. He whispered, "I can't believe it." He stared off for a moment before he blinked and looked back at her. "It appears you've opened my heart more than I knew was possible." His hand slipped to the nape of her neck, and he pressed his lips against hers—a clingy kiss, heavy with emotion. And the kissing remained that way while they used the pool as a celebratory playground rather than for its intended purpose.

32

It did not take long to track down Mary Falk. She still lived in the obscure New England town where Gale had found her last time. He'd figured she would root herself, hoping for the small chance that her son Finn would return one day. Gale mused about telling her about their son… Would she believe him?

Gale didn't expect Mary to ever want to see his sorry face again. When he found the establishment where she worked, he walked the grounds and sat on a lone bench at the foot of the lawn on the edge of the lake. He sat watching her.

The sign on the front of the one-story building tucked within many acres of scenic woodlands read, *Lakeside: A Home for Seniors.* Though the September afternoon was sunny, Mary carried a blanket to a resident who sat quietly on the back patio. Gale recognized Mary even from this distance. In her fifties now, her body was still slender under her uniform. Her flaxen hair, once long, was cut above her shoulders. She covered the man's skeletal frame with the blanket and turned to look toward the lake. Gale watched her lift her hand to her brow, shielding her eyes from the glare reflecting off the sparkling water. Though he knew he looked old sagged against the bench, he presumed she wouldn't identify him as a resident.

The beats of his heart were slowing; every inhale was a struggle. After he'd crossed the realms, he laid in the leaves for nearly two days before he recovered enough to find sustenance, followed by powerful human narcotics. He had taken a huge risk crossing so far from the portal and accepted the additional pain it caused him now.

Apparently hitchhiking was unpopular in 1989, but

he seemed a nonthreatening old man, and with little effort a driver took where he wanted to go. Dropped off at the only coffee shop in Mary's town, Gale sat in the corner of the restaurant nibbling on a sandwich and listening to each chatty customer who came in to talk with the fluffy-haired owner behind the counter. The owner's jovial voice carried across the room when she greeted every customer by their first name and then rapid-fired questions about what they were doing, who with, and what else was new. In less than two hours Mary Falk's name was mentioned.

On his second cup of tea, almost finished with the newspaper he was reading, Gale noticed a woman in a white uniform come in.

"Afternoon, Heather. You starting your shift or coming off a shift?"

"Hi, Shirley. I'm on my way in. I'll take an Italian grinder and some of those butterscotch cookies. I swear the residents only listen to me because I sneak them your cookies. Just don't mention it to the kids who stashed their loved ones at Lakeside."

Gale dropped his eyes to the newspaper while Heather and Shirley chatted about several of the seniors at the retirement home. When Shirley handed over the sandwich and cookies, she asked, "Hey, is Mary Falk working today?"

"Yeah, she's second shift, like me."

"Be a sugar and ask her to drop by. I'm running low on parsley and thyme—you know she grows the best herbs in town."

"Sure thing. Thanks, Shirley," Heather said as she grabbed the paper bag off the counter and headed for the door.

When Shirley turned toward the register, Gale was standing there before her. She looked somewhat startled.

"Oh. Can I get you anything else?" she inquired, her

double chin still visible although she looked up.

"I'm passing through town, but I'd like to stop by Lakeside to see an old friend. Do you know if there is a bus that might take me there?" Gale saw her inquisitive eyes become round. He figured she'd start questioning him immediately about who he was seeing and why.

Just then the bells that announced a new customer jingled, and a man in dungarees and a John Deere cap walked in.

"Good afternoon, Shirley." The man raised the brim of his hat an inch in greeting before he headed over to the standing cooler to grab a soda. "Afternoon, feller," he said to Gale as he reached the counter with his soda can.

"Hello. Just a second, Lou," Shirley said to the older man, who waved his hand as if to say, *Take all the time you need.* "Lakeside's bus only runs the residents into town on Saturdays. Sorry, but you're out of luck."

"Need a ride, feller?" asked the man in the cap.

Gale turned to him and smiled.

He dropped Gale off at Lakeside's front door. Gale waved a friendly good-bye until the blue pickup truck turned the bend. Then he limped away from the entrance and skirted the building. Reaching the back of the quaint establishment he spotted a bench, unoccupied and inviting. It seemed he'd expended his energy in amicable conversation. His chest was tight, and his leg throbbed mercilessly. Once seated, he wiped the sweat from his brow and swallowed two more pills. The slow throb of his heartbeat signaled the end was near. He'd made it to his final destination. He just wanted to see her face and then make it into the water. In death he wished to return to the water. The nearby lake would make a convenient grave.

The caregiver bent down, pointed to the bench, and asked the thin man something. At his feeble shrug she swiveled her head to study the man by the lake once again. She dropped her hand and stepped through the manicured grass.

Gale struggled to stand. He wobbled, but he was determined to reach the lake, only steps away. He managed to submerge his shoes in the murky water, before he heard the alarm in her voice. "Sir, stop! What are you doing?"

He faced her; she stood merely feet away. Abruptly she stopped and sucked in a breath.

Gale caressed the woman with his luminescent eyes. She still had those freckles that bridged her nose, only more of them now. Finn truly did have her eyes, so like the green forest around them now.

"I can't believe it's you!" Mary pressed her hand to her heart for a moment. With a strangled cry she stuttered, "What...what have you done with..." Overcome with grief, she covered her mouth with her hands.

"Our son is well, Mary. He's far from here...from this place..." Gale circled his hand in the air, indicating Finn was beyond this realm. "I know you didn't believe me before, but it is true. There is another place."

She glared at him through the tears in her eyes.

Gale took several steps backward; the muck under his feet sucked him into waist-deep water. She took a step forward, as if contemplating saving the old man from certain drowning.

"I'm dying, Mary. I've only come back to tell you that I am sorry. Sorry that I wasn't the man you needed me to be. Sorry that I returned to my realm and put my personal gains before you—the only woman I have ever loved. And most deeply, I'm sorry I took Finn away from you."

"Finn!" she repeated.

Gale grimaced as pain gripped his chest, soon

followed by a warming sensation. He felt the cool smooth water at his fingertips before a buzzing numbness spread across his body. He could no longer stand. He sank slowly under the water. Everything in his sight blurred for a moment before he saw Mary's face peering into the lake through the ripples.

In that instant he reflected on the two realms, wondering why Linkers had been the only ones to cross for thousands of years. Perhaps they were chosen; it was predestined for them to advance evolution so the Linkers and humans could unify the realms by creating life and mixing the races. Somehow he'd been chosen, along with the green-eyed woman watching him through the water. His whole life had been an extraordinary adventure. Now, as his soul prepared to pass into the universe, he looked upon the one thing he had connected with, the only woman he'd loved—Mary Falk.

33

Harmony has dreaded this good-bye. She could hardly see her best friend's face through the tears swimming in her eyes. She blinked, and the tears rolled in fat beads down her cheeks. "This is so hard," she whispered hoarsely.

"This sucks," Samantha agreed. The girls hugged for the third time.

Finn nodded to the guide who would escort Harmony back to the Wellness temple, where she would ultimately cross to the human realm. The guide holding the leads of two elk exchanged a micro-nod with his chieftain. He stroked the animals' soft noses during the long farewell.

"I wish—" Samantha started to say, but Harmony interrupted her.

"I know… Me too. I wish there was an easier way to cross the realms. I will miss you both so much. I love both of you."

The three friends embraced, and Harmony mounted the elk. She waved until the stone city was blotted out by the thickening forest.

The familiar struggle and sacrifice Harmony had made all too often—losing those she loved—forced her to think of the man she loved on the other side. She had Kodiak. And it was time to return to him.

For a moment the face of another man crossed her mind—Suijin the water god. She had promised him something. Promised she would spend time with him. He said he would find her, yet he'd left her alone. Perhaps she could return without his further interference. As soon as she got to the coast she would hug the rest of her family good-bye and blast her way through the broken water of the realms. As far as she was concerned, she and the water god were even.

THE VANISHING PEARL: BOOK THREE

CHAPTER ONE

1989
The Human Realm

The headlights of Mrs. Coombs's sedan reflected off the chain-link fence that encircled the old Wentworth hotel. Numerous residents of the island were involved with the preservation committee to save what was left of the turn-of-the-century Victorian hotel. Mrs. Coombs headed the committee.

Mike sat in the front passenger seat next to his mother. He and Kodiak had just returned home from a shipwreck expedition, and he had gushed over every detail involved. From the backseat, Kodiak listened to Mike's long-winded rendition about their extended trip while his mother hung on to every word. Mike talked for the entire hour they traveled from Logan airport, where his mother had picked up the two young men, to the New Castle, New Hampshire, exit, where his mother took over the conversation. She spoke over her shoulder so Kodiak could hear while keeping her eyes on the narrow street, Wentworth Road.

Mrs. Coombs updated them about the Wentworth Hotel. "We've managed to get her on the Endangered Historic Properties list. But now, once again, the new company that bought her doesn't think they can renovate her." She referred to the Wentworth-by-the-Sea Hotel as *her*, as if the building were an old friend.

Kodiak ducked his head, looking out the window as they passed by the weathered, white-washed clapboards. In the twilight the building looked darker than dark, maybe how the iceberg looked to the passengers on the Titanic. The three of them had a common passion for relics like shipwrecks and old buildings. Learning about the past gave insight to one's future, Kodiak thought. He sat back and grinned, thinking about his wife. She also referred to the Wentworth in much the same manner as Mrs. Coombs. There was no doubt the hundred-year-old hotel had an extraordinary history. Residents on this island seemed completely outraged that their piece of history was one wrecking ball away from demolition. He wondered how his wife was taking the news. He hadn't talked to her in weeks. He kept crazy hours on the expedition and took each opportunity to learn all he could, which meant late nights talking with the experts. Every chance he'd had, he tried to call her, but she hadn't answered. Bad timing, he'd surmised. Being under the water was in his blood—he was an Aquapopulean Diver, after all—though no one knew. He wanted to be included on future dives, and so he shook a lot of hands.

"What a shame," Mike grunted before he turned to look over the seat. He said to Kodiak, "Well, hopefully your return will cheer Harmony up. I know she's worked on saving that place for years."

Mrs. Coombs glanced at Kodiak in the rearview mirror. "Kodiak, please tell Harmony about the Endangered Historic Properties list. She wasn't at the last meeting."

Kodiak leaned forward. "Harmony missed the meeting?" He couldn't interpret the strange feeling that suddenly came over him. It was unlike Harmony to miss one of her Friends of the Wentworth meetings.

"Nope. I haven't seen her for a few weeks. What has she been up to?" Mrs. Coombs's curiosity was clearly piqued.

"Um, I'm not sure." Kodiak slouched against the seat, his eyes anxiously pinned on the road the headlights illuminated. "I haven't talk to her in a while." In just minutes he would be home—well, the place he now called home, the house Harmony's grandparents left her. He missed Harmony so much he practically shook with excitement to think of seeing her. He thought about hearing her voice, seeing her smile, and feeling her body beneath his. He sat up straighter on the fabric bench seat. He couldn't wait to tell his wife how amazing his trip had been. But first, he just needed to know she was okay.

Mrs. Coombs pulled her sedan in front of the Parker house. Harmony's car was in the driveway, but the house was dark. "Do you have a key?" she asked Kodiak, concern in her voice.

"Yes, I can get in. I'm sure Harmony just turned in early," Kodiak said, opening the door. "Thanks again for the ride home, Mrs. Coombs. Talk to you later, Mike." He pulled his duffle bag off the seat and swung the car door shut. When he reached the back porch, he heard Mrs. Coombs drive away. Kodiak retrieved the hidden key and let himself in. He tentatively called, "Hello! Anyone home?"

After he switched on the kitchen light, he glanced around the room for any sign of his wife. Alarmed, he spotted what he was looking for. An envelope with his name in neat, loopy handwriting lay on the kitchen table. He dropped his duffle bag to the floor and rushed to collect the envelope. With one rip, he tore it open and plucked the note from inside. The envelope dropped to the floor unnoticed while his clumsy fingers worked to unfold the paper. The letter read:

THE VANISHING PEARL: BOOK 3

Harmony Parker has captivated Suijin, the water god. With her dual heritage and unique abilities, she is unlike any living creature he has ever encountered. He wants her—but she is married to Kodiak Night. On the cusp of her reunion with Kodiak after a lengthy separation, the god steals Harmony away to his hidden island and tries to win her heart.

When Suijin interfered in her life in the past, it resulted in tragedy and death. But things are different now. Harmony's affection becomes divided between a man and a god. Also her magical power that connects her to the oceans of the realms grows further making her feel less human. She struggles to adapt to her new abilities while controlling her rising passion for her captor. Her personal battle has begun.

The Broken Water Series features three novels and one spin off. The Rare Pearl, The Forsaken Pearl, and The Vanishing Pearl can be read as stand-alone novels but are best read in order.

LEGENDS MATE is part of a multi-author stand-alone series. It tells the tale of a minor character, a scorned siren, from the Broken Water series who meets her—unlikely—mate.

Author's Note:

As an author, I often get asked what inspires me. Like other artistic people, music often enhances my muse. I love acoustic guitar and soulful lyrics. My hope is that I rouse my readers with my stories and characters, like a song stirs emotions. I bring up music, because in this story I talk about the shipwreck the *SS Edmund Fitzgerald,* which I first heard about from a Gordon Lightfoot song. As a young child in the 1970s, I fell in love with the Canadian folk singer's songs. Throughout my life, although I listen to a variety of music from 1980s, one-hit wonders to rap to radio countdowns, I always go back to Lightfoot's music. It grounds me. That said, one song in particular, "The Wreck of the Edmund Fitzgerald," haunts me. In this book, it was a natural choice for Kodiak to visit this ship's gravesite in Lake Superior. An actual expedition took place in August 1989. The *SS Edmund Fitzgerald* freighter sank on November 10, 1975, taking twenty-nine souls with her, all the men on board. While doing research for this book I came across underwater video footage of the wreck, and I was humbled watching it. Perhaps it was forsaken, but it will never be forgotten.

About the Author

Jennifer W. Smith is the author of the Landing in Love series. These contemporary small-town romances feature both sweet and sensual attractions. They always have something to do with aviation because this former flight attendant turned novelist has a flare for travel and adventure.

For adventure in a faraway land, check out her fantasy romances in the Broken Water series.

When not writing, Jennifer loves reading, talking to readers, and hanging out with her author friends. She lives in a quaint New England town with her husband and two children, along with their blue-eyed cat and rough collie.

Social Media Links

I'm always happy to hear from readers. Please let others know how you liked the book by leaving a review on Amazon.com and/or Goodreads.com (or other blogs and places you hangout on social media). A kind review goes a long way and is greatly appreciated.

AMAZON AUTHOR PAGE Jennifer W. Smith

FACEBOOK authorjenniferwsmith

FACEBOOK GROUP Jennifer W. Smith's Book Squad

INSTAGRAM authorjenniferwsmith

GOODREADS Jennifer W. Smith

BOOKBUB AUTHOR PAGE Jennifer W. Smith

PINTEREST authorjensmith

Thanks for your support!

www.ingramcontent.com/pod-product-compliance
Lightning Source LLC
Chambersburg PA
CBHW071135170626
46809CB00002B/631